T0117253

BOBBY'S CAGE

Rodney Wetzel

ARCHWAY
PUBLISHING

Archway Publishing books may be ordered
through booksellers or by contacting:

Archway Publishing
1663 Liberty Drive
Bloomington, IN 47403
www.archwaypublishing.com
1 (888) 242-5904

Because of the dynamic nature of the Internet, any web addresses or
links contained in this book may have changed since publication and
may no longer be valid. The views expressed in this work are solely those
of the author and do not necessarily reflect the views of the publisher,
and the publisher hereby disclaims any responsibility for them.

Any people depicted in stock imagery provided by Getty Images are
models, and such images are being used for illustrative purposes only.
Certain stock imagery © Getty Images.

ISBN: 978-1-4808-6766-6 (sc)
ISBN: 978-1-4808-6765-9 (e)

Library of Congress Control Number: 2018910133

Print information available on the last page.

Archway Publishing rev. date: 08/31/2018

To my sister Jacque, thanks for believing in me all along

PROLOGUE

Little Bobby lay on the bottom of his cage. The cement floor was so cold. He knew he was going to die. There were no two ways about it. His stomach had stopped hurting, his body was numb, and there was no longer that wicked smell in the air. At first, he fought against the cold, trying desperately to reach into the cage next to him, where a small ragged blanket left behind by the previous occupant still lay. But the effort ended up being just a waste of time and energy. Still, at that time, he'd felt he had to try. Now, curled into a ball on the floor of his cage, he no longer feared the cold; it was comforting, taking away all his pain. It would all be over soon.

At the age of seven his life was ending. *Thank God*, he thought. It had been a nightmare filled with pain, hunger, and abuse. "Please—let this be the end," he murmured. If only the world for him could have been different; surely this was not all there was. Gently the will to fight was fading, gliding away with the crisp fall breeze. There was something after this life. He knew this to be a fact. Richie had told him so. If only Richie was there now, to help him travel from this world to the next. He thought one more time of concentrating, putting all his will to the lock, focusing with all his might to open it and have it fall to the ground. But even if this miracle was to occur, he knew it would be in vain. He was too weak to walk, let alone climb the basement steps and bust open the locked door at the top. No. It was best the cold take him, better to embrace the end.

For just an instant, he thought he could hear footsteps in the room above him. He listened intensely for the longest time, but there was no further sound. Maybe he was dreaming. Maybe he was traveling to that other place and the sound had come from the world beyond. There was no one from this world alive in the house. Of that he was sure. Then it came again, the sound of footsteps above him. *Just my imagination*, he thought, *my mind hearing what it wants to hear*. Reluctantly, he closed his eyes and waited for the end.

CHAPTER 1

House of Terrors

Jackson, Michigan, October 20, 1998

Captain Hazel Mae Cowan did not like the way the day was turning out. True, the fall weather was amazing, including chilly nights highlighted by somewhat warm days. Jackson's tree-lined streets were alive with color. All the trees seemed to be peaking at once. No, this was a sensation she had in the pit of her stomach. She had been promoted to captain of the Jackson City Police Department exactly one year ago, and somehow, she knew her first year on the job had been just too damn easy.

As she made the turn onto Grinnell Street, she reached over to grab her coffee mug, but it was not there. Looking over, she witnessed Chief Detective Vinnie Moretti putting something in his mouth and taking a sip from her mug.

"Vinnie, really?" Hazel said.

"What? I need to take my morning pill. I have a bad thyroid," said Vinnie.

"With my cup?"

"Oh, what's the big deal? I don't have cooties, you know," he said with a smile.

"Have you ever heard of asking first?" she said sarcastically.

Vinnie grinned. "Please—may I take a small sip of your precious coffee, which, by the way, is cold as shit?"

"No. Now put my cup back down," said Hazel. "You can be such an asshole sometimes."

"True, I am an asshole. I cannot argue with you about that." He grinned.

Vinnie had started with the police force about the same time as Hazel had, way back when Kip Gilmore was still captain. That had been twelve years ago, yet it still seemed like yesterday. Captain Gilmore had been her mentor. If not for him, she might not have hung in there. It was not easy being a female cop in a conservative town like Jackson, but look at her now. Captain Gilmore had been her role model, her teacher. She hoped that she had made him proud.

He had been killed while investigating a string of murders that took place just outside of Jackson in a small town called Parksville. Both she and Vinnie had worked with him on that case. Parksville University had insisted its area be annexed into Jackson's taxing district just the year before; otherwise, none of them would have even been involved. It would have been the Jackson County Sheriff Department's case. Eventually, the case ended up in the hands of the FBI, and personally, she was never content with their findings. Hazel knew there was more to the story than was reported. But by the end, it seemed everyone wanted the whole thing brushed under the rug. Once the killing stopped, there was no public desire to rehash the brutal slayings. Still, someday she was sure she would learn the whole truth.

"I wonder if the new medical examiner will be on-site,"

said Vinnie. "I still can't get used to the term *medical examiner*. What was wrong with calling them coroners?"

"I don't know, but God help us if he is anything like the last one. That may be why the county changed the title, to get the taste of that dumbass out of their mouths," joked Hazel.

As she pulled up to the correct location, the new medical examiner's car was, in fact, in the driveway with three patrol cars parked in front of the house. "Why in hell don't they have this cordoned off? Look at all the people milling around," said Hazel as she exited the car.

"I'll take care of it," responded Vinnie. At once, he started moving people off the front lawn.

"We need this whole front yard cleared," he said. "Hicks, tape off this yard. God only knows what evidence has already been contaminated."

Hazel smiled. Vinnie was a pain in the ass, but he was the best crime scene investigator she had ever seen. *That's why Captain Gilmore gave him the camera*, thought Hazel. *He knew he had talent even before Vinnie knew it himself.*

Hazel looked up at the house. Like most houses on Grinnell Street, it was older but well kept. The home was a light blue two-story dwelling with an oversize front porch. *Strange how the worst things happen in the most normal of settings*, she thought.

Walking up the steps of the front porch, Hazel was greeted by a face she had not seen in eight years. "Sam Helmen, as I live and breathe, is that you?" she questioned while approaching him.

"Hazel, as beautiful as ever," said Sam, giving her a long embrace. "It's been forever."

"Don't tell me you're back."

"Yep, I'm your new cor—sorry, medical examiner."

Sam had been the county coroner for years before marrying and moving away. He, too, had played a part in investigating the Parksville murders. Hazel had always admired the man. Not only had the county struggled to find anyone near his talents over the past eight years, but he also was the survivor of a terrible fire that had left half his faced severely scarred. The fact that he was able to overcome his abnormality and excel in his profession was always an inspiration to her. Besides all that, he was also one hell of a nice guy.

"Oh my God, Sam," Vinnie said from the bottom of the porch steps.

"Vinnie, that you?" asked Sam. "I almost didn't recognize you with all that long hair. Still a toothpick, I see."

"I get away with the hair because I say I'm doing undercover work, and she buys it," he said, pointing to Hazel.

"That's right. You're a captain now, I hear," added Sam.

Hazel just lifted her shoulders in disbelief. "Can you believe it? Obviously, there was little to pick from. But why did they call you down to the crime scene? I mean, you'll get the body soon enough."

"That's just it. They want me to identify what's in there as actually being human. Seems there's some question as to what they found," responded Sam.

"So you haven't been in there either?" asked Vinnie.

"No. I heard you were on the way and thought I would wait till you got here. Shall we?" Sam motioned toward the front door. "So who called this in?"

"The neighbor. Said she could smell it from her kitchen," answered Vinnie.

The minute they walked through the front door, they were overwhelmed with the aroma of decaying flesh. For just a moment, Hazel had a flashback to the last time she had endured this smell. That had ended with her finding two elderly bodies in Parksville. They were decapitated with their heads placed vulgarly between their own legs.

Entering the kitchen, the three saw why there was some confusion as to whether the remains were human. The corpse, if it truly was a corpse, was sliced into neat little bundles and stacked in piles on the kitchen table. All the parts that could have identified it as human—feet, hands, genitals, most of its bones, and the head—were gone. They were all gone. It was simply a stack of unrecognizable flesh. Protruding from the wooden table in the middle of the bloody mess was an oversize meat cleaver.

"Shit!" exclaimed Vinnie. "This is the work of one sick individual."

Sam did not hesitate. He marched across the bloodstained floor directly to the table, unshaken by what he saw. With one look, he identified the mass as human. "Those ribs are human. That I know for sure," he said, pointing to two slabs of ribs placed toward the middle of the table.

Vinnie started to snap pictures. "These cuts on the right side of the table are clean, but less so for the pile on the left," he said while circling the table. He was talking into a small tape recorder in his left hand and snapping pictures with the camera he held in his right. "The blade got duller as he went around the table. See?" said Vinnie. "So the killer started with whatever parts are over here and worked his way around."

"You're absolutely correct," said Sam, surprised at Vinnie's ability to see the difference.

"We will need to label according to the placement on the table," Vinnie added. "At least we will have an idea of his process."

"And why remove some parts and not others?" questioned Hazel. "Looks like he was cutting the victim up for the freezer. Why the small bundles?"

"Captain, there is more in here," said Officer Jackson from the walk-in pantry.

Hazel walked over to the pantry door and saw Jackson holding up an old tarp. Lying on the floor were the hands, feet, disregarded bones, and head. "Shit, Sam. Come look at this."

Sam made his way to the pantry. "There's the rest of him all right," he said.

"It looks like we are all coming to the same conclusion here," said Hazel, staring up at Sam for some sign of understanding. "These are the parts one would throw away if one were cleaning game." The way the body was cut up in small packages, it seemed to Hazel someone had butchered him, literally, like someone would order a side of beef or a pig.

"Captain, I need you down here," said Officer Morris from the basement door. "You really need to see this."

"What now?" asked Sam.

"What you got, Morris?" yelled Hazel.

"Cages. A lot of cages."

Vinnie and Hazel met at the basement door. "Did he say 'cages'?" asked Vinnie.

Hazel just shook her head and started down the steps. At the bottom, there was very little light. But without any doubt, she could make out three rows of oversize cages. Each cage stood about four feet high, and each was maybe six feet long. Between each row was a small walkway.

"Where's the lights?" she asked Officer Morris, who was guiding his way with a flashlight.

"Tried it. Bulb must be burned out."

"What the fu ..." said Vinnie, coming up behind her.

Officer Morris was just making his way to the back of the basement when he came to a dead stop. "Shit, there's someone in this one!"

Hazel now ran to the back of the room. With the light from Officer Morris's flashlight, she could see a small and overly thin boy lying in nothing but his underwear on the bare cement floor. She reached in through the bars and grabbed his tiny wrist. "He has a pulse, not much of one, but something. Get those fucking EMTs down here now, and get some goddamn bolt cutters to cut this lock. *I mean now, people!*"

Everyone other than Sam and Hazel ran up the stairs.

Bending over once more, Hazel took the boy's hand and started rubbing it. It was freezing. "Sam, I have a bad feeling about all this. You don't think this has anything to do with the Parksville murders, do you? I mean, after all these years?" Hazel asked with a slight tinge of fear in her voice.

"Hazel, that case is over. The man responsible is dead. Take my word on that. This—whatever this is—has nothing to do with Parksville." Sam said this with such conviction that Hazel at once started to relax.

"Looks like there have been others down here. What the hell were they doing?" said Hazel.

Just then the room filled with light. Turning, Hazel and Sam saw Officer Hicks standing on the top of one of the cages screwing in a light bulb. "It was loose is all," he said, jumping down. "I count fifteen cages, all empty except for that one," he added, pointing to where Hazel was bent. "And look—all the windows are painted black."

Sam and Hazel looked around. It was true. All the small basement windows were painted black. "Good work, Hicks. Obviously, he did not want anyone seeing what in the fuck was going on down here," said Hazel.

Officer Jackson now ran down the steps with a pair of bolt cutters. He raced over to the cage.

"That padlock is going to be bitch to cut," said Sam.

But before Hazel could even move out of the way, the oversize Jackson had snipped the lock, which landed with a loud clank on the hard cement floor. Next came the EMTs running down the steps. Hazel and Sam moved quickly out of their way to let them work.

• • • • • • • • ● ○○○○○○○○○ ○ ○

Chad Timberlake drove his new BMW up to the front door of the Prescott estate. The colors of fall were amazing this year, and the Prescott estate's front driveway was lined in maples all ablaze with red leaves. The estate loomed large with its three stories of aged red brick draped in ivy from bottom to top. As he walked up to the front door, Martin, the Prescott's butler was there to meet him. *Martin must be in his nineties by now*, Chad thought, *and they're still working the old bastard to death no doubt.*

"Please come in, Mr. Timberlake. Her lady is on the phone and has asked me to tell you to take a seat in the Orchid Room, and she will be with you momentarily," said Martin with his hand pointing to the room off to his left.

Chad grinned. He was used to this game. Agnes Prescott was audacious, to say the least. She took sport in making those with an appointment to see her wait, sometimes up to an hour, just to show her importance. But over the past few years Chad had come to enjoy the wait. The Orchid Room lived up to its name, with the most beautiful orchids he had ever seen hanging near every window. To Agnes, it was a game. To Chad, it was a few minutes of peace and quiet.

After about twenty minutes, Martin returned to show Chad to Agnes's home office. Chad walked through the open door that was at once closed by the obedient Martin. Agnes sat behind her large mahogany desk. Her tight, wrinkled old face was pasted in makeup in a feeble attempt to make herself look younger than she really was.

Before Chad had even reached the chair across from her desk, she began. "Chad, here are the requests from the society that need taken care of. First, the Henderson family has requested that the new Blind Bull Steak House be subject to a surprise health inspection," said Agnes, reading from a small writing pad she had placed on her desk.

"For goodness' sake, Agnes, that would make the fourth this year. That's twice as many as any other restaurant in town," protested Chad, nervously taking his seat. "I mean, Larry needs to be reasonable bout this."

"They are effecting his dinner crowd," said Agnes abruptly. "As a member of the society, it is your duty to represent the society and its members and to follow my requests."

"I know, but there are limits on what I can do."

"Chad, you are where you are because of the society. Just make this happen, I will inform Larry this is the last time if you insist, but for now …" Agnes said, closing the subject. "Next, I hear they are thinking about showing that nasty *Rocky Horror Picture Show* at the Michigan Theater again; all those kids running around in their underwear—it's not acceptable."

"But, Agnes, it brings in a lot of money to the theater and—"

"And nothing. It's disgusting, and I will not have it."

"Fine. I will talk to them."

Agnes gave him a smile. She knew he would give her no more trouble. "Next—"

Before Agnes could carry on with her demands, a loud knocking came at her office door. "Madam, I am sorry, but Mr. Henderson is here; said it's most important," came Martin's frail voice from behind the door.

"Speak of the devil," said Agnes. "Show him in, please."

With that, Larry Henderson, owner and chef of the Under the Oaks Steak House, the classiest restaurant in Jackson, came bounding through the door. Half out of breath, he made his announcement, "Agnes, there are police cars outside the property on Grinnell Street."

"Fuck," said Chad.

"Language, Chad. I don't allow vulgarity in my house," said Agnes. "Please continue, Larry."

"I was driving by, and it looks like every cop in town is there," said Larry, trying to catch his breath.

Agnes stood and made her way around her desk. She was lost in thought. Both men sat quietly waiting for her response. "Larry, pass the word. I want a meeting of the society here in my house tonight. Do you understand me?" spoke Agnes at last.

"Look, I don't think that is such a good idea. Shouldn't we wait until we know a little more?" asked Chad.

"I want the meeting tonight," Agnes snapped.

"I was just thinking maybe we should—" started Chad.

"No, I want the meeting tonight. And, Chad, until it is your family's turn to wear this ring," she said, flashing a large band of silver inlaid with rubies, with one large cluster in the middle in the shape of a large rose, "we will do as I say."

Neither man uttered another word.

· · · · · · · · ● ○○○○○○○○ ○ ○

Hazel sat in little John Doe's emergency room waiting for an update from the doctors. The boy was in bad shape; that much was certain. With no family to spend these agonizing hours on his behalf, she took the mantle and held fast. For the past five hours, she had held the boy's hand as nurses and doctors gave shots, took readings, and put in one IV after another. *How much fluid can this kid hold?* she thought. The last updated had been over four hours ago, when the ER doctor had told her that it was still touch and go; he was severely dehydrated, and they were having a hard time getting a stable heartbeat. The doctor added that, at this point, he was afraid of kidney failure and, worse yet, the drop in blood pressure, depriving his small body of oxygen.

"We are moving him to the intensive care unit," said one of the nurses as she came into the room. "If you like, you can wait out in the waiting room. We will notify you when we have him all settled in."

With that, Hazel released the boy's hand, and more out of maternal instinct than anything else, kissed him on the forehead.

The nurse gave her a smile. "His pressure is finally coming up a little. I think he will be fine," she added.

As Hazel pushed the button to open the security doors at the end of the hall separating the main waiting room from the emergency room, she saw Vinnie sitting waiting for her just beyond the door. A smile came over her face; at least someone else was here for her to talk to.

"How's the kid?" asked Vinnie, with true concern in his voice.

Hazel repeated everything the doctors had been saying about the boy's condition and that they were moving him to the intensive care unit.

"You need a break; did you even eat lunch?" asked Vinnie.

"No, not a bite since breakfast," responded Hazel.

"How about us going up to the cafeteria? I'll buy," said Vinnie, not reacting to Hazel's gasp of wonderment.

"You are going to buy me lunch?"

"Oh, be nice. God only knows when the offer will come again. I can fill you in on what we know so far."

And with that, the two made their way to the elevators in the main lobby.

• • • • • • • • • • ● ○○○○○○ ○ ○ ○ ○

Sam stood looking at the piles of meat stuffed into plastic containers on his examination table, all marked by their position on the kitchen table at the Grinnell house. He marveled at the brute strength it must have taken to cut the body up so neatly with nothing more than a meat cleaver. This was no mere murder; this madman had taken his time, cutting through meat and bone. There simply was no way to determine the fatal blow, no way of knowing if the man had died quickly, or slowly as parts were being hacked off him. The head was intact, no signs of trauma and no cut marks above the neck. With any luck, the bastard got his head cut off with the first blow. It sounded brutal, but it would have been the quickest way for him to die.

My first day back and this shit happens, thought Sam. He had been downsized, to put it in the best of terms, from his last job. It seems that it was cheaper for the county in which he worked to write an interlocal agreement and share the medical examiner's duties across borders. Deep down, Sam knew this made perfect sense. He had been so bored at his last job he had often thought about moving on anyway. He was surprised when he heard of the opening in Jackson County and even more surprised when his wife, Linda, told him to apply. Sam knew it was not easy for her to leave her hometown and drag their two girls out of school to make the move, but she never let on that it affected her in the least. She was his angel. Why she had fallen in love with him was beyond him; it sure as hell was not for his good looks. Whatever the reason God had blessed him, he would be forever grateful.

Slowly and methodically, he began his work. Now that they knew who he was, maybe he could figure out some clues to help the police figure out who had killed him and why. Deep down, he had the feeling that no questions would be answered from this mess, but he had to try. *Why didn't I go into family practice like my mother wanted me to?* he thought.

• • • • • • • • • ● ○○○○○○○○ ° ° °

Hazel and Vinnie took a seat in the half-empty cafeteria. Vinnie had passed on lunch, stating he had already eaten, but Hazel knew that Vinnie was one hell of a picky eater. Every time they went out to lunch, it took him forever to pick something off the menu, and then when he would finally make up his mind, he added his special request, no onions, no peppers, none of this, and none that. It was no wonder the man was so thin. Standing six feet five did not help; it seemed to make him look even skinnier than he truly was.

"We identified the victim as one David Willmore. He was the owner of the property, twenty-six-year-old white male. After Sam cleaned the blood from his face, we could positively identify him," said Vinnie.

"He lived in the house alone?" asked Hazel, mostly to solidify what she already knew.

"Yep, he was single; no family other than his father that we know of. Get this. His father owns and operates a butcher shop on West Michigan Ave. He's been there for years."

"You have got to be kidding me right. I mean talk about irony."

"Maybe not. Seems the kid worked there as a meat cutter for most of his childhood. He moved out at twenty-one and bought that house on Grinnell."

"How does a twenty-one-year-old kid come up with enough money to buy a house?" asked Hazel.

"Good question. There is no lean on the house. Seems he paid cash," answered Vinnie. "And get this. When Jackson and I went to the dad's shop to notify him his only beloved offspring was dead, the bastard showed absolutely no remorse at all; I mean nothing. He, more or less, told us it was none of his concern, and if we needed him for anything it would have to wait until after he closed his fucking shop for the day. Can you believe that?"

Hazel just sat there in bewilderment munching on her daily special of burritos and rice. "Tomorrow, I want the father brought in for questioning. He obviously had the skills to butcher his own son. We need to see if we can determine a motive. Maybe he offed him to get the house. Check and see if there was an insurance policy or some kind of will."

"We're still going through all the paperwork found at the house. We will check with his bank as well," said Vinnie, taking notes on his little green pad.

"It would help if we could pin him to the location—prints, DNA, something. What about footprints, all that blood on the floor?"

"None, and I dusted every inch of that house. That man must have been some kind of germophobe. I mean there was so little to pick up, and his whole house smelt like bleach. I will have to wait for the lab, but it looks like all the prints match, even the ones on the meat cleaver. I think they are all his."

"The killer must have worn gloves. The man didn't hack himself to death, for God's sake," said Hazel. "What about the basement, all those cages—anything down there?"

"No prints anywhere, other than the cage the kid was in. Either I'm right and this guy was a neat freak and polished those cages or—and let's hope I'm wrong—the kid was the only one."

"Highly unlikely. Those cages were there for a reason, and now it seems the only ones that can answer that question, that we know of, are either lying in pieces in Sam's office or fighting for their life in intensive care," said Hazel with a hint of agitation in her voice. "There has to be more in that house, something."

"Some of the other cages had carpet squares, dog dishes, blankets, and a plastic bucket. We found more of each piled behind the stairs, enough for each cage. So, if he was the only one, he undoubtedly was planning on having more inmates."

"What about the boy's cage? I don't remember any blankets or carpet?" asked Hazel with a look of concern.

"Just the bucket," replied Vinnie. "Maybe he was being punished for something."

Now Hazel's face became red with rage. Vinnie had never seen her so upset. "He wasn't the first Vinnie, and if someone wouldn't have put a stop to it, he wouldn't have been the last. Maybe the bastard just got what was coming to him. Maybe the dad did us all a favor."

It was half past seven by the time Agnes Prescott called the meeting of the Primrose Society to order. Around the large round table placed in her immense office sat the elders of six of Jackson's most prominent families—each member sitting in order according to his or her family's chance to chair the society. Agnes sat at the end closest to her desk, and on her left sat City Commissioner Chad Timberlake. His family was next in line to take control of the Primrose Society and the coveted ring that symbolized that right. Next to him, going around the table, sat Larry Henderson, who owned the finest restaurant in town, along with any number of food chains that most people of the town did not know about. Then sat Earl Southworth. He owned most of the small party stores in town. The following member at the table was Barbra Wentworth, the most expensive attorney in town. The family's law firm had been ranked one of the town's biggest moneymakers for over the past forty years. Last, but not least, sat the bank president, Mark Cross. The following two chairs remained empty.

"And where is our good Dr. Hendershot?" question Earl Southworth, looking at the empty chairs.

"And our newest member?" added Barbra.

"I met with both of them this afternoon. They are tending to the business at hand," replied Agnes in her courteous yet sarcastic manner.

"And just what is the business at hand, Agnes? All we know is the house on Grinnell was raided this morning. I do hope you have more information to pass forward to the group," said Barbra.

"Dear Barbra, I seriously doubt I would waste my time or

yours if I did not," Agnes said coldly. "We know that young David is dead. He apparently was cut into little pieces."

This was met with a unified gasp from the assemblage.

"What about the basement? Was anyone still down there?" asked Chad nervously, tapping the table with his fingertips.

"Yes," said Agnes, putting her hand on Chad's to stop him from tapping. "One boy. No word on if he will make it through the night, but we have that matter well in hand."

"What do you mean well in hand?!" yelled Earl, jumping up and slamming his hand on the table. "Damn it, Agnes, a little more information would be helpful. Do we need to run to the hills or not?"

"Sit down, you old pompous ass," said Barbra. "It's called plausible deniability, fool. I for one do not want to know how it is taken care of, only that it will be and soon."

"They kept no records at the house like we agreed I hope?" asked Chad directly to Agnes.

"No, no records," she replied.

"We should have kept doing things the old way," said Mark. "We never should have used a broker for something like this, and sure as hell we should never have funded it."

"Well," said Agnes as she stood to her feet, "we did, and now we must make sure that the society endures. Once the issue of the boy is addressed, I see no further need for concern. You will all go about your daily activities as if nothing has changed. It is important that no one draws attention to themselves. I am in good faith that no one here will step out of line. In a few weeks, this will all pass."

"We need to talk about changes to the society," said Chad, avoiding Agnes's eyes.

"This society has survived because of our heritage and tradition. When you wear this ring, Chad, then, and only then, can you talk of change. This meeting is now over," said Agnes, dismissing the group with the wave of her hand.

• • • • • • • • • ● ○○○○○○○○○○

Hazel sat in the hospital room in silence. The nurse told her that the boy's vital signs had stabilized, and his blood pressure was back to normal. She then informed her that the doctors were changing shifts, and Dr. Smith would be in to check on him within the hour. Hazel gave instructions to Vinnie to send up someone to relieve her at ten and stand watch outside his door till morning. He may be the only witness who could testify as to what atrocities were taking place, and she sure as hell was not going to let him out of their sights.

I hope the doctor gets here before my relief shows up, thought Hazel. She really wanted to talk to him and make sure the boy was okay before she left. Just then, she heard the boy shifting in his bed; this was accompanied with a loud moan. As she looked over, she saw the boy staring at her as if in disbelief.

"Well, hello there," she said, walking over and taking his hand in hers. "You gave use quite the scare."

The boy did not move. Nor did he say a word. He just lay there, staring up at her face. Hazel noticed how warm his hand was now; it had been so cold in the basement. His eyes were sunken way back in his head, and his timid little face showed no signs of emotion. Hazel wanted to send a barrage of questions his way but knew now was not the time. He seemed so helpless, so alone. She reached over without looking and pulled her chair up next to the bed, never letting go of the boy's hand.

"Well, look who's awake," said the nurse coming through the door. She had been so nice to Hazel since she gotten up there to see him. Twice she'd brought her coffee.

The boy gave her a quick glance and then turned his eyes back to Hazel.

Just then a doctor, rather short in stature and plump in the middle, came into the room. He seemed rather taken back to see Hazel sitting in the chair next to the bed. "Are you family?" he asked abruptly.

"No. I am here in a professional capacity. I am Captain Cowan of the JPD," she responded.

"Oh, I see," he said, walking to the other side of the bed. "Has he spoken yet?"

"No, Doctor," responded the nurse. "He just woke up."

"Nurse, will you see if the results of Mr. Hopkins MRI are back for me please? I want to check them before I complete my rounds."

"Not a problem," said the nurse, giving him a strange look.

Something was not right. Hazel could tell. Still, the nurse obediently did as she was told and left the room.

"I am sorry, but can you step outside for a while. I need to check him over," said the doctor to Hazel.

But Hazel did not move. She sat defiantly in her seat.

"Look, I do not mean to be rude—"

"Then don't be," snapped Hazel. "It's not like I've never see a naked little boy before. I have kids of my own, you know." This was, in fact, a lie. She had always wanted children, but her career and the lack of compatible suitors had kept her from it. Still, she had a strong feeling about not leaving the boy alone, even if he were a doctor. *There was something about the way the nurse looked at him before she left.*

"Fine, fine, whatever," said the doctor, caving in. "Stay if you must, but please be quiet." He pulled a syringe out of his pocket and drew into it from a small vile he held in his left hand. "I am going to give you a little something for nausea," he said to the boy and then bent over to administer the shot.

That's when it all started. The boy turned and, for the first time, looked up at the doctor. His eyes widened, as if he had seen a ghost. The doctor had just started administering the shot when the syringe went flying out of his hand and stuck in the wall, just inches from Hazel's head.

"What the hell?" said the doctor.

The boy lay there, just staring at the doctor as if the devil himself was behind him. Without warning, the tray table between them flipped over, knocking the doctor to the floor. Two nurses came running into the room to see what had caused all the commotion.

The first nurse through the door was the same one who had been there all day. The other one Hazel had not seen until that moment. Hazel stood, but she was too scared to move.

Before the doctor could react, the doctor's entire body levitated off the ground. The look of terror on his face was beyond measure. Then, as if launched from a cannon, he flew headfirst into the outside window. Glass flew everywhere, and he landed hard on the floor, his face a bloody mess. Both nurses gave out an ear-piercing scream.

The man slowly and painfully pulled himself into a sitting position, his back against the wall. A plea for help was written in his eyes. But whatever was going on was not done yet. A large shard of glass rose from the hospital room floor. It moved across the room, ending up just inches from Hazel's face, where it hovered for a few moments. Then slowly, it turned until it was perfectly horizontal. With the jagged edge pointing toward the doctor, it shot itself straight into the top of the doctor's head, slicing off a large portion of scalp and bone before penetrating deep into the wall above his bleeding head.

Hazel could only stand there in total disbelief. Slowly, the body was pulled out from the wall, the top of head scraping against the glass as if some invisible being had grabbed him by the collar. Within seconds, the body was off the floor once again, floating limp in thin air. The doctor's arms and legs dangled toward the floor, and blood dripped from his head. For just a spilt moment, Hazel thought she could see his brains displayed through the small hole in his skull.

As the nurses both screamed yet again, the body was sent sailing, only this time it went smashing straight through the broken window. Everyone in the room could hear it landing hard on top of an unseen car below. They distinguished the landing spot to be a car because, at once, a car alarm screamed to life. Both nurses ran to what was left of the window.

In contrast, the still shaken Hazel turned her attention to the little boy on the bed. He was out cold. Hazel grabbed the syringe that was still stuck in the wall and pulled it out. She then turned. "I want to know what is in this syringe, and I want to know right now!" she yelled at the two distraught nurses, who were both sobbing as they gazed out the window at all the commotion below.

After some time, the nice nurse who had been so helpful all day turned slowly. "I will look at his chart," she said, whimpering. "My God, did you see that?" she asked, walking over to the foot of the bed. She was trying hard to stop her sobs, her body still shaking uncontrollably. "He was not due for any medication," she said, looking down at the boy's chart.

"But the doctor had just started giving him a shot, with this," said Hazel, holding up the syringe.

"Only nurses dispense medication," the nurse said, through sobs.

"Listen, listen to me closely," said Hazel, grabbing the young woman by her shoulders. "What's your name?"

"Judy," replied the nurse. "That's Sue by the window."

"Listen, Judy, I know things are crazy right now. Trust me, I am scared to death. But I think Dr. Smith was trying to kill the boy. I need to know what this is," said Hazel, holding up the syringe and trying desperately to remain as calm as possible.

"That's just it. That's Dr. Hendershot. He's not even his patient," Judy said, a look of bewilderment on her face.

"There is a crowd gathering outside," said Sue, keeping her post at the window.

"Judy, please, can you tell me what's in this. We may still have time to save the boy," Hazel pleaded once more.

"What's this?" said Sue, picking up a small vile from the

floor just below the window. "This must have been in his pocket just before …" She burst into tears again.

"For God's sake, woman, it's probably what's in the syringe. What is it?"

Nurse Sue wiped her eyes and looked down. "Oh, my God. I hope not. This is potassium chloride."

"Shit. Go get Dr. Smith, stat!" yelled Judy to Sue.

There was no need. The commotion from the room had drawn security, every nurse on the floor, some of the ambulatory patients, and Dr. Smith himself, who had just arrived when Sue was talking about the potassium chloride. Pushing through the crowd at the door, the young man at once started asking questions.

"Okay, first of all, who gave my patient a shot of potassium chloride?!" he demanded.

"It was Dr. Hendershot," replied Judy.

"Shit," said the young Dr. Smith. "Was his blood pressure dropping again?"

"No. His blood pressure has been fine for the past three hours," answered Nurse Judy.

"I want blood work done, stat," he said, turning to Nurse Sue.

"Yes, Doctor," she answered.

The front of the room by the door was now filling with onlookers.

"I'm sorry, Miss. Who are you?" he asked of Hazel.

"Captain Cowan of the JCPD," she replied.

"Captain, can you help get these people out of here for me?" he said to Hazel.

"Sure," responded Hazel, trying desperately to keep her wits about her.

She at once started backing people out of the room.

"I want a calcium chloride infusion, dextrose, and insulin diluted in water ready just in case," he yelled out to both nurses. "Do we know the dosage?"

"This is what is left," said Hazel, handing him the syringe.

"My God, that's enough to stop the heart of a raging bull," replied Dr. Smith. "But that still doesn't tell me how much the boy got. Are we sure he was even stuck?"

"I saw him put the needle in, but I don't know how much, if any, he gave the boy," said Hazel, still motioning for people to vacate the room.

"Nurse," Dr. Smith said to the still sniffling Judy, "I need you to compose yourself. Can you do that for me?"

Nurse Judy gave him a half-hearted nod of her head.

"Prepare another room, and I want him monitored for any signs of slow or irregular heartbeat, seizures, or shallow breathing. Did you get all that?"

"Yes, Doctor," she replied.

"Now, for God's sake, can anyone tell me what in the hell just happened in here?" he asked in a loud firm voice.

"I can," said Hazel, "at least what I saw."

Dr. Smith looked at her with his stern eyes and gave a nod of his head for her to begin.

• • • • • • • • • ● ○○○○○○○○○○ ○

Agnes was sitting up in bed drinking her chamomile tea and enjoying a rather raunchy romance novel when the phone rang. *Whoever could that be this late?* she pondered and then reached over to pick it up.

"Agnes, this is Earl. Fredrick is dead," came the voice on the other end. "They think he was murdered at the hospital, but it's unclear as to what really happened."

"They think, what do you mean they think? Slow down and start at the beginning, for goodness' sake," Agnes said with more than just a touch of concern in her voice.

"Look, I just hung up with his wife. The woman is beside herself. It appears he was pushed out of a patient's window at the hospital. I am on my way right now to pick her up. Sorry, but that is all I know."

"What about the boy? Is he dead?" asked Agnes, grasping for straws.

"Who the hell knows. I will try and find out when I get there."

"Do that, Earl, and let me know," she said sternly.

"Will do. Got to go," said Earl, and the other end of the phone went silent.

Agnes sat on her bed contemplating for the longest time. Their one chance to get to the boy was maybe gone. *But, still, what does the boy even know? Nothing that can tie that house to the society. But still ...* Agnes thought long and hard. There was still another issue that she knew needed addressed, one her feebleminded comrades had over looked. She made up her mind what her next step needed to be. "It's time for the big guns," she said out loud. Still holding the phone, she began to dial.

• • • • • • • • ● ○○○○○○○○○ ○ ○

At the same time that Agnes Prescott was dialing her phone, Hazel was finally pulling into her drive. This had been the craziest day of her life. As she shut off the engine and grabbed her purse, a feeling of dread came over her. It was all too much to take in—the house, the boy, the doctor, and the endless questions. She tried but could not get the images of what she had seen out of her head, especially the look of panic on the doctor's face when he was first lifted off the ground.

Though unexpected, it was nice to see Officer Brian Hicks standing in the door of her back porch dressed only in his shorts.

"So, how is the kid?" he asked.

Hazel simply walked past him, across the porch, and into the house, where she plopped her purse down on the table and continued her way to the living room. "Can we talk about anything else other than the case tonight, Hicks?"

"You know, eventually you will need to use my first name," he said, following her into the living room with two large snifters of wine.

"No, because then I will slip up and call you Brian at work," she said, sitting softly on the sofa and kicking off her shoes.

She and Brian had been dating for a little over two months, and over his objections, they'd agreed to keep it strictly between themselves. Even though there were no rules about her dating one of her direct reports, she knew if word got out, it would cause nothing but trouble. Besides, she knew this thing with Brian would not last. He was a great guy, but the last thing she ever wanted was to get romantically involved with another cop. When Brian's father died a couple of months before, she'd felt a need to give him comfort. That had turned into dating and then a little more.

Brian handed her one of the snifters of wine. "There is leftover takeout in the fridge if want me to warm it up for you," he said.

"You are the sweetest guy," said Hazel. "But I'm good."

"Well how about I carry you upstairs and do nasty things to you?" he asked, quickly moving his eyebrows up and down.

"Not tonight," she said. "But if you could just hold me, that would be nice."

Hicks walked over to Hazel and sat next to her on the coach and then he put his arm around her. She laid her head on his shoulder, and she began to cry.

Brian looked down and grabbed her by the chin, softly lifting her head so her eyes met his. "What's wrong?"

"I don't know. It's just been a long day."

CHAPTER 2

Sam's Dilemma

In the early morning, just before dawn, Sam Helmen sat waiting for his breakfast. Linda had just poured him his second cup of coffee and was finishing his eggs, over easy, and buttering his toast. "Linda," said Sam, "I know this maybe out of left field, but if you knew a certain police captain would object to you doing something, even if you knew it may help prevent future murders, would you do it?"

Linda turned and gave him that look of cut the bullshit. "What you really want to know is whether pissing Hazel off by going behind her back is okay if the outcome is what you want?"

Sam smiled. "Okay, okay, yes. There is someone I think I need to talk to, but I am not sure that Hazel will approve."

"Now, Sam, you know what I am going to tell you, but here it is anyway. Talk to Hazel, even if you are not asking her permission; let her know what you are intending to do." She walked over and put her arms around his neck. "Sam, you are the most honest person I have ever met. You're not good with lying about anything. I know it, and everyone who knows you knows it too."

"Well, there were things about the Parksville murders I never told anyone," said Sam somewhat impressed with himself.

"I know. You never even talked about it with me, and that's okay. But I know you, Sam. Keeping this from Hazel would drive you nuts. Just go talk to her." With that, Linda walked back over to the stove to flip his eggs.

Sam sat lost in thought. *What if I call first and then tell Hazel? She might be mad, but at least it will be done.*

With that, he got up and walked over to the phone hanging on the wall and dialed a number he knew by heart. Sam had met Phillip Parker when he'd assisted their good friend Captain Kip Gilmore of the JPD during the Parksville murders. Sam and Phillip had been good friends ever since. Hazel had always felt Phillip had taken part in Kip's demise, but Sam knew different. Whatever it was doing all the killings so long ago, Phillip had been a part of putting an end to it. Phillip had never told him the whole story, and Sam had not asked. He knew that Phillip had been there the night Kip died, knew there was more to the story that Phillip kept to himself, and yes even knew that something unnatural had taken place. After hearing about the occurrence at the hospital, he had a feeling Phillip would be the man to talk to.

Linda smiled as she put his eggs on a plate with his toast. "I will be in the other room. Tell her when you're done," is all she said as she walked into the living room. Once there, she yelled for the rest of the Helmen family to emerge for breakfast. Linda always made sure Sam had his privacy when talking to someone on the phone about work.

Sam was starting to worry he had called too early in the morning, but he knew that Phillip Parker was an early riser. As the phone rang with no answer, he was about to hang up when a familiar voice came on the line.

"Hello. This is Franky."

It was Franky Lake, Phillip Parker's good friend and confidant. "Hello, Franky. It's Sam. I am back in Jackson—can you believe it?—moved back just a couple of days ago."

"Oh, Sam, that's great. We've missed you," said Franky.

"Hey, is Phillip around? I need to talk to him."

This was followed by an unusually long pause.

"Franky, everything all right. Did something happen to Phillip?" Sam asked at last.

Again, there was a long pause. "I can't go into details right now, Sam, especially over the phone," came Franky's now quite voice. "I can just tell you that Phillip and one of our good friends from Dublin are both missing."

"Missing? How long?" said Sam with concern in his voice.

"Well, about three months. He disappeared down in Tampa, Florida. We got people looking but ..."

"Oh, Franky, I am so sorry to hear that. Is there anything I can do to help?"

"We filed a missing person's report, hired a private investigator; nothing yet. Do you think talking to Captain Cowan could help?"

A million thoughts now rushed through Sam's head. "No!" said Sam, a little too loudly. "Now would not be the time. You know she still suspects you and Phillip of being part of Kip's death. I don't think now is the time to let her know he is missing. That would just raise more questions than we need asked right now. We will talk to her, I promise, but let's just hold off for now."

"Whatever you think is best. We can do lunch, and I can

tell you more," Franky responded in half a question, half a statement.

"That would be nice, but for now please try and keep a low profile. I will explain later."

"Will do," replied Franky. "God, it's so nice hearing your voice again."

As Sam hung up the phone, he had a sickening feeling. He closed his eyes and said a quick silent prayer for Phillip and his safe return. In regard to this case, he knew he was on his own.

• • • • • • • • ● ○○○○○○○○○ ○ ○

Hazel marched into her office, avoiding everyone she met on the way. As she passed Vinnie's desk, she whispered, "My office, now please."

Vinnie looked up and, without saying a word, got up to follow Hazel.

Once inside her office, Hazel shut the door behind them. "You are not going to believe what I am about to tell you," she said, taking her seat behind the desk.

"Man, there are rumors flying around the office that someone killed the kid's doctor, threw him out of a window, and you saw the whole thing and did nothing, on and on," said Vinnie, preferring to stand rather than sit. "I mean, wow, the accident is all over the news this morning. The major is wanting us to make a statement to the press. It's been crazy."

"Well if you shut up for a minute, I will tell you the whole story, but for God's sake keep it between us."

Vinnie just stood there staring at Hazel for a moment and then took a seat. Hazel's mood was somber to say the least. He could sense the determination it was taking for her to retell her story.

For the next thirty-five minutes, she went over her ordeal the night before. She told him about the doctor's failed attempt to murder the kid and then the doctor being confronted by some indiscernible force, about the shard of glass severing the top of the doctor's head open, and finally about the invisible intruder flinging him out the window. Vinnie sat without interrupting once. He knew if anyone else had told him this story, he would have walked out halfway through, but this was Hazel. Hazel had her shit together more than any person he had known his whole life. He did not question, because if Hazel said it, it happened.

"Well," said Hazel when she was finally done, "how fucking crazy am I?"

"Where there any witness that saw it?"

"The nurses in the room told the exact same story to the hospital administration."

Hazel leaned back in her chair waiting for Vinnie's smart-ass comment, but the first words out of his mouth were, "Maybe the kid has one hell of a defense system. Maybe he knew that bastard was going to kill him somehow and—"

"And what? It sounds crazy," said Hazel, getting up and looking out the window.

"There are stories about people with—oh, what do you call it?—ESP. Maybe this kid is some kind of fucking mutant with super brain power," said Vinnie, putting his fingers to his head and then making it look as if his mind had just blown up.

"Believe it or not, that's what Dr. Smith said." Hazel did

not turn around but kept her concentration out the window, as if turning and looking Vinnie directly in the eyes would make it seem too real. "I've got to get back up to that hospital. If we are wrong and the kid is, in some way, merely an honest bystander, then his life could possibly be in jeopardy. I doubt the doctor acted alone. There is a reason someone wants him dead, and I want to know what it is."

"Well, you are not going alone. I am going with you," said Vinnie.

Hazel did not put up an argument. In fact, she was glad he had volunteered. She would feel safer with someone else along this time. "Tell Hicks and Jackson I want them to pick up the butcher this afternoon and bring him in for questioning before we go. I don't care if the bastard has to close shop early or not. I still think he knows more than what he is telling, and I want a few minutes alone with him to make him talk."

"Will do," said Vinnie, who turned and walked out to relay the message and grab his coat.

•••••••••●○○○○○○○○○○

Agnes Prescott was finishing applying what she aptly called her war paint. Her morning regiment took over a half hour to complete. Lilly, her maid, was in the oversize walk-in bedroom closet putting away laundry and listening, as she did every morning, to Agnes's endless list of things she wanted done that day.

The vanity at which Agnes sat at was an antique, dating back to the Victorian era. Its natural wood finish clashed with the otherwise white decor—white sheets with a white comforter, white curtains, white carpet, and all white furnishings. The vanity's impressive mirror swiveled between two arms reaching halfway up its length from its base. Throughout the years, all the staff had learned to never touch the mirror. Even when cleaning it, it had to be placed back exactly in the position Agnes had left it.

"Lilly, you will need to drive me into town today. I am meeting Ms. Wentworth for lunch at Under the Oaks," said Agnes. She heard a sigh come from the closet. "Now none of that. Martin is just getting too scary to ride with, the old bat."

"Yes, Ms.," came a defeated reply.

As Agnes turned to respond to Lilly's less-than-enthusiastic response, her mirror moved upward a good inch.

"Damn, when we get back, I need Martin to tighten this mirror." Agnes said this more to herself than Lilly.

All of the sudden the mirror, all by itself, spun completely around, barely clearing the back wall, and stopped right back in its original position. Agnes now jumped back, knocking over her stool. As she did so, she stepped on something with her bare feet that sent a shockwave of pain up her spine. Looking down, she saw a child's toy, a race car. "Lilly, get in here now!"

"Yes, Ms.," said Lilly, running back into the bedroom.

"Did you see that?" mumbled Agnes.

"See what, Ms.?" she responded and walked over to where Agnes now stood by the bed.

Agnes looked at her for a moment and then back to the mirror and then back to Lilly. "Nothing, nothing." She stood there for a moment, trying to take in what had just happened. *It was all in your mind, you crazy old woman,* she thought to herself. *You are driving yourself crazy with all this nonsense going on; starting to see things that are not real.*

"Now how did this get in here?" said Lilly, reaching down and picking up the toy from the floor. "This belongs in the nursery."

"I stepped on the damn thing. Hurt like hell!" Agnes bellowed.

"Sorry, Ms., I don't know how it could have gotten in here. We haven't had kids in the house since your grandchildren were small," Lilly said sheepishly.

"I better not hear of any staff thinking they have to right to bring their nasty little children or grandchildren, nieces, nephews, or any other goddamn child in this house, and especially in my bedroom. Do I make myself clear!" snapped Agnes.

"Yes, Ms., but I can tell you there have been no children, none," said Lilly, slowly backing up. "I would tell you, I promise."

"Good, because it will be you out on the streets if it happens again, understand?" With that, Agnes turned and walked out of the bedroom, yelling back over her shoulder, "Remember we are leaving for town at noon."

· · · · · · · · ● ○○○○○○○○ ○ ○

Arriving at the hospital, Hazel and Vinnie made their way to the main elevator on the first floor. As they entered, there stood Nurse Judy, who Hazel had met the night before. She was not dressed in her scrubs but, rather, in a nice pair of jeans and top.

At once, she smiled at Hazel. "Hi. Are you going to the meeting as well?"

"What meeting is that?" asked Hazel.

"The hospital administrator told me to come in. He has some questions. Seems there is some detective that wants to get my statement," said Judy, taking time to give a smile Vinnie's way.

"Oh, I'm sorry. This is Detective Moretti."

With that, Vinnie offered his hand.

"But I took your statement last night. What detective is wanting this?"

"Hell if I know," she responded, shaking Vinnie's hand, the smile never leaving her face as she gazed up at him.

As the door opened up to the second floor, Nurse Judy started to walk out. But Hazel grabbed her arm. "Just a minute. I am going with you."

Vinnie looked surprised, as they had just pushed the button for the fifth floor where the boy's room was. "Vinnie, please wait for me in the car. I will be down shortly," said Hazel.

"But—" responded Vinnie.

"I'll explain later. Now, please, just wait for me in the car," said Hazel, letting go of the elevator door and letting it close. Slowly Vinnie's confused face disappeared, and Hazel turned her attention to Judy. "Who all is in this meeting, do you know?"

"Not a clue."

As they made their way down the hall, they talked about the night before. Hazel could see the look of uneasiness in Judy's face as she recounted the events. At the end of the hall was a large lobby area that seemed out of place for the rest of the uniform hospital appearance. This section looked more like an office waiting room one might see at some big corporation. A receptionist sat at a single desk next to a large door with a sign that said "Board Conference Room."

"Are you two here for the meeting this morning?"

"Yes, we are," answered Hazel before Judy could respond.

"Go on in," said the receptionist, pointing to the conference door. With that, she returned to her computer.

Hazel followed Judy into the room. At once, everyone around the table looked up. There were three individuals dressed in white lab coats, Nurse Sue dressed in her scrubs, and a man dressed in a cheap suit. At the head sat a man who Hazel recognized at once as Samar Khatri, the hospital's chief administrator.

"Officer Cowan, how nice of you to join us, though I don't remember seeing you on the invitation list," said the man in the cheap suit.

It took her a moment to recognize the man. He had lost a lot of weight and shaved off his gruesome mustache. It was Agent Alex Bibens of the FBI—the same man who had investigated the Parksville murders. "Agent Bibens, so nice to see you again. But that's Captain Cowan now," said Hazel with a sarcastic grin.

"I'm sorry, Captain, but this is no longer your case," said Bibens.

The woman who was dressed in the lab coat sitting between her two male counterparts spoke up. "No, please let her stay. She was there last night, and that is what this meeting is all about, isn't it?"

"I don't know," said Bibens, shaking his head in objection to Hazel remaining in the room.

"Well I do. Your department is in charge of the murder investigation, Agent Bibens, but my department is in charge of the boy. The more we know about his actions last night, the better we can prepare his new lodgings," said the lady in the white coat.

Bibens shifted in his seat. "And you are allowing three suspects in a murder investigation to hear each other's story before I have a chance for a formal investigation."

"Oh, for god's sake, I don't care who attends this meeting and who doesn't," said Samar Khatri. "I just want that boy out of my hospital as soon as possible. I talked to Captain Cowan last night. Trust me, you will get more out of her than you will these two." With that he pointed to the two nurses. "She was the only one who had her wits about her last night. If not, one of my doctors would have committed murder, in my hospital. I don't know what powers this young man has. Nor do I care." He said this in the direction of the three white coats. "And I don't give a damn as to why someone wanted him dead." This time, he was looking directly at Bibens. "I just don't want anyone else in the hospital, staff or patients, to get hurt. So, come in and sit down, Hazel, so we can get this done. You two can have your federal agency pissing contest later."

From that moment on, it did not matter who thought he or she was in charge; in his hospital, no one other than Samar Khatri would lead a meeting.

Hazel sat quietly at the table as the two nurses gave their accounts of what had occurred the night before. Hazel was amazed at how well they could recall the prior night's events. The white coats did not seem at all shocked or amazed at their telling of the story. The white coats then asked Hazel an unusual set of questions, like how much she thought the doctor weighed, how fast he had traveled across the room, how large was the piece of glass that had sliced the top of his off. They were not questions about what Hazel thought had taken place, but more about the mechanics of it all.

The group then turned their attention back to the two nurses. When both nurses had completed answering the questions posed by the team of three, they were allowed to leave the room. Both jumped out of their seats and headed for the door at a quickened pace. Hazel had seen the look of concern on their faces when Bibens made his statement about three suspects. From that point on, they'd seemed upset and shaken. She was glad to see it was over for them, at least for now.

"Who are you people?" Hazel finally asked after the two nurses closed the door behind them. This she asked directly to the white coats sitting at the table.

"You are not the one asking questions here," said Bibens.

"No, no. It's all right, Agent," said the female, turning her attention to Hazel. "We are with a federal agency that is not well known. And we, well to put it plainly, deal with unexplained phenomenon. We were contacted by Dr. Khatri last night. You see, he once held a position within the agency."

Hazel saw Samar nod his head.

"This is Dr. Moore on my left," she said pointing to an elderly gentleman, "and this is Dr. Johns on my right." This time, she pointed to a heavyset gentleman in his early thirties. My name is Dr. White; you can call me Nancy. We are here to see how the boy is able to do the things he is apparently doing. He is not the first child with extrasensory perception we have dealt with."

"I thought all that ESP stuff went out with the '70s. I mean I didn't know people still believed in it," said Hazel with a look of confusion on her face.

"Some people are born with a gift," responded Nancy, "though this one seems somewhat extreme."

"So, you think it was the boy who was responsible for all the shit that happened last night, don't you?" asked Hazel.

"Yes. We also think he killed the man in the house. We think he is trying to defend himself. I mean, God only knows what took place in that basement," responded Nancy.

"I, on the other hand, am not buying any of this. I am here to solve two murders," said Bibens, facing Nancy, "and thanks for giving three of my prime suspects an out." With that, he grabbed his notepad and started walking toward the door.

"How did you hear about this, Agent? I didn't call in the feds on this," asked Hazel before he could reach the door.

"Oh, no, Officer, I mean Captain"—this he said with a high level of sarcasm—"I will not be answering any of your questions today, but you will be answering mine," he added without turning around. Then just as he was ready to close the door behind him, he turned and looked Hazel directly in the eyes. "You still look as hot as ever, by the way." And with that, he was gone.

Hazel got a little shiver running down her spine.

"I detest that man," said Samar.

Hazel turned and faced the white coats. "So, where are you taking him, the boy?"

"Sorry, but we cannot say," said Dr. Moore.

"Wait, just wait," said Nancy. "Tell us a little more of your side of the story, Captain. Then we can make decisions as to who might have access to that information."

• • • • • • • • • ● ○○○○○○○○○ ○ ○

Outside the hospital, Vinnie was getting a little more than impatient. He knew Hazel had her reasons for making him return to the car, but that did not make the waiting any easier. He was just weighing his options of going into the hospital and poking around when he saw a man in a cheap suit walk directly in front of the car. Unlike Hazel, Vinnie recognized him at once; it was Agent Bibens. Something at that moment told him to turn away, so if the man looked, he would not see who it was inside the car. Vinnie doubted if the man would even remember who he was, but for some reason Vinnie held tight to the belief it was best not to be seen.

"What a dick," said Vinnie as the man got into his car and drove away. He knew that Kip had had no love for the man. And according to Hazel, he'd hit on her every chance he got last time he was in town.

Just a couple of minutes later, Hazel appeared at the passenger side door.

Opening the door to let herself in, she asked Vinnie, "Did you see who just pulled out of here?"

"Yeah, the FBI's finest," responded Vinnie.

"Did he see you?" asked Hazel.

"No. I made sure he didn't. Why?" Vinnie asked, not really wanting an answer.

"He was in the meeting. Afterward I saw him lurking outside the kid's open door. He just stood there, like he was studying him. I just never trusted that bastard. I just want to keep our options open, if you know what I mean."

"You want me to tail the FBI, don't you?"

"I just had a feeling it was him. The minute I heard a detective wanted to question the nurses, which I knew was not the case, they must have meant agent, I just knew it would be him. So I thought it best he not see you in case ..."

"You want me to tail the FBI, don't you Hazel?" said Vinnie, only this time it was clear he wanted his question answered.

But all he got in return was a smile.

"Shit, you have got to be kidding me."

"I just want to know where he is going, what he's up to," said Hazel. "I think he still has the hots for me, so I plan to use that if I need to."

"Hazel, do you hear yourself? The man is with the goddamn FBI," said Vinnie.

"Yes, but he is still an asshole. If you can't handle it, then—"

"Shut up. You know I will, but damn," Vinnie said, starting the car. "What about the boy?"

"Oh, get this. Samar has the boy under heavy sedation. He called in some special federal agency last night that deals with this kind of shit—you know, like you said, people with ESP. They are taking him to Parksville University. Seems they are modifying an old science lab there. They want me to try and communicate with him because I held his hand at the hospital, and nothing happened. They think I may have a comforting effect on him, some kind of mother figure."

"And you agreed to that?" exclaimed Vinnie.

"Yes, yes, I did," she said, avoiding making eye contact. "Bibens will shit himself if he knows I have access to the kid. He said that I and the two nurses were suspects in a murder investigation. Can you believe that bullshit?"

"Hazel, this is not a game. If that kid has some kind of power, you may be getting in over your head. If he killed the doctor—"

"I don't know, Vinnie. I know it all sounds so crazy, but I don't think the kid meant to hurt anyone."

"Tell that to the good doctor."

"They think he killed David Willmore as well," said Hazel reluctantly.

"And you want to go have a chat with the nice young man?" asked Vinnie.

"Call and see if Hicks and Jackson have left yet to pick up old man Willmore."

"Hazel, you can't interfere with an FBI investigation. Did you share your information about the father?"

"I didn't know he was on the case when I gave them that order, now did I. As for Bibens, let him follow the trail. If he asks, I will tell him whatever he wants to know. But it is not my fault if he doesn't ask, is it?"

"As a matter of fact, yes, it is. It's called withholding evidence."

"Oh, just shut up and drive. I have no evidence of anything, yet."

Vinnie just shook his head. Once on the main road, he grabbed his radio and asked dispatch if Hicks and Jackson had left yet. He was informed they had arrived at the butcher's shop, but the suspect was not there. They were en route to his residency on Sandstone Road. Hanging up the radio, Vinnie turned to Hazel. "Funny how he wouldn't close early yesterday even though his only son was found dead, and today he doesn't even bother to show up for work."

"I know. I'm thinking the same thing. Floor it," said Hazel.

· · · · · · · · ● ○○○○○○○○ ○ ○

Barbra Wentworth was driving back to her estate. Her lunch with Agnes Prescott was a bore as always. First, they'd had to put up with Larry Henderson making a big deal about his latest creations; Agnes in her usual phony enthusiasm hung to every word. She let him pick out her lunch, her wine, and her desert. Barbra, on the other hand, ordered her T-bone, medium rare, with a side of baby carrots. She was not returning to her office that afternoon, and a good hearty lunch would lead to a nice nap and then maybe some alone time in the hot tub. For over an hour and a half she had listened as Agnes ambled on and on about this event she went to and who was there to another event she'd attended with so and so. Barbra was bored to tears. *Agnes, always playing the part of the sophisticate,* she had thought to herself more than once. Everyone knew that, in her younger days, she had been the biggest whore this side of Michigan Ave. She'd had two or three abortions that Barbra knew of, and at least three STDs. The two children she did have were out of wedlock. She refused to marry either father, lest they get their fingers on her money. Agnes would never willingly give up her family name anyway. That would have disqualified her from remaining in the society and stripped her of the promise of someday becoming its chair.

Barbra, on the other hand, could have cared less if she ever took that position. She hoped she was long gone before it was time for another Wentworth to be at the head of the table. She did not like children and didn't want any. She didn't care if, when she passed, her nephew, Brice, got her spot. He was a good kid. Besides, no man was ever going to plant his seed in her; she detested the thought of a male touching her. Only another woman would ever feel her passion, and God knows there where a lot of them in town who had.

Just as Barbra started to make the turn onto Fourth Street, her foot reached for the break to slow down. Only something grabbed her by the ankle from under the driver's seat and pulled her foot back. Looking down, Barbra saw the bluish hand of a child with a tight grip. She screamed and inadvertently swerved right into someone's front lawn before she slammed on the break with her free foot. When she looked down again, the small hand released her and disappeared again under the seat.

Barbra slammed the car into park and jumped out, leaving her driver's side door wide open. Now standing in the middle of a stranger's front yard, she started screaming violently into the air. From a good distance, she looked in the car's back seat, expecting to find a child crouched on the back floorboard, but there was nothing. Slowly, she opened the back door and then jumped back as if Satan himself was going to besiege her, but there still was nothing there. The front seat and back seat were both completely empty.

That was when the owner of the house came out blaring at the top of his lungs. Barbra didn't hear a word he was saying. She was still in shock.

Within just a few minutes, two cop cars appeared out of now were, their lights flashing. Slowly Barbra began to regain her composer. As her mind started to clear, she realized that, if she told anyone the truth, they would lock her up in the nuthouse. She blurted out the first thing that came to into her head. "A snake—there was a snake in my car." She walked over to the man whose yard she had just violated. "I am so sorry. There was a snake in my car; scared the hell out me. I am so sorry. I will pay for any damages, I promise."

The man just gave her a strange look. As the cops came into the yard, she repeated her story to them.

Both were clearly suppressing a grin as she gave her explanation. "What kind of snake was it ma'am?" asked one officer with a slight chuckle.

"I don't know. A snake is a snake," was her only response.

The other office took out his flashlight and looked under both seats. "Well, he's gone now, whatever kind it was."

· · · · · · · · · ● ○○○○○○○○○○ ○

It was close to five when Hazel returned to her office, where she found Sam waiting patiently for her. After the day she'd had, she was glad he was there. Sam always seemed to bring reason to madness.

"I hear I got another one coming my way," said Sam as she approached.

"Come on in, Sam," said Hazel.

"You look exhausted," said Sam as Hazel unlocked her office door and walked inside.

"I am exhausted," responded Hazel. "Come on, and I will fill you in."

"Good. Then I will update you on the other two and my visit with the FBI."

"Bibens came calling then?" said Hazel, putting down her purse. Instead of walking over to her desk she sat next to Sam in one of the two chairs in front of her desk. She laid her head on Sam's shoulder. "Sam, the whole world is turning to crap."

"You will get through this, I promise. Now tell me— what happened at the Willmore house?" Sam asked.

"Vinnie and I arrived shortly after Jackson and Hicks. They were standing outside as we pulled up. Seems they had knocked numerous times but got no response, even though his car was in the driveway. It was Vinnie who walked around the back to find the back door wide open. We went in, guns drawn. The place was torn apart. I don't know what they were looking for, but the place was completely sacked. Mr. Willmore was lying dead on the floor of his bedroom; the bedroom window had a nice little bullet hole, which means whoever shot him did so from outside the house. They must have been one hell of shot as well. Willmore had been shot squarely between the eyes. There was no sign of forced entry. Strange, but It looked as if he was in the process of packing. There were two suitcases on the floor. Obviously, whatever was taking place on Grinnell Street, he was involved, and he was getting ready to flee. We left everything as it was and call Bibens. It's in the FBIs hands now."

"Yeah, I had a little visit from him this morning, demanding a final report on the butcher's son and the doctor from the hospital. He said I needed to stop any communication with you on the murders and that, from now on, I was to report my findings to him directly," said Sam, hanging his head. "But to hell with Bibens. There's not much to tell anyway. I am putting down the cause of death for David as a blow to the neck with the meat cleaver. As for the doctor, I am pretty sure landing on the car did him in. The fact you could see his brains from the hole in his skull tells me he was probably not long for this world to begin with, but it was the fall that sealed the deal. Snapped his neck. The scalp on top of the glass confirms that it was the object that, indeed, made the wound to the top of his head. Other than that, I really don't know more than anyone else."

"Thanks, Sam. I don't think you will find much with our good butcher. The shot was clean."

Sam got up and patted Hazel on the shoulder. "Let Bibens deal with this one, Hazel. He is the world's biggest asshole, but let him take on this headache. You have enough on your plate."

Hazel looked up at her old friend, "Okay."

"Okay," repeated Sam. And with that, he gave her a smile and left, shutting the door behind him.

A million thoughts were now running through Hazel's mind as she sat alone in her office. *Maybe I would be better off just handing this over and forgetting about it. After all, like Sam just said, it's the FBI's headache, not mine*, she thought. A vision of Captain Gilmore's face when he was forced to call in the feds came clearly to her mind. She had been standing in his office when he'd made the call. He'd looked defeated, like he was giving in on a fight that was his alone to fight.

Just then, a knock came at her office door. She opened it only to find Hicks standing there. In his hand, he held a single red rose. "For you, Captain," he said. "Don't worry, no one saw me."

Hazel pulled him into her office and shut the door and kissed him long and hard on the lips. "Take me home and tuck me in, Hicks," she said.

"I am not off for another two hours, but I will be there. You can count on it. And no talking about the case, I promise, Captain," Hicks said with a large smile on his face.

Hazel kissed him once more.

CHAPTER 3

A New Cage

Mark Cross walked down the stone path leading from the back of his house to the woods and a small clearing he had constructed as an outdoor barbeque area, complete with awnings and fifteen well placed picnic tables. There were two complete BBQ grills constructed out of red brick, one of which ran off a natural gas line running from the house, the other used only for charcoal. Off to the left was a little band staging area they had used for many weddings, family reunions, and parties. Then there was his three-foot-high above-ground cement pit, which he had built himself for pig roasts. His son, Mark Junior, was holding his homecoming dance after-party here, and Mark wanted to make sure everything was ready for the big day. The generator was housed in the storage shed, and along with the usual garden tools, there was any number of lounge chairs, tablecloths, outdoor games, and other party necessities. At night, all the colored lights hanging from the trees above seemed to give the isolated area a surreal atmosphere, like something sprung from the pages of Tolkien.

He had chosen this time of day to do his inspection because he knew seventeen-year-old Tina Robertson, his next-door neighbor, cut through this way to catch her morning bus. He had been working on that piece of ass all summer. His approach was easy enough but took a long time to develop. Let them think they were the ones who wanted it and then act like you had done everything you could to prevent it. He knew Tina was hooked; all he needed now was to confirm a date and location, hopefully right there tonight if all worked as planned. After all, he would need to return later and make sure the generator was working, as well as all the lights.

Thank God Barbra is so good at what she does, thought Mark. He had never been caught pursuing his desire for young girls, but it would only take once to make his life hell. That he knew for certain. Still, the fact that Barbra would defend him made his adventures a little less frightening.

Mark walked over to the pit and pulled off the tarp covering it. The rotisserie rod was clean, and the pit had been shoveled. He grabbed the hand crank and attached it to the rod. There was no use hooking up the motor without electricity, but at least he could make sure it was spinning easily. He gave it a few good turns and put the hand crank down. They were cooking a small pig, so he knew there would be no issues. He reached over and grabbed the tarp once more to cover it back up, but as he did so he noticed an abnormality in the tarp as it came to rest on top of the pit. Clear as day, there appeared the outline of a child's head and shoulders standing just on the far side of the rotisserie rod. Had he left something there? *What could possibly be making the shape in the tarp?* Mark thought to himself.

Then Mark saw the shape move—not much, just a little. But he knew for a fact it had moved slightly toward him. Mark screamed and, grabbing the tarp, pulled with all his might, sending it flying over his head. When he looked, there was nothing there, just the pit. An uneasy feeling came over him. He walked back toward the house, not bothering to replace the tarp. Even the thought of missing Tina Robertson was no longer an issue. He only wanted to go back to the safety of his house.

• • • • • • • • ● ○○○○○○○○○ ° °

Vinnie stopped at Dunkin' Donuts for a cup of coffee. It was a lot closer to his house than Starbucks, and the lines were never as long. He had learned through years of experience that, at this particular location, you got in and out a lot faster walking in, rather than waiting in the extended drive-through.

The moment he walked through the door, he spotted Sam two people ahead of him in line. "Sam, are you buying doughnuts for everyone back at your office?" asked Vinnie mockingly.

Sam turned and saw Vinnie smiling back at him. "We I'll be damned. They do let you out occasionally, huh. Grab your coffee and have a seat with me for a minute." Then Sam turned to place his order.

By the time Vinnie got his coffee, Sam had a nice table picked out in the back.

"Well, well, how are things going now that your back?" Vinnie asked as he approached.

"Please, if I knew I was walking into this mess, I would have moved to Idaho," joked Sam. "No, really it is rather nice being home. I missed Jackson."

"Well, I guess we can't discuss the Bibens investigation," said Vinnie, taking his seat. "There is definitely some crazy shit taking place; that's for sure. To tell you the truth, I am glad it's in the feds' hands. Hazel may disagree, but let them deal with this shit; that's my philosophy."

Sam looked up and smiled at him, "You are so full of shit your eyes are brown. I bet Hazel has you doing something on that case right now."

Vinnie just smiled. "Well, she has suggested I follow Bibens to see what he's up to."

Sam smiled. "You know you can get your ass into a hell of a lot of trouble with that one."

"I still haven't said I would," said Vinnie with a grin. "But today I am going out to Parksville and talk to Professor Parker."

"What? Phillip Parker, why?" responded Sam, giving away his concern.

"Relax," said Vinnie. "I know Hazel has this thing about him, but I like him. I know he was helping Captain Gilmore, not plotting against him. I am going to be completely honest with you, Sam. Something unnatural took place back in Parksville; I feel it even now. I know deep down Parker was there the night Gilmore died, but maybe he honestly can't say what really happened."

A look of relief filled Sam's face. "Have you ever said that to Hazel?"

"What? That woman is as black and white as they come. With her, facts are facts—like when there was no clear explanation of what happened to Captain Gilmore, she had to find someone to point her finger at. Unfortunately, it was Professor Parker and Franky."

"You know Franky Lake, I mean Professor Lake?" asked Sam, taken aback by Vinnie's comments.

"I didn't back then, but I got to know him years later from the YMCA. We both held gold memberships; he used to work out there about three times a week. Nice guy. We ran laps together in the evenings. And before you ask, no, Hazel didn't know that ether. I keep my personal and professional lives separate. Hazel's great, and I think the world of her, but my life is my business."

"So, you haven't talked to him recently?"

"No, not for over a year. Why?"

"Phillip Parker is missing. Franky told me the other day on the phone," said Sam, looking down at his half-empty cup. "I promised him I would help find him when this was all over. The last thing we need right now is Hazel and Bibens catching wind of this."

"Missing, how long?" said Vinnie.

"He's been missing for months, went missing down in Florida of all places."

Vinnie sat lost in thought for a few moments. "Okay then," he said, standing up. "I guess that changes my game plan for today. Sorry, Sam, but I guess I have someone I will need to tail."

Sam smiled. "Go get 'em, tiger."

• • • • • • • • ● ○○○○○○○○○ ○ ○

Hazel had no sooner walked into her office then she received a phone call form Dr. Nancy White asking if she would be able to join them at the college. She stated she had some very interesting things to discuss with her and asked if she would still be willing to meet with the boy. Hazel had agreed with very little hesitation. She felt a connection to the boy, the way his depressed eyes had stared up at her in the hospital. There was nothing malicious in those blue eyes, only a deeply rooted sadness the likes of which she had never seen before.

Her instructions were clear enough—take University Trail till it ended. There, in the farthest reaches of the university sat the Science and Technologies Building. Enter through the main doors, take the main hallway to the very end, and there would be a set of double doors on her right. Once there, she would need to ring the bell, so someone could let her in.

Hazel navigated all of this without an issue, until she reached the double doors. At first, she could not find the buzzer to the door. Finally she spotted it on the opposite wall next to a small voice box. As soon as she pushed the little red button on the bottom, a voice came through the box. She recognized it at once as belonging to Dr. White.

"Hello, can I help you?" came the voice, very polite and professional.

"This is Captain Cowan. I am outside the doors."

"I will be right down."

With that, Hazel heard a click at the other end. Within minutes, she heard a latch on the double doors being slid open, and then Dr. White appeared. "Captain, come on up. We have been waiting for you. Just follow me upstairs, and we can give you a quick briefing."

Hazel walked into a small room with yet another large and secured door directly across from the doors she had just entered. To her right was a cement staircase following the wall up to the second floor. She followed the good doctor up the steps to yet another sealed door that the doctor opened with her key card. As she walked into the twelve-by-twelve square room, she was amazed at the large amount of equipment neatly stacked against every wall. On the far side, directly across from the door was a wall made of glass. She knew at once what she was looking at, for her office used the same one-way mirrors in their interrogation rooms.

"Welcome," said the elderly Dr. Moore, who had been busy sitting and staring at a computer screen. "Dr. Moore, but please just call me Jim. I was never a fan of titles." With that, he stood and walked over to Hazel and shook her hand.

"And I am Dr. Johns, but you can call me Albert," said the younger robust man, who had been working on a TV screen placed above his working space. "Sorry, this damn thing has been giving us trouble all morning."

"Nice to see all of you again," said Hazel, somewhat surprised at all the niceties. She did not know what to expect when she arrived, but obviously, her assumptions that she would be spending the afternoon with a bunch of stuffed shirts was wrong.

"Here, please have a seat," said Nancy as she wheeled a chair over to the wall of the glass.

Before Hazel sat, she looked out of the glass. The room where the boy was placed was two stories high. The team, situated on the second floor, had the view of the entire room, looking directly down on the boy, who was sound asleep on the bed placed in the dead center of the room. There was a couch, two chairs, a nice dresser, and a small TV and stand. Hazel realized the trio had gone to great measures to make the room look more like a small apartment than a lab. The only thing crazy was all the furniture and equipment they had placed in the room was against one wall, with no clear rhyme or reason to their placement.

"The boy's been sleeping on and off most of yesterday evening and this morning," said Nancy with a look of sympathy in her eyes.

"Yeah, but the little guy's still been busy," said Albert.

"Play the tape for her, Albert," said Nancy.

With that, Albert pulled out a VHS tape and slapped it into a player on his desk. The TV screen above his head that he had been working so intensely on sprang to life. "Now, I am going to speed this up because this all happed over the course of eight hours. But it seems the little guy did not like the way his room was set up."

Hazel sat glued to the TV screen. Every time the boy was awake and sitting up in his bed, another piece of equipment or furniture slowly made its way to the far wall. This was all completed with the boy never once leaving the bed. The large dresser and couch moved with ease, sliding across the floor as if on wheels. But, as Albert so enthusiastically pointed out, the scrape marks left behind on the newly polished tile floor would prove otherwise.

"So, you are telling me," said Hazel at last, her voice trembling just a little, "that the boy is doing all of this, moving all these bulky items, with just his mind?"

"This may well be the greatest document case of telekinesis ever recorded," said Jim with a huge smile on his face.

Hazel, still shaken at what she had just seen, was amazed

by the look on Jim and Albert's faces. Their faces did not show fear, but wonderment and excitement.

"Poor little guy. God only knows what he has been through," said Nancy just above a whisper. Hazel could tell her enthusiasm was somewhat curtailed by her genuine concern for the boy.

"Wait, there's more," said Albert. "This morning, we got the thermal image cameras working." With that, Albert replaced the VHS with another one. "This is from this morning."

"See," said Jim as the new tape began, "you can make out the boy sitting on the bed, but look over to the left. See the heat signature on the other side of the room. It looks almost human, doesn't it?"

Hazel gazed in amazement. If she had not known better, she would have sworn there were two people in the room.

"Now look here," said Nancy, standing up. With the pen in her hand, she pointed to a very narrow strip, almost unnoticeable. If Nancy hadn't pointed it out, Hazel would have missed it all together. The dim white line ran from top of the boy's head to the other figure on the other side of the room. "See the boy's connection to the other figure; we think they have a special connection."

"I see," said Hazel, still confused about what she was looking at. "But what does this all mean?"

"This morning, we got a small amount of audible chatter from the boy—the only thing he has said since he has been here," said Jim.

"Two words," interrupted Albert. "Quiet, Richie. That's all he said."

"We summarize that, in his isolation in the basement, the boy created an imaginary friend; only with his extraordinary gifts, the young man was able to focus his telekinetic energies into bringing his friend, well to put it plainly, to life," said, Nancy staring down at the boy. "He made his friend as real as he possibly could, giving him his own identity."

Hazel was lost for words. She sat back in her chair, and she too now stared down at the boy lying so helplessly below her. *No. It isn't real. How could any of this be real?* A child with an imaginary friend made up in his own mind, which he feeds with physic powers, making him strong enough to rearrange an entire room. It was too much.

"Look at how he makes him move," said Jim, pointing back up at the screen.

The second figure now floated across the room next to the boy. Hazel watched as the boy on tape started to giggle, like he had just heard a funny story, and then the figure that was Richie simply moved away and through the locked door, the very thin line that connected them stopping at the door.

"It seems Richie is not bound by the room's security, but you can still see the connection. We have no idea if the boy can see what is on the other side or what is taking place once he leaves the room."

All of a sudden, the figure reappeared and took his spot along the far wall. The boy, seeming exhausted, simply lay back down and feel to sleep.

"Amazing, isn't it?" asked Nancy of Hazel.

Hazel did not answer right away; her entire belief system was being torn apart, and she needed some time to collect herself. She thought about the brutal murders that had taken place. If the boy could move heavy furniture with ease, how hard would it have been to heave a doctor out the window? It was all just too crazy for her to comprehend.

"Look, I know this all maybe coming as a shock to you, a little more than what you signed on for, but please take some time and think about it. There is so much we need to know," said Nancy. "We know we may be sitting on a time bomb. But when all is said and done, he is still just a little boy." Nancy reached out and took Hazel's hand. "We will understand if you do not want to help us; it's frightening. But it seems to all of use that you have bonded with him in some way, and you may be the only one who can help him."

"Does Bibens know about all this?" asked Hazel, avoiding Nancy's eyes.

"He knows we are here in town and that we are studying the boy; that's all he ever needs to know. Our agency has been around for a very long time. We have earned our right to be anonymous. We do not answer to the FBI and they do not answer to us."

"And what happens to me if I say no?" asked Hazel.

"Nothing," responded Jim. "Look, you could go tell everyone and their brother about what you just saw. You can talk about the agency and our secret mission to discover the unknown. We have dealt with that for years. No one will believe you; trust me. Or you can simply go on with your life like none of this ever happened. It's up to you."

"We have tried speaking to him through the intercoms. He will not even acknowledge us," said Albert. "Without any prior contact with him, the risk of him reacting negatively to us popping in for a chat is greatly increased."

"We cannot make this decision for you, but we wanted to make sure you knew everything we did so you made one based on the facts," said Nancy. "The choice is yours, and you need to take some time to make your decision. There is a real danger here. We all know that."

The vision of sitting in the hospital flashed across Hazel's mind—the look in those boy's eyes. From somewhere deep inside her, she knew, whatever had happened, the boy was not to blame. There was no way he'd killed anyone; of that, she was sure. With all the courage she could muster, she stood and looked at the group. And much to their surprise she said, "I'll do it. I need to know the truth."

• • • • • • • • ● ○○○○○○○○○ ○ ○

Larry Henderson was hard at work on one of his signature dishes—seafood stuffed red peppers. As he cut the portobello mushrooms, he heard his name called from the other side of the kitchen.

"Larry, can you give me a hand with this?" It was Mrs. Henderson, who was battling with an overly stubborn lid to an olive jar.

Setting his butcher knife down on the cutting block, Larry walked over to his wife, mumbling something about a hundred staff and her having only him to yell for. Once he had completed this meaningless task, he returned to his cutting block, only to find his favorite butcher knife gone. Looking over at the prep table, he saw it lying next to one of his line cooks. "Antonio, why did you take my knife?"

Antonio turned and looked at Larry and then down at

the knife, "I didn't take your knife," he said and went back to chopping salad.

Larry walked over to the table and grabbed his knife. "Whoever used my knife, please keep your hands off it. Now I will need to rewash it!" yelled Larry to everyone within earshot. With a loud grunt, he walked over to sink and placed the knife in the hot water. He walked over to where the cleaning cloths were stacked neatly above the automatic dishwasher and returned to the sink. Though he searched every inch of the bottom. The knife was not there. Once again, it was missing.

And once again, he turned, only to find it still dripping wet next to Antonio. "Very funny, Antonio, but I have had enough of your bullshit."

"What the hell are you talking about?" asked Antonio, picking up the large bowl of salad he'd just cut and heading for the dining room. "You're losing your mind, old man."

Once again, Larry walked over and grabbed the knife. He quickly washed and dried it and then walked over and placed it back on the cutting board next to the mushrooms. Then he grabbed a towel and started to dry off his hands.

"Larry, I have another jar," came the voice of Mrs. Henderson once more.

Larry turned. "Damn it, woman. Can't you ask someone else to help you for once?" he yelled back and then turned back to his mushrooms, only to find that, once again, the knife was gone.

Looking over at the prep table, he saw his knife, only this time Antonio was nowhere in sight. Larry tuned to see where the young smart-ass might be. And that was when the knife went whizzing past his head and impaled itself deep in the wall just inches from Larry's nose.

Larry backed away, screaming. Everyone in the kitchen turned to see what was going on. "Where is that fucking little Antonio? He tried to kill me."

"Antonio is out front, Larry. He's filling the salad bar," said his wife.

· · · · · · · · · ● ○○○○○○○○○○

"The damn thermals are down again," said Albert, looking at the screen. "Shit, and I just got them up this morning."

Hazel, who was just getting ready to make her journey down the steps and into the boy's room, stopped and turned around.

"I don't like her going down there not knowing what's going on with Richie," said Nancy.

"We will have to wait until I can get them working again. I only hope it's not a problem with the cameras. We would have to utilize Sleeping Beauty to get in there," responded Albert.

"Sleeping Beauty?" questioned Hazel, still standing by the door.

"Yes," said Jim, turning around. "This red button over here will fill the boy's room with a mild sleeping gas. We installed it in case of emergencies."

"No, no, no. Don't do that. I will be fine, I promise," said Hazel, with reservation in her voice. "Besides, the boy has to eat." She held in her hand a sack lunch for the boy. The tray they had place through the slot next to the door was still untouched.

"Again, Hazel, are you sure you want to do this?" asked Nancy.

"I'm sure. Look I have been sitting in here for two hours waiting for him to wake. I still have another job, you know," she said jokingly.

Nancy smiled. "Okay. I will be standing right outside the door, and I will be in there in a heartbeat if you call."

With that, the two of them descended the stairs to the bottom floor. Once there, Nancy again used her key card, and the bottom door unlocked. She then heard the tag beep again and saw Nancy reach in and retrieve the morning tray form the small shelf mounted on the wall just inside. As soon as she pulled the tray free, she relocked the slot with her badge. They were taking no chances.

Hazel took a deep breath and then opened the door and slowly made her way inside. The door was immediately closed behind her by Nancy, only this time there was no sound of the lock.

Inside, Hazel looked at the boy, now sitting up in his bed. He stared intensely at her as she made her way into the room. Hazel was afraid to utter a word. She had been working so hard on what she might say, and now, nothing came to mind.

The boy lay back down on the bed. From across the room, one of the dining room chairs skidded to place next to his bed. There he lay, reaching out his hand. *Just like the hospital,* thought Hazel.

Slowly, she walked over, sat in the chair, and held his hand. Neither said a word for the longest time.

Finally, Hazel spoke in the gentlest voice she could find. "How are you?"

The boy did not answer but instead shrugged his shoulders.

"My name is Hazel. I've met you a couple of times."

"My name is Bobby," said the boy in response. His voice was extremely weak and shallow. Hazel could barely make out his words.

"Do you like it here?" asked Hazel softly, while looking around the room.

The boy seemed to ponder the question for a moment and then looking up to the ceiling. "It's bigger than my last cage," he said at last.

"Do you remember much about the last place you lived?" asked Hazel.

"Don't want to talk about it," said the boy, now looking away.

Hazel gave him a smile. "That's okay. We can talk about whatever you want."

He tuned so that he was facing her. "What's that?" asked the boy, looking down to the brown bag Hazel still had clenched in her fist.

"It's for you. It's something to eat."

"Why is it in there and not a bowl?" said the boy, a look of curiosity filling his face.

"This is what we call a sack lunch," said Hazel. "See." Reaching into the bag, she pulled out a tuna fish sandwich wrapped in plastic wrap. "It's really good. Want to try some?" She started to unwrap the sandwich to the amazement of Bobby. "Here. Go ahead and take a bite."

Bobby took the sandwich, turned it over in his hands, and then smelled it. Reluctantly, he took a bite. The boy's face seemed to illuminate. Hazel watched in delight as, within seconds, the sandwich was gone, and the boy was reaching into the bag for other hidden treasures. There was a can of pop, which Hazel had to open for him, a large yellow delicious apple, and a chocolate chip cookie. Each offering brought a bigger and bigger delight to the boy. When the boy had consumed all there was to consume, Hazel put all the wrappings back into the bag. "How was that?" asked Hazel.

"Good," responded Bobby, wiping his mouth with the back of his hand.

"Wait, wait. Here's a napkin to wipe your face with." Hazel handed him one of the napkins she had spread across her knee. "Bobby, do you know your last name?" asked Hazel.

"What's a last name?" Bobby questioned, while looking up at Hazel with those big blue eyes and thick pouty lips.

"Never mind. Do you know how you got here?"

Bobby thought a moment. "No. I was asleep I think."

"Bobby, why do you think you're here?" asked Hazel, brushing the hair out of his eyes.

"I don't know," he answered with a shrug of his shoulders.

"Do you know how you're able to move things around without touching them?"

"Don't want to talk about it," he responded, avoiding any eye contact.

Hazel knew she was losing him. "Okay, maybe you can tell me later. Is there anything else I can get for you, maybe some more blankets?" asked Hazel but got no response. "Do you want me to help you get off the bed, so you can walk around a little?"

"No. I want to go to sleep now." And with that, the boy simply rolled over and closed his eyes.

"Okay. Well then, can I come back and visit you again sometime?" asked Hazel.

"Tomorrow would be nice," said Bobby.

"Okay, tomorrow then," said Hazel with a caring smile. "They will put food through that slot next to your door again. You need to eat, okay."

The boy did not respond, so Hazel simply patted him on the back and made her way to the door.

"Remember tomorrow," came Bobby's meek voice once more.

Hazel smiled and knocked on the door to let Nancy and the others know she was coming out.

On the other side, she was met with a hug by Nancy. "You are the bravest soul I have ever met in my life," she said.

Hazel smiled, surprised at the sudden show of affection. "Sorry I didn't get more information from him, but he just shut down."

"Are you kidding me? You were great. You made a strong connection with him. I could tell by what I heard over the speakers. You did everything we could have hoped for and more." Nancy reached over and locked the door with her card. "I think he trusts you. That's what we hoped for."

As the two women made their way back upstairs, the conversation continued.

"He just seems so tired all the time. I mean he looks exhausted, like every little effort wears him out," said Hazel.

"And he has yet to move off the bed. I don't think he is

comfortable yet with that much open space to move about," replied Nancy.

As they made their way through the door of the lab, both men stood and clapped their hands. "You were awesome," said Albert, walking over and shaking her hand.

"Yes, job well done," continued Jim. "I am still not comfortable with you going down there without the thermo cameras though. Albert will need to work on those before tomorrow."

Albert, ignoring Jim, walked over and looked through the glass to the sleeping boy below. "I wonder how long he was in that cage. The poor little guy must be scared to death. You helped relieve some of that fear; I could tell."

"Well, if it is okay with the group, I would like to work on getting him off the bed tomorrow. Putting food out across the room will not help if he is afraid to go get it," said Hazel.

"Agreed," responded Nancy.

"I have made up my mind about one thing already, and I don't care if anyone agrees with me or not," said Hazel, not looking at anyone in particular. "I don't think that boy has killed anyone. I just don't see it."

"Hazel, please don't jump to any conclusions," said Jim. "I agree it is hard to believe the boy is capable of those terrible deeds, but still, you cannot let down your guard. Remember, there are still two dead bodies connected with this young man. We must take every precaution. The last thing any of us want is for you to push too hard and get hurt."

"I agree with Jim," said Albert.

"As do I," added Nancy.

Vinnie felt like he had wasted his entire day. He had driven past the house on Grinnell Street, only to find two young wannabe FBI agents roaming the grounds outside of the house. Next, he went to the hospital and then the butcher Willmore's house, but there was no sign of Bibens. Finally, he happened upon the agent's car at the butcher's shop. Since then, Vinnie had spent the entire afternoon in the insignificant restaurant directly across the street. From this location, he could see Bibens's car and the front of the building. Bibens had only emerged twice, both times carrying out boxes of what looked to be files and placing them into the back seat of his car. *Why the butcher's shop? What is he looking for?* thought Vinnie.

The restaurant was pleasant enough, and his waitress was very nice, coming back to his table every few minutes to check on him. He was afraid she would get annoyed with him just sitting there and not ordering much, but if she was, she sure didn't show it. More than once, she stopped by for nothing more than a quick conversation.

Still, the hours seemed to drag as Bibens continued to investigate the butcher shop. Finally, around four thirty, he emerged one more time, this time stopping to lock the front door. He returned to his car, threw one more box into the back seat, and was gone. Vinnie paid his bill and headed home. There would be no more tailing today; if Agent Bibens was planning on going through all the paperwork he had just thrown into his back seat, that would keep him busy for the rest of the night.

He wouldn't have spent the day there unless he thought there was something there. What is he looking for? Lost in his thoughts, Vinnie tried to play out scenarios in his head. *The father knew what was taking place on Grinnell Street. Maybe he was the mastermind behind the whole operation; that's why he was killed, to keep him quiet. Then maybe, just maybe, the shop would be the place to look for evidence.*

For the first time, Vinnie realized he needed to look beyond the murder and concentrate on all of this as if it was just another illegal operation. Maybe the cages weren't there for someone's twisted personal enjoyment but for the sale of children. The thought made him shudder. If it was a business, someone was keeping the books. And what better place to hide them than a legitimate business?

CHAPTER 4

A Bump in the Night

Brian Hicks and Devin Jackson walked out of the restaurant shaking their heads. Larry Henderson was still bellowing at them from the door. "I want you two to find out who the fucker is trying to kill me. I want them behind bars."

"Yes, Mr. Henderson, we will be looking into it I promise," said Jackson, getting into the patrol car.

Hicks looked over at him with a doubtful look and got in as well. They had arrived on the scene just over twenty minutes ago. Larry Henderson had called claiming someone had tried to murder him. The knife, stuck squarely in the wall, was the only evidence the man could produce. But when questioned, not one employee stated they saw what had happened. The only person who was anywhere near Larry when the knife went flying was Mrs. Henderson. Both men knew immediately that there was no way that frail, old woman could have hurled the knife with enough force for it to sink that far into the wall. As big and strong as he was, it had taken a few minutes for Jackson to pry it lose.

"You believe this shit?" said Hicks. "You think someone is really trying to kill him?"

"Why? I mean there is no motive, and why do it in a busy restaurant?" answered Jackson. "This whole town is going fucking crazy if you ask me."

"How do you think we write this one up?" asked Hicks.

"Hell, if I know," said Jackson. "I'll leave that one up to you. I'm off tomorrow, remember."

"Shit, that's right. I will get stuck with Harris tomorrow."

"Better you than me. He doesn't exactly like working with a brother, if you know what I mean."

"He doesn't like working with anyone; trust me. I don't think it's because you're black. I think it's because he's an asshole," said Hicks with a grin.

"Bullshit. I can tell. That's why I remind him all the time the town was named after me."

"You tell everyone that. You know it's named after a white president, don't you?"

"No shit. Thanks for the history lesson, snowflake," said Jackson, starting the car.

"So, any big plans for tomorrow? You and the wife taking the kids somewhere?" asked Hicks.

"Hell no. Her mom has the kids tomorrow. We are going up to Frankenmuth and getting some fried chicken."

"Man, I haven't been up there for years, not since I was a kid."

"You know what my wife asked me last night—if I wanted another kid. Can you believe that? Like three isn't enough. I told her *hell no!*"

"Another kid?" responded Hicks, surprised. "I thought, after the last one, she said there was no way in hell she was ever going to have another one."

Jackson pulled onto West Ave. "She did. But, man, when a woman gets to a certain age and starts thinking her time is running out to make babies, she starts getting all crazy."

Hicks laughed. "You think she's there."

"Man, I know she is. And what about you? When you going to join the ranks? You even seeing anyone?"

Hicks paused. "Well there is someone I am seeing, and I think I am going to ask her to marry me."

"What? Who?" asked Jackson, taken aback by Hicks's revelation.

"I can't tell you yet. Let's just say she makes me very happy."

"What do you mean you can't tell me? What's the big secret? Is it someone I know? Is it that big girl down in lockup?"

"No, it not Amanda. I'll tell you, as soon as she says yes," said Hicks. "You think the Lions have a shot this year?"

Jackson gave him a suspicious look but decided to let him have his way and let it go, "*Hell no!*" he exclaimed.

• • • • • • • • ● ○○○○○○○○○ ○ ○

It was dusk by the time Hazel left her office. Her communication with Vinnie about Bibens's actions that day had left her in a bit of a funk. She had known from the moment she saw the basement that this was no singular nutjob. If there was one cage, that would have been different, but multiple cages meant someone was making money, and she knew Old Man Willmore had been involved. If only she had gotten her hands on him before he was murdered. Maybe she had underestimated Bibens, though she strongly doubted it. *If he did find the books,* she thought, *let's at least hope he has enough sense to keep them under wraps until the case is solved.*

Not long after she had hung up with Vinnie, Jackson

and Hicks called in their report from the restaurant. Hazel was not sure how to feel about that one. After spending the morning and afternoon with Bobby, she wondered if the boy did have something to do with all the strange happenings around town. Even if Bobby was not doing it directly, could it be possible that Richie was able to travel so far?

Hazel felt the night air brush against her face as she walked out the front door. It was cool and refreshing, the way fall should feel. She knew Brian was not coming over tonight, and for that she was glad. He had told her that morning he was partying with an old friend from high school and not to expect him. She needed a break, time to think. Besides, she knew he would be asking her questions about why she had been gone from the office most of the morning, and that she did not want to answer. Just a couple of days ago, Hazel would have told anyone willing to listen that all of this was impossible—a boy able to move items with his mind. Even now, after seeing it with her own eyes, she was having a tough time coping with the reality. Hazel liked things cut and dried, a rational explanation for everything. If not, life did not make sense; cause and effect was all she was ever able to cling to.

Hazel remembered when she was young and how her and her father had spent endless evenings at the Cascades. The man-made waterfalls had beautiful colored lights that changed patterns to the music and fountains spraying high into the night sky on each side. It was truly one of the most beautiful sights Hazel could remember ever seeing. The first time she saw them she thought them magical. But her father, in the way some fathers do, explained to her how everything worked—about the gallons of water used, about the lights carefully placed, and about the timers and the angles. In his own way, he was simply passing his knowledge on, but to Hazel it was explaining away the magic.

Like her father before her, Hazel started looking for the cause and effect in everything in her life. Life's mysteries had answers; you just needed to find them. Still, to this day, every Fourth of July with its elaborate fireworks over the falls, every winter to sled down its banks, and every spring for the hot air balloon festivals, Hazel spent her spare time at the falls. The magic was not in the water, but in the love of a father. At the age of sixteen, Hazel had lost her father to a stroke. She had been the one to find him lying facedown on the back steps of their two-story home, and it had torn her apart. The image of her father lying on those steps was forever embedded in her brain. Maybe that was why she had felt such a strong need to support Hicks a couple months earlier when his father died.

Hazel got in her car and headed for home. It would be quiet there tonight. And maybe, just maybe, she would be able to relax and put the outside world aside for a while. *A warm bath, smooth jazz, and some scented candles will be just the ticket to make everything else fade away,* she thought.

· · · · · · · · · ● ○○○○○○○○○ ○ ○

"Thermo cameras are up," said Albert, rather pleased with himself. "Richie is back in there."

"Jim," said Nancy, shaking the man's shoulders, "you're snoring. Go back to the hotel and get some sleep."

"But I got first watch tonight," he said, half-awake.

"Albert and I will take first watch. You go get some sleep," said Nancy in her motherly tone. "Just be back here at four so one of us can get some shut-eye."

"Nancy, you might want to come and see this," said Albert, in somewhat of a panic.

"What is it, Albert?" said Nancy, trying to help Jim out of his chair.

"Richie's gone again, only this time ..."

"Only this time what?" responded Nancy, walking over to the monitor. The thin line connecting Bobby and Richie now ended at the glass windows of the lab. "Shit, he's in here."

"Looks like he finally came to visit," said Jim now wide awake.

All of a sudden, the atmosphere in the room seemed to change. All three scientists were completely silent. On the table in the middle of the room, which they had used for research, lunch, dinner, and any other number of things, the pages of Nancy's case notes started turning over on their own, one page at a time.

"Shit," said Albert. "He's in here with us."

After a short time, it seemed as if the entity was bored with the notes and moved on to Albert's workstation. The monitor that was tracking his moves inside Bobby's room now started to flicker; the picture was dark and blurred.

"It's some kind of electrometric charge," said Albert, pushing his seat back. His desktop, which was on one of his games at that moment, also started flashing on and off. "He's taking it all in."

Nancy looked out the window at Bobby's silent physique lying below. The way he was turned, it was hard to say if he was asleep or just resting there, motionless. More papers, this time from Albert's workstation, floated gently into the air and then were neatly returned to their resting spot.

All three scientists remained still, as slowly, the entity moved around the room, picking up paper clips, staplers, the phone, and other objects along its way. Then, as quickly as it had started, it all ended.

Albert looked back at the monitor. "He is back in there with Bobby. Look," said Albert.

All three gazed at the screen in amazement. There he was, a faint smudge of reddish light at the end of Bobby's bed.

"That was intense," said Jim at last.

"Wait. He's moving again, only this time, he's going out the front door."

Nancy walked over and picked up the case notes. "I think he was just curious. I mean, look how neat everything was put back. At least he knows we don't mean him any harm."

"Richie? Or Bobby?" asked Albert.

"Albert, you know as well as I do that Richie is just an extension of Bobby. See." And with that, she pointed out the window at the boy, who was now lying on his other side. His eyes were wide open. "We must never forget that all of this is inside his head."

"What if he has some kind of split personality, and Richie is the manifestation of his dark side?" asked Jim.

"I thought about that, but I don't think so. Millions of kids have make-believe friends when they are young," replied Nancy. "I had one myself, Becky. The fact a child has an imaginary friend has no correlation with split personalities."

"So, Bobby now knows who and what is up here. Maybe

that will help us communicate with him," said Albert. "If we can get Hazel to convince him we are nothing to be afraid of, we could move forward."

"Agreed," said Nancy.

"Maybe," said Jim, unconvinced.

"Jim, go get some sleep now. I think our young man is done with us for the night. There are all kinds of things in the science department he can look at. I am talking to the dean tomorrow and having her cancel all classes in this building until further notice. We will think of something—asbestos or some shit like that. But I want to make sure everyone is safe. Besides, could you imagine if he pulled this stunt in a room full of students?"

"How far is his range? I mean, how far do you think Richie can travel away from Bobby?" asked Albert.

"In all honesty, I don't know. No one has seen anything like this," responded Nancy. "Let's just hope his range doesn't go beyond this building."

· · · · · · · · · ● ○○○○○○○○○ ○ ○

Agnes Prescott was sleeping soundly in her king-size bed, drooling endlessly into her silk pillowcase. She had taken a little something to help her sleep. Things had been crazy since the news had come out about the raid on Grinnell Street and then the death of Dr. Hendershot. As she lay there in her golden slumber, the quiet of the night was disrupted by the faint sound of a child's chuckle in her ear.

Agnes sat up, gasping, and frantically looked around her bedroom, sure she would see a child standing by her bed. But there was nothing. The sound had stopped, and Agnes was just getting ready to write it off as a bad dream when there came the sound of a child's footsteps running down the hallway just outside her room.

Agnes pulled back her satin sheets and sat on the side of the bed. There was no doubt there was a child running up and down the hall; again, she could hear the giggles, as if the child was at play. Agnes became infuriated. One of her staff had brought a child into the house, and now it was running wild and unattended through her house in the middle of the night. *But how? Why?* None of it made any since.

Still, there was a child out in the hall, and she was going to put an end to whatever this was. Quickly, she got out of bed and put on her night robe. As she opened her bedroom door, the sound immediately stopped. There was only silence.

After seeing nothing in the dark hallway, Agnes turned and headed toward the staircase. If a child was in the house, it could not have gone far. A feeling of trepidation came upon her as she walked the quiet hall toward the main stairway. She felt like someone was testing her, challenging her to take another step. *Is someone trying to get to me, scare me, make me go crazy?* she thought as she moved onward, reaching along the wall for the switch to the large chandelier hanging in the middle of the entrance hall.

As the room illuminated with the glow of electric light, Agnes screamed. At once, staff started to appear from their rooms—the downstairs maid, the upstairs maid, Martin, and even the cook all came running to see what in the world was going on. At the top of the stairs, just above the landing, hung the oversize painting of Agnes. Only now, the face had been ripped to shreds. The implement that had caused the damage was easy to distinguish, because it was still stuck through the neck on the painting. It was the pair of scissors she kept in the nightstand next to her bed. They were stuck clear through the painting and into the wall behind.

Agnes looked over the banister down to the first floor at all the staff who had gathered and then to Lilly, standing just two doors down from hers. The terrified look on everyone's face was enough to convince her that none of them had done this appalling thing. There was a stranger in her house.

Through a shrill plea she requested, "Will someone call the police? Martin, take the staff and search the house."

· · · · · · · · · ● ○○○○○○○○○ · ·

As Agnes's staff searched the estate, across town, Earl Southworth was just getting ready for bed. It had been a brutal day, and he just wanted his porn, a quick jerk, and then sleep. Earl had just ended it with wife five, and the hunt for number six was not going well. All but the last one had given him children, and still she was the one who had given him the most headaches, taking him to court over and over, looking for that golden payday. Barbra's firm had managed to keep her at bay over the past nine months, but the bitch was relentless. There was no way he was giving her this house. It was the only thing he managed to keep his hands on through the years, and after a two-year marriage that bitch wanted it handed over to her like she had done something to deserve it.

The Southworth estate was beautiful in its simplicity. The house was one story and laid out in a perfect V formation. In the middle were the large open living room, dining room, and kitchen. Off to the left were three guest bedrooms, two staff quarters, three bathrooms, and a game room. On the right were the laundry, the pantry, Earl's office, a bedroom that he had converted into a large walk-in closet (this he had done for wife number three), the master bedroom and bath, and then the workout room. He had built the house the way he wanted it, custom for his taste. And no half-witted, double D bimbo was taking it from him, no matter how well she gave head.

Earl jumped into bed wearing nothing but a pair of boxers adorned in red and blue hearts. He reached over to grab the new magazine he'd purchased that morning filled with Asian porn. Next, he reached into his bedside table and pulled out his bottle of joy jelly. *Maybe an oriental chick for wife six*, he thought to himself.

Just as he was getting settled in and had found a page he liked, the door to his bedroom slowly opened. Earl looked up. Seeing no one there, he figured he had forgotten to close it all the way. It was not uncommon when the air-conditioning kicked in for the door of his bedroom, if not completely closed, to swing open. Reluctantly, he got out of bed and made his way over to shut the door. The last thing he need was for one of the maids to walk by while he was choking his chicken. Earl shut the door and, this time, made sure it was locked. Swiftly, he made his way back to his bed and grabbed for his magazine. Then something he had never imagined occurred. The door unlocked itself and, once again, opened.

This time, Earl was reluctant to move. All thoughts of pleasing himself were now completely gone. Gradually, he got up and ambled toward the door. This time, he did not close it but walked through it out into the hall, half expecting to see someone standing there. The hall was empty. Then he noticed every door down the hall was wide open—the laundry, the pantry, the walk-in. Earl suddenly broke out in a cold sweat. He made his way to the middle of the house. Glancing down to the opposite hallway to the left, he looked in horror as every door, including the one that led to the service quarters, stood open. Now, standing in the middle where he could take it all in at once it was clear, someone had opened every single door in the house. How this was done without waking up any of his staff was beyond him.

Then, out of nowhere, starting at the far end of the left hallway, all the doors, one after another started to slam shut with a loud bang; door after door came booming shut. As soon as it reached the middle of the house, it started again on the right-hand hallway, all the way down to the workout room. Earl could hear both the maid and the cook screaming from their rooms. Then, just like with the doors, every window in the house, starting with the farthest left, exploded inward—window after window imploding with a great force. Shattering glass filled the hallways, the living rooms, the bedroom, and everywhere in the house there was a window. Earl ducked just in time to avoid the shards of glass from the panels on both sides of the front door ripping into his face. Again, he heard the screams from his staff.

Earl could do nothing. He just stood there in the center of his house without moving or speaking. And in his fright, he left a large puddle on the floor beneath his feet.

· · · · · · · · ● ○○○○○○○○○ ○ ○

Hazel awoke and rolled over to the spot that Brian usually occupied. She never thought it would bother her not having him there, but it did. She had grown accustomed to rolling over, putting her arm around him, and pressing her breast against his warm back and her pelvis against his nice warm buttocks. She missed rubbing her hand across his bare chest, smelling the remnants of yesterday's aftershave, and feeling him breathing against her. *Funny*, she thought, *all those years waking up alone, and now it seems so different.*

She remembered when she was young and would wake up early just to sneak into bed with her father. Mom was always up early and busy with breakfast, so that left just the two of them. He would place his large arms around her, holding her tight. She never felt safer in her whole life than snuggling against her dad. She remembered the first time they had all gone to the Michigan Theater to see an old movie that her mom had always wanted to see. Hazel had thought it the most beautiful place in the world. It was so big, and everything was done in such detail. But when the theater staff had turned down the lights, she'd instantly became overwhelmed with fear. The beautiful theater had now become ominous. Her dad, sensing her fear, put his arm around her, and all that fear had simply melted away. Just knowing he was there was enough. He was her protection, her guardian against all the dreadful things in this world. Maybe she was coming to feel just a bit of that with Brian.

Hazel got up to the sound of the coffeepot rumbling in the kitchen, which meant her coffee was ready. Thank goodness she'd bought the model with a timer. It was a full hour earlier than her usual time for getting out of bed, but she knew she would have to make an appearance at the office before she went back to the university. Hopefully last night had been quiet, and she would get out of there on time.

In what seemed to Hazel to be no time, she was showered, dressed, and had her coffee cup in one hand and her purse in the other. Once in her car, she was eager to start the day. She always liked her morning drive to the office. It gave her time to think, time to reflect on open cases and staff issues. This morning, however, the only thing on her mind was Bobby. For some odd reason, she could not wait to see the boy again. He had touched her deeply. Perhaps it was his kind face or the fact she knew that, whatever they boy had gone through, it was horrible and nothing a child should endure. Whatever it was, she felt a bond with the child—a bond she had never felt with a niece, nephew, cousin, or child of a friend. He was special.

Her arrival early at the office was not what she suspected. Vinnie, who was notorious for coming in late, was already at his desk going through files. As soon as she walked through the door, he was on her tail. "Wait till you read the reports from last night—some of the craziest shit I have ever heard of."

"Vinnie, there damn well better be a coffee in my hand before you say another word."

Vinnie continued, taking no notice of her threat. "The Prescott estate was vandalized in the middle of the night. Larry Henderson, the owner of Under the Oaks—"

"I know who he is, Vinnie," said Hazel, still walking toward the break room and the coffeepot.

"He swears someone tried to kill him with a butcher knife, but no one saw it happen."

Hazel poured her coffee and walked toward her office.

Vinnie, unabated, continued close behind, "And get this; the Southworth estate had every one of its window busted in the middle of the night—every single one of them. And again, no one saw a thing."

"Damn," said Hazel, finally sitting down at her desk, sipping on her fresh brew. "All this happened last night?"

"Yea, funny, huh. And all of this just seemed to happen to some of the richest people in town. Don't that seem a little out there to you?"

Hazel slowly started to process the onslaught of data being thrown at her so early in the morning. "The Prescott family, the Henderson family, and the Southworth family, all in one night."

"And get this," continued Vinnie. "Yesterday, Barbra Wentworth drove her car into a complete stranger's front lawn, swearing there was a snake in her car, one that no one other than her saw." Vinnie threw his hands up in the air. "I mean, take into account what happened to Dr. Hendershot, and it looks like Jackson's most elite are under some sort of siege or something."

"Do we have anything connecting them all together, some country club or organization they all belong to?" asked Hazel.

"I haven't found anything yet, but I will keep looking." Then Vinnie paused, closed the door, and sat down across from Hazel. "How did it go with the kid yesterday; does he really have that ESP thing?"

"It's true," said Hazel. Vinnie was the only person in the world she would ever trust with this information. "I saw it myself."

"Do you think maybe he had something to do with all this? I mean—"

"I know what you mean, but I don't see how. He's never met any of these people. God only knows how long he was in that fucking basement. Besides, you're talking about a lot of power, to terrify everyone clear across town from a lab outside the city limits."

"Well, I guess you're right about that one. I don't know, but I think Bibens may have some of the answers. I still don't trust him though."

"Nor do I," said Hazel. "Nor do I."

Vinnie smiled and got up to leave, but Hazel stopped him. "Vinnie, I was walking through the college trying to find the lab where the boy is being held, and I saw the craziest thing hanging on the wall. It was a picture of you in a basketball uniform. It said something about holding the university's highest scoring record for a single season."

"No one has broken that yet? Shit that was a long time ago," said Vinnie very nonchalantly.

"Vinnie, you are my best friend in the world, and I still don't know a damn thing about you outside of work—where you live, who you date, what you do, nothing."

Vinnie just smiled and walked away. "I will try and see what all these rich bastards have in common." Then he opened the door and was gone.

CHAPTER 5

A New Life

Sam was in the process of examining the body of David Willmore Senior when Agent Bibens walked into the examining room. "Agent Bibens, and how are you this fine morning?"

"I am doing wonderful. And yourself?" responded Bibens.

"Good. How can I help you?" said Sam, returning to the dead body lying on the table.

"Well, I was wondering if there was any new information about our friend here, any clues to who could have kill the poor bastard."

"Cause of death was a single gunshot to the forehead, some sort of rifle I would guess. The bullet was lodged in the back of his skull."

"What did the ballistics report say?"

"Don't know yet. I look for cause of death. Ballistics will send me the report when it's done. There were no prints on him, no signs of a struggle, pretty cut-and-dried case really. I would say, unless they find the murder weapon, we will need to rely on your team to find the man who did this."

"Then why are you still working on him?" asked Bibens sarcastically.

"I am doing my job, Agent, just making sure I did not miss anything."

"Well, my team and I went through his whole house, and I can tell you, there was nothing. I think this one may go unresolved unless we get a break somewhere," said Bibens.

"Well, let's hope we get one then. Is there anything else I can help you with?" asked Sam in an obvious attempt to get him to leave.

"No, I guess not. But you will inform me immediately if you find anything, right?" Bibens phrased this as an order more than a question.

"You will be the first to know," said Sam with a smile.

As Bibens left the room, Sam felt an anger building up inside of him. *That egotistical son of a bitch, just who does he think he is?* thought Sam. Then it occurred to him. *Why didn't he ask about the other victims? Why the interest in only the senior Willmore?* After two very bizarre deaths, Bibens's only concern was for the one victim whose cause of death was the most obvious. Hopefully, that meant he was on to something, and this whole thing would soon be over. But deep down, Sam felt this was far from the truth.

When Sam had read the FBI's final report given to the local police after the Parksville murders, he had known that Bibens was a fool. He drew his conclusions from unsubstantiated data that any decent detective with half a brain would have thrown out. It appeared to Sam that Bibens didn't really give a shit about who had really committed the murders, as long as it was him getting the credit for them ending.

• • • • • • • • ● ○○○○○○○○○ ○ ○

Hazel was somewhat concerned when she got to the science building and there were no cars in the parking lot. Thankfully, Nancy, anticipating her arrival, stood waiting at the front door of the building.

"Hazel, what great timing. I was just getting back from the hotel—my turn to sleep, thank goodness. And I had a feeling you would be arriving soon, so I waited."

"Not long I hope," said Hazel, following Nancy as she unlocked the front door.

"No, to tell you the truth, I had just reached the door a few minutes before I saw your car pulling into the lot," said Nancy, locking the door behind them. "We had a visit last night from our friend Richie in the lab. We thought it best that the building be closed off for today. That gives us today and the weekend to know a little more about his abilities to travel, as it were."

"So, he came into the lab? Were you all in there when it happened?"

"Oh yes," said Nancy. Not another word was said as they walked down the hall.

Unlocking the door to the lab area, Nancy continued. "Gave us quite a start seeing all my notes floating around and things moving on their own." Walking up the stairs, Nancy turned and smiled at Hazel. "I am so glad you're here. I was afraid you might not come back."

"Me too," responded Hazel with a grin. "It's the boy. I think he needs me."

"We all need you. We tried communicating with him a little last night, after the visit from Richie, but nothing. You are still the only one he has said a word to."

Albert and Jim both looked up as the women entered the room. "Hazel, glad to have you back," said Albert. Then looking over at Jim, he added, "You owe me a five."

"He's kidding. I knew you would be back," said Jim with a big smile. "He has been awake all morning; still has not moved off the bed, but he is moving around a lot. It seems he is feeling a lot better."

Hazel walked over to the glass and saw the boy fidgeting on the bed below. "He is acting kind of strange. You said he still hasn't gotten off the bed; do you mean in two days?"

"Yes. Why?" ask Nancy.

"Can you let me in right now?" asked Hazel of Nancy.

"Well I think you need briefed. Hell, I need briefed after being gone for five hours," said Nancy.

"You can fill me in later, please, I must get down there." With that, Hazel made her move out the door and down the stairs. Looking up at Nancy who was close behind her, she said, "How could I be so stupid?"

"What's wrong?" asked Nancy.

"He doesn't have a bucket?" responded Hazel, waiting for the door to open.

"A what?" asked Nancy, opening the door.

Hazel did not answer. She walked over to the boy, who seemed to be in distress. Hazel picked the boy up in her arms. "You need the bucket, don't you?"

The boy nodded his head as she carried him through the door clearly marked bathroom. She placed him down on the floor right in front of the toilet and lifted the lid. The boy looked up at her confused. Hazel pointed down to the water below, "Bucket," she said.

The look of confusion disappeared, and the boy threw down his bottoms. A strong stream shot out over the top of the toilet before the boy got control and pointed it down into the water below. When he was done, the boy pulled up his pajama bottoms and just stood there, unsure what to do next. Hazel reached around him and, to the boy's amazement, flushed.

"Now, remember, the seat goes up to pee and down when you—"

"Poop," said Bobby.

"Yes," said Hazel, "when you poop. Do you know what this is for?" She pointed to the toilet paper roll.

The boy started to giggle. "That's for wiping your butt when it's dirty."

"That's right. This room is called a bathroom, and I want you use it when you need to. Understand?"

The boy started to smile, and then a strange look engulfed his face as he looked around. As Hazel watched his facial expressions, she noticed panic slowly overtaking the boy. *This is the first time he has been off the bed*, thought Hazel. *After all that time in a cage, the open space must be overwhelming.* She bent down and held the boy in her arms, "You listen to me, Bobby. No one is going to hurt you here. You understand?"

The boy, near tears, gave her an unassured nod of his head.

"Today, we are going to check out your new living space." This she said grabbing the boy's face in her hands so that he was looking directly in her eyes. "I am here, so I promise nothing will ever hurt you in here, okay?"

"Okay," came the boy's soft and unsure reply.

"Take my hand. We are going for a walk."

The boy reached up and took Hazel by the hand. For the moment, it appeared to Hazel that the panic had subsided a little, and the boy was no longer on the verge of tears.

"This is the shower," said Hazel, walking over and pulling back the walk-in shower curtain. "Nancy, Albert, can you hear us in this room?" There was no response, so Hazel stuck her head out into the main room. "Nancy, can you hear me?"

"Loud and clear. Are you two okay in there?" asked Nancy.

"Yes, we are fine. Can you send down a bath towel and maybe some new pajamas for Bobby?"

"Sure. I will send it through the slot."

"Maybe some shampoo and conditioner. I don't see any down here."

"There should be a little bag in there under the sink with toiletries—soap, shampoo, toothbrush, toothpaste, and whatnot."

"Thanks," said Hazel. Then looking down at Bobby, she smiled and walked him out into the main room. Bobby looked at the bed like he was going to make a mad dash, but Hazel quickly turned his attention away. "See this over here? This is all the furniture they put in here to make you feel at home. This is the couch and chairs. This is a TV. We will hook that up for you later and move this furniture back to where it needs to be." Then Hazel walked the boy over to the small table mounted to the wall with the locked slot going to the outside. There was a tray of that morning's breakfast sitting there untouched. No sooner had they made their way over to this location then the flap opened, the tray disappeared, and through the wall came a new pair of Spiderman pajamas and a towel.

"See, this room is bigger than you are used to, but it is still just a room. You can feel safe walking anywhere you want to in here, okay?"

"It's too big," said Bobby, looking away.

"Look, honey, you just need time to get used to it. Besides you can't spend your life on the bed."

"Is this my new life?" asked Bobby, looking up at Hazel with those big blue eyes.

Hazel was lost for words. Did anyone know what was to become of him after this little experiment was over? Finally, she said the only thing she could think of, "Oh, sweetie, this is just a start. We just need to get you used to a real life again; that's all." With that, she took him by the hand and walked him back toward the bathroom. "Let's take that shower now, shall we? Sorry, but you are a little stinky."

"That's because I farted," joked the boy and then snickered.

"Well come on, fart master. We need to get you cleaned up."

"Fart master? I'm no fart master. I'm the fart king," said Bobby and then let one rip as he walked along. This was followed by even more giggles.

"Wow, now you really do stink," joked Hazel.

As the two of them made their way into the bathroom,

Hazel noticed a change in the boy. The fear appeared nearly gone. He seemed, for the most part, energetic and happy.

· · · · · · · · · ● ○○○○○○○○ ○ ○ ○

"What's up with the thermal cameras?" asked Nancy, returning from downstairs.

"Richie is in there. You can barely make him out sitting on the bed. He hasn't moved all morning," responded Albert. "Absolutely no reaction to Hazel."

"Good. Seems like, when the boy is feeling good, Richie's presence is minimal, but when the boy is exhausted, Richie starts his shit," said Jim.

"Thank God he's quiet for now. I worry about her," said Nancy, obviously talking about Hazel. "She is amazing, the way she gets him to open up."

"She got stuck on one question, though," said Albert. "What is going to happen to him when we are done? You know, we only have him for so long."

"I don't know," said Nancy. "Unless we can prove he is not a danger to people—"

"And how do we prove that?" asked Jim. He was by no means being sarcastic, and Nancy did not take it that way.

"We need to know if his imaginary friend is an evil reflection of his other half, or if Richie is really as harmless as Bobby."

"As you so nicely put it the other day, they are the same person," alleged Albert.

"I know what I said, and our directive still stands. If we think he is a danger to human life, our orders are clear. We use Sleeping Beauty, make the call, and then they will come and take him away. I just don't see any indication that that is the case. His powers are far beyond what we expected, but I have seen nothing to indicate he is a danger to anyone."

"What about the doctor?" said Albert.

"And the man that was chopped up?" added Jim.

"I don't know. I just don't think this child could have done those things, even in self-defense," concluded Nancy.

"God, I hope you're right," said Albert. "I like the little bastard."

"Me too," said Jim.

• • • • • • • • ● ○○○○○○○○○ ○ ○

Bobby jumped back as the water came on in the shower, an immense smile on his face.

"Okay, buddy, this is how we do this. You hold out your hand and feel the water." Hazel took his hand and stuck it in the water. "When the water is warm enough, like right now, then you get in."

Bobby started to make his move, but Hazel grabbed him before he got the chance. "Hold on. You need to take off those pajamas first."

Bobby wasted no time in pulling off his top and bottoms. "Now?" he asked, all excited.

Hazel reached her hand under the showerhead. "Okay. You're good to go."

Bobby walked under the water; a large smirk covered his face. "It's warm," he said.

"First things first," said Hazel lifting one arm and starting to scrub his armpit. Then she turned him and did the other, trying her best not to get soaked herself. "Now take this," she said, handing him the soap, "and wash you privates."

"What's that?" asked Bobby.

"Your butt and pee pee," said Hazel.

"What's a pee pee?" Bobby asked.

Hazel pointed to the desired location on the boy's body. "You know, your ..."

"That's my dick," said Bobby.

"Well, we are going to call it a pee pee, okay?" asked Hazel.

"Okay," said Bobby, doing as instructed.

Next Hazel had the boy move on to his legs and feet while she scrubbed his head with the shampoo. Once he was clean from top to bottom, Hazel said, "Okay, now you can play for a few minutes, but let me get out of the line of fire."

With that, she closed the curtain to keep from getting drenched herself. She could hear the boy slapping his feet in the puddles of water on the floor. *He is actually enjoying himself*, thought Hazel. She wondered how long it had been since the boy had had a chance to play. She almost didn't want the moment to end for him, but she still needed some answers. "How did you bathe in the basement?" asked Hazel, hoping the boy would not shut down.

"The Man—that's what we all called him—he would come and take our rugs and then make us take off our clothes. He'd spray some soap in our hands and then spray us with the hose," responded Bobby, matter-of-fact like.

This is a good sign, thought Hazel. *He is talking about the basement.* Still, she didn't want to press to hard. Maybe she should wait until she was in the main room where it was all being recorded, but the iron was hot, so she pressed on. "My goodness, how long did they keep you down in the basement?" she asked as if the question was not that important.

"I don't know. Since I can remember," said Bobby still splashing around, a torrent of water bouncing off the shower curtain.

"Wasn't it lonely down there?" asked Hazel.

"Sometimes," came the response.

"Okay, buddy. I think you're done," she said and reached in to shut off the water. She half expected an objection to this, but as she pulled back the current, the boy stood there smiling up at her.

"Thank you, Hazel, that was sooooo great—a lot better than the hose. That was always so cold. I hated it."

Hazel grabbed the towel and started to dry the boy off. "Bobby, did you ever see any other adults beside the Man in the basement?"

"Sometimes men would come down there. They would make us all stand in front of our cages, and they would walk around looking at each kid. Some even wanted us to open our mouths, so they could look at our teeth."

"What did the men look like who came down to look at you?"

"All kinds—black, white, some that wore funny hats made out of cloths wrapped around their heads. Those ones looked mostly at the girls. I don't know who they were, but some of them were bad men I think. They would put their hands down our pants and feel around."

"Do you know what these men wanted?" asked Hazel, aware she was pushing.

"I don't know," said Bobby, shrugging his shoulder. "But sometimes after they were done, we would wake up the next morning and some of the kids were gone. There were always kids coming and going."

"What do you think happened to the kids that did not come back?" asked Hazel.

"The Man said they were adopted, taken to live with their forever families. But I think he was lying."

Hazel finished drying off the boy and helped him put on his Spiderman pajamas. "Why do you think that?" Hazel saw the look in the boy's eyes change. She was losing him again.

"I don't want to talk about it," said Bobby.

"Ok, honey. That's fine. We will only talk about things you want to talk about today."

"I'm hungry," said Bobby, once fully dressed.

Hazel stuck her head out of the room, "Nancy, can we get lunch down here?"

"On its way," came the response.

"You know the people upstairs are really nice. If you ask, they will get you what you need," said Hazel.

"I'm scared. I don't know them."

"Well, you didn't know me a few days ago either."

"That's different. They are not you, Hazel," said the boy as he walked by himself into the main room. In no time, the slot opened, and a tray appeared on the table.

"There is your lunch, honey. I want you go get it yourself this time, okay?"

"Okay," said Bobby reluctantly. "But you will watch me, okay?"

"I will watch every step. Grab it and bring it back to the bed. I will be there waiting."

With that, the boy made his way to the tray, looking back every few feet to make sure Hazel was still watching. He grabbed the tray and ran back to the bed. "I did it, all by myself."

"I am so proud of you, my little man," said Hazel. Looking down at her watch, Hazel jumped off the bed. "Honey, I need to go to work now. Remember, if you need anything, just ask."

Bobby looked up at her with doubt in his eye but nodded his head.

"I want you to do this for me before I go, okay?" asked Hazel and then whispered in the boy's ear.

"No. I just want to eat my food now," was his response.

"Please, Bobby, do it for me," said Hazel and gave him a huge smile.

Then to the amazement of everyone upstairs, the boy said loud and clear, "Nancy, can you open the door for Hazel? She needs to get out."

"Yes, honey. I will be right down," came the response over the intercom.

"I am so proud of you, my little man," said Hazel, pinching the boy's cheeks.

Bobby looked up at her, beaming from the compliment.

• • • • • • • • ● ○○○○○○○○ ○ ○

Agnes was just getting ready to eat her lunch on her veranda. The day was unseasonably warm for October, and not knowing how long it would last, Agnes had decided to eat outside; it may well be her last chance until spring.

"Madam, I am ever so sorry to bother you, but there is a group of people here to see you. I told them you were just sitting down for lunch, but they did insist that they be seen at once."

"And who is it that is in such a hurry they cannot wait until after I dine?"

"Well, madam, it's Mr. Timberlake, Mr. Henderson, and Mr. Southworth," said Martin timidly. "Shall I make them wait?"

"No, no. Go ahead and let the horde in. But, Martin, show them to my office please."

"Yes, madam."

"And, Martin."

"Yes, madam."

"Have Cook cover my food so it stays warm. Hopefully this will not take long," said Agnes.

"Yes, madam," said Martin and then turned and left.

Agnes huffed as she got up and walked across the veranda to the french doors at the far end that opened into her office. No sooner had she taken her seat at the head of the table than all three men came bursting in all together, talking loudly to each other.

"Gentlemen, please, please, calm yourselves and have a seat at the table," said Agnes, more than just a little annoyed. Coldly she watched as each man became silent and found his spots at the round table. "Now can someone tell me why you all needed to see me, and during my lunch."

"I came to see you to let you know that they canceled *The Rocky Horror Picture Show*. I ran into these two at your front door," said Chad.

"Well, I'm here because someone tried to kill me with a butcher knife yesterday. Something has to be done Agnes!" yelled Larry. "I think someone is trying to take out the society."

"Calm yourself, Larry. We are not going to find solutions to anything if we don't remain calm," snapped Agnes. "There will be no yelling at this table. You know the rules."

"Fuck your rules, Agnes. Something broke every window in my house last night. I am not here looking for your solutions, I'm here to give warning," said Earl, never bothering to even look in Agnes's direction. "We are all cursed. First it was Fredrick; now it's after the rest of us."

"Relax, Earl. Calm yourself. Look, my house was invaded last night as well," started Agnes. "But I've thought about what took place, and I've decided someone is trying to get us to play our hand. Someone knows something about the society, and whoever they are, they are having their way with us. Mark my words, they will come forward and ask for monetary compensation. When that happens, my man will take care of it. Until then, we must remember they are only trying to wear us down, frighten us into submission."

"Well they're doing a pretty damn good job of it, Agnes!" exclaimed Earl. "Look, I'm telling you what happened at my house last night was, was …"

"Oh, for God's sake, man up, Earl," said Agnes, keeping her voice under control. "This is a case of blackmail, plain and simple. Someone, somehow, knows what the society has been up to, and they are trying to reach their payday; that's all."

"You think so?" asked Larry.

"I know so," said Agnes. "And they are not going to get away with this."

Earl leaned back in his chair and offered a sinister smile. "You are not listening. What happened at my house was not done by any man or woman. The spirits of those we have wronged are seeking revenge, *and they're fucking pissed off*! We will not make it through this, any of us."

"Calm down," said Chad at last. "We are all under a lot of stress. I know right now it seems like the world is coming to the end. But for once, I have to agree with Agnes. We need to stay calm. We need to look at all our options."

Agnes now turned on Chad with a frozen glare. "And what options are you considering Chad?"

"Look, Agnes I didn't mean—"

"I don't care what you mean. I told all of you once, and I will tell you all one more time—I will take care of this. But you must stop whining like a bunch of children and stay the course. With all of us running to the police, it won't take them long to link all of us together. That's what this son of a bitch wants—us to panic so they can swoop in and clean us all out."

"You're right," said Larry. "I'm sorry. I will do my best."

Earl just smiled and stood up. He gave the group one final look up and down and then shook his head. As he walked out the door, he repeated what he had just said a moment before. "We will not make it through this, any of us." With that, he was gone.

"We need to keep an eye on him," said Chad.

Agnes leaned back in her chair and stared straight at Chad. "Is he the one we need to keep an eye on, Chad?"

With that Chad stood, glared at Agnes for a moment, and then walked out behind Earl.

• • • • • • • • • ● ○○○○○○○ ○ ○ ○

Vinnie had spent all morning in the office going through arrest records of every Prescott, Southworth, Henderson, Wentworth, and Willmore he could find. He was going through the last of the Wentworth's file when Hazel walked into the office.

"Vinnie, in my office please," she said as soon as she saw him at his desk.

Vinnie at once got up and followed her, closing the door behind them. "How did it go with the boy today?" asked Vinnie.

"Really good actually. I got him to open up a little today," responded Hazel. "He even started talking about his time in the basement. There is now no doubt left in my mind; whoever was behind those cages, they were kidnapping and then selling kids on the open market. From the way he described the men who came in, I would say some were dealing in the white slave market, the way he described them inspecting their teeth. The rest were probably perverts and sex traffickers. Regardless, it must have been a big moneymaker. I am sure no one took that kind of risk without expecting a high return. What do you think a child would go for? I mean, how much would a person pay for a child?"

"I don't know. Makes me sick just thinking about it," said Vinnie with a shiver. "How long do you think he was down there?"

"I don't know, but it was a long time. The kid didn't

even know what a toilet was." Hazel sat behind her desk and put her feet up on its edge. "I still don't think the kid had anything to do with any of the murders, powers or no powers. I can see it; it's just not possible."

"Well, while you were playing with the child, I worked on old case records," said Vinnie.

"And?"

"And nothing. I mean everyone uses Barbra Wentworth as their attorney; some minor arrests, not one conviction."

"Well, she is the most high-priced lawyer in town, right?"

"The Willmore family is a little more interesting, though. They too have used her as their attorney. Seems the young Willmore got busted a number of times for petty theft; no convictions."

"Interesting. You wouldn't think a small-time butcher could afford a Wentworth." Hazel put her feet down and leaned in, "Sounds a little fishy to me."

"That's what I thought," said Vinnie. "Anyway, I am going back on the road and looking for Bibens in the morning. Can't take another day in this office."

"Tomorrow's Saturday. I thought you were off," said Hazel.

"I'll flex if it's okay. I still think Bibens knows more than we give him credit for."

"That wouldn't be hard," joked Hazel. "Tomorrow is my day off as well, and I'm spending it at the university. I think there is more we can learn from Bobby."

"Is that the only reason you're going back?" said Vinnie with a smirk.

"No. You know that's not the only reason, I want to help

this kid, I think he's worth the time. He may be some miracle of nature. But to me, he's just a sweet kid."

• • • • • • • • ● ○○○○○○○○○ ○ ○

"Nancy, come here and look at this," said Albert.

"What? Problems with the thermals again?"

"No, come look at the connection between Bobby and Richie," said Albert pointing to the screen. "Can you see the connection? It's wider. And look at Richie. He's growing in color and mass."

As Nancy looked at the screen it was obvious that, as the connection grew wider, Richie seemed to flourish. "Interesting; it's almost like Bobby is feeding him power."

Without any warning, the thermal cameras went completely down. "*Shit!*" exclaimed Albert. "Not again."

"Quiet, listen," said Nancy, grabbing Albert by the arm.

"That's enough, Richie," came Bobby's voice through the intercom.

Looking down through the glass, Nancy saw Bobby lie back on his bed. All day, the boy had been wide awake and active. Now he looked like he was totally wiped out.

"I need to get some sleep now, Richie. Please let me get some sleep," came his voice once more through the intercom. "In the morning, we are moving all the furniture back the way it was, okay?"

Nancy wished Hazel was there. She'd had to run off before she could brief them about their conversation in the bathroom, but had sworn she would be back first thing in the morning to fill them in. She hated to do it, but with time limited, she would need to pressure Hazel about asking

Bobby about Richie. After Hazel had left, the boy would not even respond to her over the com. She had asked him if he wanted dinner. "No," was the only thing he's said. After that, nothing. Hazel was the key—the key to understanding how and why the boy had created Richie and the key to Bobby's future.

"Well, that was a strange exchange between them. He has not said a word to Richie all day," said Albert.

"Albert, I love you with all my heart, but if you don't get these fucking thermals operational, I am going to put my foot right up your ass."

Albert chuckled. "You got it, boss. I will get them working tonight. I promise."

· · · · · · · · ● ○○○○○○○○ ○ ○

Barbra Wentworth walked through her front door, carelessly dropped her briefcase, on the floor of the hallway, walked directly into the kitchen, and poured herself a healthy glass of red wine. As she walked through the stately living room, wineglass in hand, she stripped off every stitch of clothing she wore, dropping articles off every few feet on the hardwood floors. Once completely naked, she opened the glass doors to her backyard and the crisp nighttime air. She shuffled her way onto her raised deck, walked all natural over to the hot tub, turned on the jets, and climbed in.

"This has been the week from hell," she said out loud to no one else but herself. As she put her feet on the footrest of the hot tub, made with special jets pointed directly at her feet, she sighed. This was it, the only spot in the world she could truly relax and shut the world out. When she'd left the office, her first thought had been to call one of her female acquaintances to meet her tonight for a little rumble and tumble. But the moment she had gotten into her car and headed home she had known tonight was just not that night. She took a good sip from her wineglass and laid her head back on her bath pillow. This was what she needed— solitude, a chance to meditate and let all her stress bubble out of her body.

As she lay there listing to the motion of the water, a faint sound caught her ear. It was almost inaudible at first, hidden behind the sound of the jets. She sat and listened carefully. Something was moving in the bushes behind her house. Barbra sat up and looked on one side and then the other at the bushes lining both sides of her house and meeting on each side of her deck. She saw no movement in either direction. *A rabbit,* she thought, *nothing more than a rabbit.* The hairy vermin had infested her property, eating their way through her beautiful garden. Just then came the sound once more, only louder and closer. It was definitely coming for the bushes on her right side, under the kitchen window. A bunch of possibilities now ran through her head—a raccoon; a skunk; or, worst of all, a possum. She hated the thought of any of them but especially the possum; to her, they were nothing more than giant rats.

Quietly she climbed out of the hot tub. This was not her first encounter with unwanted varmints. Still on the deck, she walked over to the back of the house and grabbed the hose. She turned it on, grabbed the nozzle, and sprayed full force into the bushes. Nothing happened. No drenched rodent came out running for its life. No raccoon hissed in protest. Nothing. She then tried the left side, just in case the critter had slipped under the deck to the other side. Again, nothing.

Whatever it was, it's gone now, she thought. She turned off the hose and returned to the hot tub, and none too soon; it was getting chilly out there with the cool night air blowing stiffly against her wet birthday suit. Normally, it was a straight walk into the warm house. Even in the middle of winter, she made it with no problem. But it was not so when sneaking across the deck to make a major attack, only to end up having the chilly water from the hose blow back into your face. The warmth of the water was like ecstasy, and again she started to relax. But then came the other sound. The sound of a child's laughter.

Before she could even raise her head from her pillow, she was splashed in the face with water from the tub. She was sure someone, or something had just jumped in the tub with her. But when she wiped the water from her eyes, there was nothing there. *That's enough of this shit*, she thought and started to rise.

She was just turning to take the steps out of the tub when she felt something pushing her hard back into the tub. She slipped and fell backward, landing hard on her backside. In a panic, she got back up and frantically looked around for her attacker, but once again saw nothing. Out of desperation, she tried once more for the steps, only to once again be pushed back in.

Barbra was at a loss. There was nothing there. What the hell was happening? Then she felt it. The water was getting warmer; it started burning her feet and inner thighs. Barbra screamed and headed for the other side of the tub. She would pull herself out there. Then came the laughter, the laughter of a child. Barbra stopped and looked back over her shoulder. There by the steps sat a naked child with its feet dangling in the water. From where she stood she could not tell if it was a boy or girl, for it had its legs together, and its shaved head looked straight down, staring at the bubbles. Its skin was pure white, like that of a corpse.

Barbra screamed one more time and then turned and made a dash for the other end. As she finally started pulling herself out, there came a swift blow to the side of her head, knocking her back in once more. The water was much hotter this time; she could feel it scalding her skin. Again, she rushed for the steps, and yet again, she encountered resistance. She felt someone grab her by the hair on her head and pull her straight back into the now boiling water.

Barbra screamed once again, only this time it was not out of fear, but complete and utter pain.

CHAPTER 6

Soup

At two in the morning, Albert was still trying to bring the system on line. "I give up. This equipment sucks," he said, throwing his hands up in the air.

"Nancy is due back in a few hours. I would suggest you find the problem," said Jim.

"I have tried everything I can think of. The damn thing has a mind of its own, I swear."

"Well, we might have a backup system for detecting Richie's presence," said Jim. "Look." With that, Jim pointed to his computer monitor. "The reading from the censors we installed."

Albert got up and walked over to Jim's screen.

"See here. No changes whatsoever in any of the readings other than this," said Jim, pointing to a line of numbers.

"Ozone?" asked Albert.

"Ozone," said Jim. "It's still way below a hundred parts per billion. That's why we haven't smelled it. But look at how it changes. I did a comparison to the times we knew Richie was in the room and when we knew he wasn't, and look."

"Shit," said Albert. "He must be omitting some sort of kind of electrical charge or something."

Jim opened another file on his computer. "I pulled this from last night, when the line between Richie and Bobby doubled in diameter—you know, just before your thermals took a shit."

"Damn, it doubled," said Albert.

"At least we will know now when he is here and when he has gone on one of his little adventures," said Jim, leaning back and basking in his achievement. "By the way, your cameras are back on line."

Albert turned, and sure enough, the cameras were back on. "You have got to be kidding me," he said.

"Is Richie in there?"

"Yep, clear as day."

• • • • • • • • ● ○○○○○○○○○ ○ ○

Hazel was awoken at five in the morning by the sound of the phone on her nightstand. At first, she thought it part of her dream. But then, eyes still closed, she reached over to the nightstand, accidently knocking her alarm clock to the floor, and grabbed the phone. After just a few brief minutes, she responded with a "Got it. I'm on my way. Call Vinnie. I want him there too."

With that, she hung up the phone, retrieved the alarm clock from the floor, and then reached over and smacked Brian squarely on his uncovered bare buttocks.

"What the hell?" he said, still half-asleep.

"You didn't hear the phone?"

"What? No. What's going on?" he said, rolling over, and put his arms around her waist.

"Get up. I want you to go with me. The cleaning lady found Barbra Wentworth floating dead in her hot tub this morning."

"What? Aunt Barbra's dead?"

"Aunt Barbra?" said Hazel, confused.

"Well, she wasn't my real aunt. I grew up with her nephew, Brice; they lived next door. He always called her Aunt Barbra, and so I started calling her that."

"I forget you came from that side of the tracks, little rich boy."

"Funny," said Brian, sitting up. "My family is rich, not me."

"Whatever. I'll believe it if you want me to."

Brian found his shirt on the floor next to his side of the bed and pulled it on over his head. "What happened anyway?"

"I don't know, but you and I are going to find out. The call just came in, and I want to get there before Bibens."

"Hazel, now you know you will need to inform the feds. It's their case."

"We don't know if it has anything to do with their investigation until we get there. For all we know, she slipped and hit her head or something. Now get your ass up, and let's go." With that, Hazel hurried to the bathroom.

"My uniform is in my locker at work," he yelled, pulling up his jeans.

"I don't care," came the response from the bathroom.

"I expect overtime for this. I wasn't due at the station till ten," he said, only half-joking.

Hazel emerged from the bathroom and walked swiftly over to her closet. From there, she grabbed her desired attire. Brian, who had just started making his way to the bathroom, was cut off by Hazel as she walked right by him and back into the lavatory, shutting the door.

"Come on, Hazel. I gotta take a leak. You just can't wake a man up in the middle of the night and not give him a chance to drain the vein."

"Use the downstairs bathroom."

• • • • • • • • ● ○○○○○○○○○ ○ ○

As Vinnie pulled up to the Wentworth estate, every light in the house was burning bright. Parking in the driveway, he saw a black SUV. *The feds are here already*, he thought. Next to the SUV was the medical examiner's vehicle, with two men from Sam's crew standing next to it, and Sam's car.

"Hey, guys," said Vinnie, getting out of his car. "Is Sam already here?"

"He's behind the house," said one of the men. "We are just waiting for the word to clean up that mess."

Vinnie gave the man a questioning look and then proceeded to the back of the house.

Before he even made it to the backyard, he heard Sam arguing with one of the junior FBI guys he had seen the other day at the Grinnell house.

"Look, I'm telling you this woman was in boiling water for at least two to three hours. Look at how her flesh is just falling off the bone," he heard Sam say.

"Right, old man. You mean to tell me this hot tub malfunctioned and started to boil and she never bothered to just get out? Sounds a little crazy to me. Besides, I felt the water when I got here—ninety, maybe ninety-five, but definitely not boiling."

Instead of moving forward, sure that Junior would make him leave, Vinnie simply stopped and listened for a moment.

"Okay, first of all, that's sick. It's like sticking your finger in a bowl of human soup. Second, you may have contaminated my evidence," said Sam, using a tone Vinnie had never heard from Sam. Usually, Sam was the levelheaded one, but Vinnie could sense his frustration. "I will be glad when Bibens gets here and keeps you two idiots from doing any more damage."

Just as Vinnie had made up his mind to go around the corner and make himself known, he heard yet another vehicle pulling into the drive. Slowly, he made his way back around the house and peaked around the corner. It was Hazel and Hicks.

"Hazel, Hicks, over hear," Vinnie said in a quiet voice, waving his hands for them to come in his direction. Vinnie tried to make sure to respect Hazel's authority and always referred to her as Captain around the staff, but this time it simply slipped his mind.

"How did the feds find out so quickly?" asked Hazel as she approached.

"Fuck if I know," said Vinnie. "But Bibens has yet to arrive, just his junior leaguers. They don't even know I am here yet."

"Where's Sam?" asked Hicks.

"Out back giving them hell for messing with evidence," said Vinnie. That's when he noticed Hicks was out of uniform.

Hicks saw a look of enlightenment on Vinnie's face and shook his head, while he gave him his patented "don't ask" look, but to no avail.

"Shit, you two are—"

"Yes, but keep it to yourself, Vinnie," said Hazel in a nasty tone.

"Why?" said Vinnie, shrugging his shoulders like it was no big deal.

"We are not ready for everyone to know, okay?" said Hazel just above a whisper. "Do you have a problem with that?"

"No, no," replied Vinnie, moving out of the way for Hazel to move on past.

Hicks walked up and patted him on the back. "Tried to warn you, man."

Not showing any of the patience that Vinnie had displayed, Hazel walked straight to the back of the house, across the backyard, and right onto the deck. "Sam, nice to see you. What do we got?"

Sam turned. "Hazel, good to see you."

"Just a minute," spouted the junior FBI agent. "Bibens gave us strict orders—no local PD. He doesn't want you guys messing with the crime scene."

"Right, like you know what the hell you are doing," snapped Sam.

Hazel investigated the hot tub. "No, that's fine. Now that we know the FBI is on the scene, there is no reason for us to stick around," she said and walked back over to Brian and Vinnie, who were still making their way to the deck. "Have a good day, Sam," she said over her shoulder.

Brian and Vinnie did an about-face as she passed them going the other way.

"That's it?" asked Brian.

"I found out what I needed to know," responded Hazel. "Trust me. That was no slip and fall."

"Sam said that that hot tub must have been boiling for hours for her to be in that shape," said Vinnie.

"That's impossible. I got a hot tub at home. And trust me; they get hot, but they don't boil water," offered Brian.

"You're both right," said Hazel. "I saw her. She has been in boiling water. That hot tub looked like a giant pot of chicken noodle soup, chunks of meat floating everywhere. Sam is going to have a hell of a time getting her remains out of there. And you're right too; no normal hot tub would ever get hot enough to make the water boil, so ..."

"So, what?" asked Vinnie.

"So, I don't know. Maybe the kid is responsible." Hazel reached down and opened the door to her car.

"Wait, what kid? The one from the basement?" asked Brian. "You know where he is, don't you?"

Vinnie gave Hazel a hard glare before walking to his car. Hazel knew that look; "keep your mouth shut."

"He's alive. That's all I know," she said, not looking at Brian.

"Is it true he can make things happen with his mind?" asked Brian, getting into the passenger's side door.

"Where did you hear that?" asked Hazel.

"I am a cop, you know. It was all over the hospital the night it happened. If you remember, I had to respond to that call."

Hazel hesitated for a minute. She looked over at Vinnie's car, whose headlight had just come on. "I don't know, Hicks. Maybe."

"You're hiding something from me; I can tell," said Brian, putting on his seat belt. "You know more than you're telling. But I am not going to press; it's not my place. I may be your boyfriend, but you're still my boss, and I know what need-to-know basis means."

Hazel did not say another word. She simply put the car in reverse and backed out. Not another word was exchanged until they pulled back into Hazel's drive.

"I may as well report in," said Brian, reaching over to give Hazel a kiss.

"See you tonight?" she asked.

"Sure," he replied and headed for his car.

Hazel got out and walked to her back door. She knew Brian was upset, and she could understand why. But again, this was what she had feared from the start. She knew better than to get involved with a direct report. Hazel made up her mind right there and then to end it with Brian. As long as he was a cop, there was no future for the two of them.

• • • • • • • • • ● ○○○○○○○○○ ○ ○

Nancy walked into the lab around six in the morning. She had overslept and was sure that Albert, the next in line for downtime, was more than eager for a break. She was happy to see the thermal cameras were back up and working and even happier when Jim told her that they now had a backup system for monitoring Richie's movements.

Around seven, she got the boy's breakfast but wondered whether it was even worth the effort. So far, he had only eaten with Hazel there. Still she could not let him go without.

Making her way down the stairs, she thought about the

briefing that Jim and Albert had given her about the boy. He had gotten up twice to use the bathroom, and the rest of the time, he'd slept. This morning, he had not moved and inch, lying sound asleep on his bed. Unlocking the flap, she slid in his breakfast of toast, oatmeal, and juice. She closed the flap and walked back up the stairs. *He's acting like he did the first day he was here*, she thought.

As she entered the lab, she walked across the room and sat in her chair by the glass. To her surprise, the boy was sitting up on the edge of his bed. *The sound of me delivering breakfast must have woken him*, she thought. Nancy watched in amazement as the container of juice she had just delivered lifted itself off its tray and started floating toward Bobby. "Jim, can you see Richie in the thermals?"

Jim looked over at Albert's station. "He is over by the bathroom door. He's a lot more defined today, easier to see."

So, he can move things without Richie, thought Nancy. *He has not been focusing all his talents on his imaginary friend. He can use them independently*, she concluded. She watched as the boy opened the plastic juice container and then downed the juice inside, leaving the rest of the morning meal untouched. When he was done, Hazel saw him replace the container back on the tray without even leaving his bed.

"You just saw that, right?" said Jim.

"I saw it," replied Nancy. "He can move objects without Richie."

"What do you think that means?" asked Jim.

"I don't know," responded Nancy. Just then, the buzzer for the door went off, making both of them jump.

"Hazel must be here," said Jim.

Without saying a word, Nancy got up and headed for the stairs. She was happy Hazel was there. For some reason, she felt more secure having her around.

"Good morning, Nancy," said Hazel as Nancy let her in. "How is Bobby this morning?"

"Sleeping," said Nancy. "He hasn't moved much since you left him yesterday."

"Really? He was full of piss and vinegar yesterday."

"Well todays he is acting more like the first day he was here," said Nancy. "We have a lot to talk about this morning."

As the pair made their way into the lab, Jim stood and offered his welcomes to Hazel. Hazel at once noticed how tired both he and Nancy looked. This was taking a lot out of them, she could tell.

"Please, sit with me at the table and let me fill you in," said Nancy, gesturing toward the table. "You want some coffee?"

"Oh, that would be great. This morning has already been crazy," said Hazel.

Jim stood up. "I'll get it. Cream, sugar?"

"No, black please."

"Black it is, even I can't screw that one up." With that, Jim walked over to the coffeepot, grabbed a large coffee mug, and poured Hazel a generous amount of coffee.

"First of all, let me fill you in about how Bobby transfers his energy to Richie," started Nancy.

"We got it all on tape if you want to see it," added Jim.

"You mean he feeds him his powers?" asked Hazel. "I thought you said that Richie was a manifestation of his powers, that his powers created Richie."

"He did, but it seems that he needs to be, I don't know, recharged for lack of a better word," said Nancy.

"That thin line that connects them—remember we showed you on tape?" cut in Jim, returning with the coffee. "It gets bigger. I think it's when he makes the transfer."

"Are we sure Bobby is giving it to Richie? Or is Richie simply taking it from Bobby?" said Hazel.

"Let's hope not. For that to happen, Bobby would need to have some sort of split personality. He would be thinking as two distinct individuals," said Nancy.

"That would mean that sweet child down there may not be as innocent as we would like to believe. If Richie has his own personality, for all we know, it could be something not so nice," said Jim.

"Hazel, you have been doing a great job with the boy. I know that you two talked out of range of intercoms while in the bathrooms yesterday, and I know you had to leave before we got a chance to debrief, but did he say anything about Richie while you were in there?"

Hazel took a sip of her coffee. She thought about everything that had transpired between the two of them the day before. "No. But, guys, he was making such good progress. He talked about his time in the basement, about his life down there. He talked about the men who came to buy the children."

"What? Buy children?" said Jim.

Hazel looked at the shock on both of their faces. She had forgotten that their focus had been strictly on the boy's abilities and not his history. "From what he told me in the bathroom, there is no doubt whoever was holding him in the basement was kidnapping and selling kids on the open market."

"Fuck, that is sick," said Jim. "I am so glad Albert's not here. As sensitive as he is, he would be upset for days if he heard something like that."

"But nothing about Richie?" said Nancy.

"Not a word," said Hazel, standing up and walking over to the glass with her coffee mug in hand. "You need me to ask him, don't you?"

"Yes," said Nancy, getting up to join her. "Decisions need to be made about him, Hazel. If he is a danger to others, he needs to be placed somewhere safe—safe for him and for everyone he may come in contact with."

"You mean locked up somewhere," said Hazel, "a new cage somewhere else."

"If need be, then yes," said Jim. "If he was responsible for the death of that doctor, he could kill more innocent people. We are all getting to love the little bastard, but if that's what it takes, then yes."

To Jim and Nancy's surprise, Hazel did not offer any rebuttal to their argument.

"But, if I can show he is not capable of those things and that Richie is nothing more than an extension of the boy, then what?" asked Hazel, not expecting any answer and not receiving one.

"What I don't get," said Jim, "is why the boy never used his powers to free himself in the first place. I mean, he had the gift. Why not use it?"

"Stockholm syndrome?" offered Nancy.

"No. He was no way attached to the Man, as he called

him, you can tell. Something else was keeping him there. Maybe the fear of getting caught, or the fear of a life outside, the unknown, a life that he couldn't remember," said Hazel. "Whatever the case, he didn't, and now he may be locked in a cage the rest of his life."

"I hope, for all our sakes, that is not the case," said Nancy. "But we will not know without answers. I am sorry all this is being put on you, Hazel. I truly am." With that she put her arm around Hazel, who was close to tears. "But we need to know if that little boy down there caused the death of a man, possibly two."

"Make that three," said Hazel. With that, she proceeded to tell Nancy and Jim about the apparent murder of Barbra Wentworth.

• • • • • • • • • ● ○○○○○○○○○○ ○ ○

It was a good thing that Vinnie had decided to go back to the Wentworth estate when he did. Earlier he had thought it a waste of time. *Bibens will be there all day,* he'd thought. *I have better things to do with my day off then sit parked watching the FBI fumble through this.* Still, something deep inside had urged him to keep tabs on what was going on.

Just as he was approaching the estate, he saw Bibens car pull out of the drive and head the opposite direction. He at once followed. *I wonder if the FBI even looks out for someone tailing them,* he thought.

Vinnie followed Bibens all the way across town to the home of Agnes Prescott. There Vinnie watched as Bibens pulled through the gates and up to the house. Vinnie found a spot across the street in the sun and waited. This was something he had not counted on. Had Bibens made the connection that Jackson's elite appeared to be targeted? Surely someone had told Bibens by now that Agnes Prescott and Barbra Wentworth were good friends. The two women were always seen around town together.

Since the time he, Hazel, and Hicks had left the Wentworth estate that morning, the weather had turned. The air was getting cold, and the sky showed signs of an early snow. He knew his warm, sunny parking spot would not last long as he watched the clouds move quickly in. The thought of having to turn on the car and run the heat was disheartening. Vinnie hated winter. He hated everything that went with it—the ice; the cold; shoveling snow; and, most of all, the slippery roads. More than once, he'd thought about moving out of state, to the south somewhere or maybe out to the West Coast—anywhere that wasn't Michigan.

As Vinnie stared up at the gates of the Prescott estate, he wondered what the connection was. *Why these particular wealthy families? There are obviously richer, more powerful people in town, the mayor for instance. So why them? The key is their connection with the Willmore Family; it must be. Barbra acted as their personal attorney before the younger Willmore even bought the house on Grinnell. Why? How far back does this connection go?*

After about an hour, Vinnie saw Bibens pull out of the gates. He drove right past Vinnie's car and headed back in the same direction they had both come from. Vinnie turned his car around and followed Bibens straight back to the Wentworth estate. *He left an active investigation to go and talk to the victim's best friend?* He pondered the situation. This

time, he did not stop. He kept driving right past Bibens, past
the Wentworth estate, and headed downtown. He needed
some time at the library for research.

• • • • • • • • ● ○○○○○○○○○ ○ ○

Sam left the Wentworth Estate around noon. He gave his
crew clear instructions to lay out what they had and let it dry.
Sam would be back that afternoon to find whatever he could
from the decimated remains. He doubted any answers would
be found from the corpse—nothing like boiling the body to
clean any traces—but he did know where he hoped he might
find some answers. As he drove out of town, his mind was
reeling. He knew that, once again, he was trying to explain
the unexplainable. Nothing about this case conformed to
any sense of reasoning. Once more, he found himself in the
middle of something he could not wrap his mind around. It
was just like the Parksville murders; only this time people
were not found half-eaten, but more butchered and cooked.
If there was a connection, there was one person he needed to
talk to, and that was Franky Lake.

Sam had purposely kept himself from learning all the
facts about the Parksville case so many years ago, even
though he was more than certain Professor Phillip Parker
would have explained everything in detail if asked. He
trusted Phillip, implicitly and there was little doubt that
Phillip trusted him as well. Sam knew the reason he had not
asked; he was scared—scared that learning all the details
would rock his foundation of beliefs and security. If evil had a
face and a name, he would just as soon not know it. But now,
he had no choice. He had to know because it was happening

again. He could not, in good conscience, turn a blind eye; if he could keep people from dying, he would have to face his fears.

Sam turned into the parking lot of the Fine Arts Building at Parksville University. He knew Franky, not as well as Phillip of course, but Franky had always seemed levelheaded. Yet, his hands trembled, and droplets of sweet formed on his forehead as he got out of his car and made his way inside the building.

After finding the room that Franky Lake was in, Sam waited patiently outside the door for his class to end. Though it was a mere twenty minutes, it seemed like forever to the nervous Sam. *What if he tells me to go to hell?* he thought. *What then?* After all, he had not seen the man in years.

As students poured out of the door, Sam made his way in. He stood by the door while Franky completed his conversation with a student, something about midterms. He was amazed at how much more mature he looked than he had the last time he'd seen him. This was enhanced by the goatee Franky now sported on his face.

When Franky was done, he looked up and saw Sam. "Sam, so nice to see you. It's been years," said Franky with a humongous grin. He walked over and shook his hand.

"You too, Franky. You got a minute?"

"Actually, I am done for the day," said Franky, "at least with instruction. Come in and have a seat."

Sam reached over and shut the door and then sat next to Franky who had placed himself in the first row of student chairs. "Franky, I would not ask this if I did not have to, but things are taking place in Jackson that kind of remind me of that ordeal you went through in Parksville."

"You want to know what really happened, don't you?" asked Franky. "I am not sure what Phillip has told you, but I know he would want me to help you in any way I can."

Sam noticed Franky's transition from joy to sadness when he mentioned the name of Phillip. "I need to know what you two have gone through. I need to know more about the evil you faced and what really happened to Phillip."

"Okay, Sam. But first you will need to tell me about what's going on in Jackson. I need to know if it has anything to do with Phillip and where he may be."

Sam stopped and paused for a long time. Giving information about an FBI investigation to a civilian would cost him his job if discovered. *Maybe even earn me jail time*, he thought. Still, this time, he had to do something; if not, he feared the killings would never stop. Finally, he reached out to shake Franky's hand. "Deal," said Sam. "But please remember, this is just between us."

· · · · · · · · ● ○○○○○○○○ ○ ○

Hazel had waited all morning and into the afternoon for Bobby to rise from his slumber. At last she could not wait any longer. "I am going down and check on him; it's not right him sleeping this long."

"I agree," said the newly arrived and refreshed Albert. "Richie is now by the wall were all the furniture is. He is pretty pronounced today."

"Let me grab the lunch I made for him, and I'll walk you down," said Nancy. She walked over to the small refrigerator in the corner and pulled out a prepacked brown paper bag, and with that, the two of them headed out the door and down the stairs. "There is one thing I forgot to tell you. This morning, I saw Bobby retrieve a juice from his morning tray."

"You mean he finally got out of bed without me here?" asked Hazel, somewhat surprised.

"Well he did go to the bathroom a couple of times, but the juice he got while still sitting on his bed. Richie was nowhere near him or the tray," said Nancy, waiting for a sign of understanding from Hazel.

"So, he doesn't need Richie to move objects?" asked Hazel.

Nancy, who had just unlocked the door, gave her a nod of her head. "It appears so."

"Interesting," said Hazel. She paused a moment and then made her way through the door. At first, she was hesitant to wake the boy. Even though she knew he was not a danger to her, she didn't want to startle him. "Bobby, you awake?" This she said just above a whisper, but it was enough. She heard him stir and then roll over in bed. As he looked up at her, Hazel could tell the boy was confused and disoriented. "It's Hazel, honey. You've been sleeping all day."

"Hazel?" asked the boy.

"Yes, honey. It's me. I'm here to see you." With that, she walked over and sat next to him on the bed. He looked exhausted and was having a hard time waking. "Are you feeling okay, dear?"

"Just tired," he replied, pulling himself up to a sitting position.

"Are you hungry? I brought you lunch."

"That's okay. I'm not really hungry right now."

Hazel knew she was supposed to be asking about Richie, but she knew the boy well enough to know that, in his current state, he would simply shut down and not talk to her at all. Besides, at that moment, she was more worried about his health. She put her hand on his forehead. "You don't feel warm. Does your belly hurt?"

"No, just tired," responded Bobby, struggling hard to keep his eyes open.

"Do you want me let to you sleep and maybe come back later?" she asked of him.

"Yes please, maybe tomorrow," was all he said.

Hazel took the hint. He wanted to be left alone to rest. "Okay, buddy. I will see you in the morning, okay?"

"Okay," said the boy, who simply rolled back over on the bed.

He didn't even say goodbye, thought Hazel, making her way to the door. *That is so unlike him.*

· · · · · · · · · ● ○○○○○○○○○ ○ ○

Earl Southworth found out about the death of Barbra Wentworth while watching the TV mounted above the bar at the Rooster Bar and Grill. It was not uncommon to find him sitting there on weekdays during lunchtime, and usually for some time after. Owning a retail dynasty came with its perks. He watched in silence as the pretty lady on TV talked about an apparent accidental death of the renowned attorney at her estate the night before. *Accidental my ass*, he thought as he motioned for Marty the bartender to bring him another rum and coke. *No accident blew out all my fucking windows.*

"I'll buy this one," came a voice over his shoulder.

Earl didn't need to turn around. He knew who it was. "Well, Chad, aren't you afraid a voter will see you here during the day for piss sake?" huffed Earl.

"No. I am not running for reelection. Remember, it's your turn next," said Chad, pulling up a stool so he was sitting right next to Earl.

"You heard about Barbra, I take it?" asked Earl, still placing his gaze on the TV screen. "You believe any of the accidental death bullshit?"

"Yes, I heard. That's why I'm here, to make sure you're all right," he said.

"Better than fucking Barbra," he said sarcastically and then laughed.

Marty approached with Earl's rum and coke. "You want anything?" he asked of Chad.

"Crown, on the rocks," said Chad, reaching for his wallet.

"Put that away," Earl said to Chad. "Marty just put them both on my tab."

"Will do, Earl," said Marty, walking away to pour the Crown.

"More of us are going to die. You know that, don't you?" asked Earl just above a whisper. "We are going to pay for our sins and those of our fathers."

Chad held his tongue as Marty returned with his drink. He gave Marty a nod of his head, as the drink was the size of a good double. "You are talking nonsense. I'm not stupid. I agree her death was anything but accidental. Still, I don't believe any evil entity is targeting the society."

"So, you're siding with Agnes on this," said Earl, taking a

swig of his drink. "First time you two have seen eye to eye on anything. You know she thinks you're trying to put an end to the society after all these years. You know that, don't you?"

"And she would be right. It is time for all this to end, Earl. I only have a short time before I govern over the society. And when I do, I will put an end to the whole dismal thing."

Earl looked down into his glass. "You know she thinks you will eventually go to the cops, don't you?"

"And why the hell would I do that? She's paranoid; always has been."

"It's okay. I've thought about it myself," said Earl, turning for the first time to look Chad in the face. "But now it doesn't matter; the police or God himself cannot help us. When we are all dead, the society will end. That will be the end of it, Chad. That's when all of this will stop."

"We need to find out who is behind this and stop them, Earl. It's that simple. Someone is trying to break us apart, make us weak." With that, Chad grabbed his drink and downed it in one big swallow. "We got a fight on our hands, Earl. You got to keep your shit together. If Agnes even thinks you're going off the edge, she will end you. I'm more afraid of that crazy old bitch than I am of any fucking ghost, and you should be too." Chad stood, patted Earl hard on the shoulder, and left.

"Bring me another Marty," said Earl.

• • • • • • • • ● ○○○○○○○○○ ○ ○

It was close to four in the afternoon when Hazel returned to the office, and if she would have known what awaited her, she would have just gone straight home and called it a day, but she had a strong urge to confide in Vinnie everything that was going on. She was having a bad day to say the least. She had been awakened early with yet another murder; she had decided to end things with her boyfriend; the boy was none responsive, she'd had to apologize profusely to Nancy for not addressing the issue of Richie with Bobby even though it was so important; and now that she had decided to finally spill her guts to someone, the one person she trusted enough to tell wasn't even there.

When she first arrived, things were fairly quiet, but that didn't last for long. It wasn't ten minutes before Officer Sandy Miller showed herself at her door. "Come in, Miller," said Hazel.

Sandy spent a lot of time in her office. She was young, pretty, and the office snitch. Anything that was going on in the office, she knew about it. Hazel was always getting an earful of gossip whenever Sandy appeared at her door. Still, it would be a nice break to hear about anything other than the case.

"Thanks, Captain," said Sandy as she closed the door behind her.

Hazel thought it odd that she was carrying her oversize purse around in the office. Usually the female officers left their purses in their lockers. "What can I do you for?"

Sandy looked down at her shoes for a moment.

This is going to be a good one, thought Hazel, *She is still making up her mind if she wants to tell me or not.*

"Well, Captain, it's about Officer Moretti ..." she started.

"What about him, Miller? Spit it out."

Officer Miller reached into her purse and pulled out

what appeared to be some sort of magazine. "My mother is moving to Arizona later this month, and she was going through some of her things, you know, cleaning out all the crap she didn't need. And well ..."

"Miller, I am busy. What is it you need to say?"

"Well, my mom is kind of a freak, if you know what I mean."

"Miller, the point."

Sandy handed over the magazine. "Mom gave me a stack of these *Fun Girl* magazines. Open it up to the centerfold."

Hazel did as Sandy asked and then slammed the magazine shut and put it down quickly on her desk.

"God really did bless him, didn't he?" said Sandy, her face turning beet red. "I didn't know what to do when I saw it. I mean ..."

"You did the right thing," said Hazel. Then Hazel leaned back in her chair; her face resembled someone who had just witnessed a horrible accident.

"It's an old magazine. Maybe no one will ever see it."

"Thanks, Miller," said Hazel after an extended pause. "I want you to keep this to yourself. Not a word to anyone. I will handle this. You got me?"

"Yes, Captain," said Sandy and then hurried toward the door.

"Remember, not a word."

With that, Sandy nodded and walked out of Hazel's office.

Hazel knew that, if this got out, Vinnie may well be off the force. She didn't know what to do. At first, she thought maybe it was a mistake. It was just someone who looked like him. She lifted the magazine once more. She wanted to make sure. But it was like looking at your brother walking out of the shower. Finally, she got up the courage and opened it.

There he was, leaning against an artificial lamppost, wearing nothing more than a fedora. Sandy was right. God had truly blessed him.

"Captain."

Hazel jumped and threw the magazine on the floor at her feet. It was, of all people, Vinnie standing at the door.

"You okay?" asked Vinnie, walking in.

"Yeah, yeah. I'm fine," stuttered Hazel.

"Look, I can come back," Vinnie said, a look of worry on his face.

"I said I'm fine. Just get your ass in here," snapped Hazel.

Just then, Sam showed up at the door as well. "Sorry, I'll wait," he said, looking at Vinnie already standing in her office.

"No. I want the both of you in here. And shut the door. I have something I need to talk to both of you about. I can't keep all of this to myself any longer."

"I can't stay but a minute. I got a body to examine," said Sam.

"Trust me. That can wait," barked Hazel, trying desperately to avoid direct eye contact with Vinnie, or his crotch.

She started telling both men about what all she had been going through at the university. Both men sat quietly while she filled them in on every detail about Bobby, Richie, Albert, Jim, and Nancy. When she was done talking, she leaned back in her chair, staring at the both of them as if she was waiting for someone to speak up.

Nothing—no response from either man.

Finally, she could not take it any longer. "Well, any thoughts on this?"

"Amazing," said Sam. "I don't know what to say. I am still trying to process all of this."

Vinnie stood up and leaned forward on her desk, "My God, Hazel. You have got to be careful. I mean you are risking your life here."

"He's right," added Sam.

"Look, don't worry about me. I'll be fine. What I want to know is, What do we do with all this information?" asked Hazel.

"I say there is not much we can do about it one way or the other," said Vinnie. "I don't mean to sound crass, but we have the FBI working on the case and another federal agency working with this Bobby kid. The only thing we can do is keep doing what we are doing—you working with one agency, Sam working with the other."

"And what about you?" asked Hazel.

"I am going to focus on this," said Vinnie, placing the items he was carrying in his hands onto Hazel's desk. One was a folder of pictures, some taken off an old microfiche printer; the other was an old hardcover book. "It's hard to be rich and not get yourself in the papers."

"You lost me," said Hazel.

"Me to," added Sam.

This is a history of Jackson dating all the way back to its founding," said Vinnie, pointing to the hardcover book. "And these," he said, pointing to the folder, "are newspaper articles going back to the twenties."

"Okay, "said Hazel. "What's our hook here?"

"Well, we all know this lady," said Vinnie, opening the folder. There was Agnes Prescott's picture taken from a current article. "Look at her right hand. See her ring?"

"You mean the rose-shaped one. What are those rubies?" asked Sam.

"It's beautiful," said Hazel.

"Well, here is the same ring in 1864, except it's on the hand of her great-great-grandfather, Herman Prescott," said Vinnie, opening up the book, which he had obviously taken the time to label with Post-it notes.

"So, maybe it's a family heirloom. It did look a little big on her hand," said Hazel.

"I thought so too, at first. Then I happened to see it again, only this time it was on this man."

Vinnie pulled out the next picture from the file. "This was taken fifteen years ago."

Hazel gasped when she looked down. The ring was now on the hand of a younger Dr. Hendershot.

"Here is his great-great grandfather wearing the same ring," said Vinnie, now referring to the book.

"So, what does all this mean?" asked Sam.

"I am not going to bother you with all of these pictures, but I have found different Wentworth, Prescott, Southworth, Hendershot, and Timberlake family members throughout Jackson's glorious history all wearing this same ring at different times. I am sure there are more families, but some of the pictures I just couldn't reference."

"That means these families are all connected and have been connected for some time," said Sam.

"Well, out of the families I have identified, two current family members are dead, one reported the windows blown out of his house in the middle of the night, and one reported a home invasion where nothing was taken but a pair of scissors were nicely placed in the throat of her portrait. I would say I have something to work on here. I am going to start with our good friend City Commissioner Chad Timberlake. Maybe he can add a little to the story, or maybe Earl Southworth."

"Don't step on Bibens's toes," warned Sam. "He can be a prick; believe me."

"No worries. Besides, I don't think he has even made the connection yet," said Vinnie.

"Don't underestimate him," stated Hazel.

Vinnie just chuckled. "Trust me; I don't. I found him visiting the Prescott estate just this afternoon. I am going to get on that piece-of-shit computer of mine tomorrow and start going through all the reports of missing children in the area, see if there is a connection to any of the families as well."

"Vinnie, you're one hell of a detective. I hope you never leave," said Sam.

Hazel just smiled and then glanced down at the magazine by her feet, making sure it was still there and unseen.

"Thanks, Sam," said Vinnie. "I will keep you all updated. But for now, that's all I have."

"Good work, Vinnie," said Hazel, and then turning to Sam, she added, "I'm sorry, Sam. You came all the way over here, and I never did ask what you needed,"

"It will have to wait," said Sam, standing and putting on his coat. "I got a body I got to examine. I have no doubt Bibens will be at my door first thing in the morning wanting answers."

CHAPTER 7

Sweet Dreams

Sam was tired, and his brain hurt. The drive home had been a blur. His mind was so full of endless possibilities that he did not remember one second of the trip. After his meeting with Franky, he had felt confused and disheartened about the fate of an old friend. Sam knew that Phillip and Franky both had gone through some crazy shit, but by the time Franky was done telling his tale, Sam was lost for words. The whole thing was so unbelievable—flesh-eating witches; it was beyond possibility. Still, he believed every word Franky said. After all, Sam himself had played his part in that horrifying tale.

Both he and Franky had summarized from what they knew that the events taking place in Jackson probably had nothing to do with Phillip Parker or the Parksville murders. Sam knew no matter how hard Franky wanted to make a connection—the thought of finding Phillip was overpowering him—the answers Franky wanted were simply not there. Yes, something beyond the norm was taking place, but it was very doubtful it had anything to do with Phillip Parker.

So, if this was something different, what was it? Was the boy that Hazel talked so passionately about truly capable of such things? And if so, why? What was the motive? Again, the connection was not there. Maybe some of Jackson's finest were involved in the operations on Grinnell, but Sam knew the kid had never seen them. None of them would ever dare show his or her face there; they would never implicate themselves in such things, even if they did have a hand in it.

As he pulled into the drive, he saw Linda standing the doorway with a big smile on her face. As Sam approached her, he did not feel that usual comfort of coming home to her. After a long hard day digging through the remains of human tissue, it was always his comfort to come home to her warm embrace, the kids landing kisses on his scarred cheek, the family meal, vegging by the TV until bed, and then spooning his wife at night until they were both sound asleep. This was what made his life complete—a life he'd thought he would never have. But tonight, nothing could ease his troubled mind.

•••••••••●○○○○○○○○○○

Hazel had mixed emotions when she walked through her front door and Brian was not there. She was relieved and disappointed at the same time. She thought it best to end things quickly but was glad she could put it off for another day. It was going to be one of the hardest things she had ever done. He was so kind and sweet. If only they had met under different circumstances, maybe things would have been different; maybe the two of them would have worked as a couple. But it was no good dwelling on what might have been. She had gone over her speech a dozen times and still had no idea what exactly she was going to say when the time came.

Just as she was getting ready to take her nightly shower, she heard a car pull up her drive. "Shit," she said out loud and hurried to retrieve her nightgown. Hazel had faced many dangerous situations as a cop. She always held up well under pressure. But now she felt her knees shake, and her stomach was tied up in knots. Looking out the window, she saw it was indeed Brian's car. Throwing on her nightgown, she slowly made her way downstairs and to the front door.

When she opened the door, there stood Brian, a large bouquet of flowers in one hand and an envelope in the other. Before she could utter a word, Brian handed her the envelope.

"This is my letter of resignation with a two-week notice," he said, avoiding eye contact.

"Brian, I can't take this. I won't take this."

"Sorry, boss. You have no choice," responded Brian as he made his way inside. "I told you a long time ago the only reason I became a cop in the first place was to piss off my old man. Well, he's not here anymore, so I'm done."

"But—"

"Look, I will be totally honest with you. I was going to leave the force after Dad died, but I stayed because it gave me a chance to be near you. Now I am afraid that me staying a cop would only drive us apart. I love you, Hazel, plain and simple."

"But, Brian, you're a good cop."

"And I will be a great businessman. I already told my brother I am coming back into the family business. Trust me; he is more than happy to have me take the reins. After all, Dad left me the business, not him."

"I don't know what to say," responded a tearful Hazel.

"Look, once I'm not a cop, I will never ask you about your work. If you want to share with me, that's fine, but otherwise—"

Hazel grabbed him around the neck and gave him a long, passionate kiss.

"I love you Hazel Mae Cowan," he said in response.

"Does this mean I can't tell you what to do anymore, Hicks?" Hazel asked sarcastically.

"You got two weeks, lady. Then I don't have to take your shit anymore. And don't call me Hicks."

With that, Hazel laughed. "I love you too, Hicks."

• • • • • • • • ● ○○○○○○○○○○

Agnes stood naked in the open night air, a cool breeze rushing across her bare skin. Behind her was a large twisted oak, long bare branches looming far above her. At first, she thought it an open field. The ground was flat, and the tree stood completely alone. Slowly, through the darkness, she could distinguish stones rising from the ground. They were all in rows and no more than a few inches high. Then she realized they were not simply stones, but headstones, lying flat upon the ground as if pushed over one by one. She gave a gasp as she realized she was standing in the middle of a cemetery. Only she did not know how she had gotten there or why in the world she would be disrobed. Over her head, the squawking of a crow, nestled somewhere in the tree above her, filled the air with sound. The clamor gave her a chill, and she wished she were home once more, safe in her own bed.

Unenthusiastically she walked over to the first row of headstones in front of her. Looking down, she noticed that all the headstones were unmarked—empty spaces where names, dates, and relationships should have been etched in stone. As she proceeded forward, she saw more of the same thing—row after row of headstones, all with clean slates, not one clue given as to who had been laid beneath the ground. Her fear continued to grow, panic rushed through her. Her heart was pounding in her chest. She felt her body shaking and could do nothing to stop it.

From under the ground, she started hearing the painful cry of children suffering beneath her feet. The moans grew louder and louder; she could hear them pleading for help, for someone to release them from their earthly tombs. Agnes's breath became deeper, faster, her eyes going in and out of focus. At first, she didn't even notice the tiny fingers that began to protrude through the blacken soil, digging and clawing their way to freedom, digging and clawing their way to her. Once she did notice the tiny appendages, Agnes could no longer hold back her terror, and she screamed into the night air.

She sat up in her bed, still breathing hard. She realized it was all a dream, a nightmare. She looked around at the comforting sight of her white-on-white bedroom, still shaken from fear. *Thank God, it was just a dream.*

"Did you like what you saw?" came an unnerving voice from the foot of her bed.

Agnes turned and saw a boy sitting in the club chair by her bedroom door. His head was shaved, his complexion was a whitish shade of blue, and his eyes were sunken and dark. The look of death was upon him.

"They will never know peace. Nor shall you." With that, the boy came flying across the room directly at Agnes. His faced resembled that of a viper posed to strike. Inches from him ripping her face apart, Agnes screamed again. That's what finally woke her, the scream.

The room was again full of sound; only this time it was her staff rushing into the room.

"It's that fucking boy. He's behind all this," was all the staff could get from her.

••••••••• ●ooooooooo o o

Vinnie sat on the floor of his bedroom, pictures scattered everywhere across the room. There were pictures of the outside of the Grinnell house on his bed, the basement on the floor, the kitchen on his dresser and nightstand, and pictures of the rest of the house tucked sporadically here and there. Dressed only in a pair of Hanes boxers, he had been examining each photo on the floor. Then he would move to the bed, cross the room, and then go back to this spot. *There's nothing*, thought Vinnie, *no kiddie porn anywhere, no satanic symbols or literature, no Nazi pamphlets, no illegal drugs, no nothing.*

Vinnie reached over and to his nightstand and pulled out his last joint, which he had been saving for a special occasion. Hopefully, there would be no random test planned for the month. He needed something to slow his mind down, to keep it from running off track. He knew he would not sleep unless he had something to take the edge off, so he lit his joint and leaned back against the bed. He had bought a pound of weed way back in college and had managed to make it last until this very moment.

Surely the upper crust was making their cut from the operation, he thought. *But why the risk? They all had more money than they could spend in a lifetime. What could possibly even get them hooked up with such a nasty deal anyway?*

A million thoughts ran through his head. The effects of the pot did little to keep his mind from trying to drill down deeper and deeper. He looked once more at the photos in front of him, and something caught his eye—the slightest difference in cages. Vinnie grabbed the magnifying glass he'd left on the bed and grabbed one of the photos from the floor. It was almost unnoticeable, but it was there. Vinnie went from picture to picture, and it was clear; two of the cages had the initials COJ etched across the top bar just above the cage door. *Why? What was so special about those two cages? Were they set aside for a certain buyer?* Then he remembered the boy's photo.

He jumped and grabbed the only photo remaining in the folder he kept them in. Vinnie gave out a loud, "Shit," as he gazed down at the photo of Bobby lying in his cage. It had the mark. *He was the next one to be sold to the special buyer.* Vinnie looked at the photo of the other cage right next to Bobby's, which also had the mark. The carpet, the blanket, and the bucket were all still there. *They must have just sold the other child,* he thought. *The items had not yet been removed.*

Vinnie took another long hit of his joint and then leaned back against his bed. *Bobby was the last child left in the cages. The rest were gone. Two cages bore a special mark, and the other child next to him with that same mark was just sold. What does this all mean? Obviously, it was time to restock, so how do you replenish that many children? They can't all be local. Hell, they can't all be from Michigan. That many children missing around the same time in the same state would have brought a statewide manhunt. No, they must have been collecting children from across the country.* "Fuck," said Vinnie out loud, "COJ, City of Jackson. These cages were marked for kids snatched from Jackson."

Vinnie got up and started pacing the floor. *For some reason they wanted to keep track of the kids they snatched from Jackson. Why?*

Obviously, they didn't want to sell them locally and have them discovered by a family member or something. But then, why take kids from Jackson at all? Obviously they had the ability to collect children anywhere. Why the risk? Unless there was a call for Jackson natives, a special request. But why?

• • • • • • • • ● ○○○○○○○○ ○ ○ ○

Chad Timberlake was awakened in the middle of the night to the sound of glass shattering somewhere on the first floor of his luxurious home. He sat up in bed and listened quietly for another sound. He heard nothing but the sound of this wife's wave machine. Slowly, he got out of bed and walked soundlessly out into the hallway. He closed the bedroom door behind him and turned on the hallway light.

It was still silent. Not a sound did he hear coming from anywhere in the house. Walking to the end of the hall, he turned left toward the stairs. He was about to turn and take the stairs but then thought about his sixteen-year-old son, William, so he continued across the top of the stair landing and headed down the hall on the other side toward his son's room. Stopping by his son's door, he gently opened it and saw him sound asleep. He slowly shut the door, turned, and walked back to the stairs.

A strange uneasiness came over him, a sickening feeling down deep in his gut. Just as he took his first step downward, there came a soft knocking on his front door.

"I have contacted the authorities, I can assure you," he said down the stairs, hoping to dissuade any intruder lurking in the darkness below.

Slowly, he descended, eyes fixated on the front door. His way forward was dark, until he was able to reach over and turn on the overhead light in the main hall. There on the floor was the oversize snow globe they had purchased in Holland, Michigan, the year before. It usually sat on top of an antique milking stool that his wife had refurbished and displayed as an ornamental plant stand. Now it lay shattered on the tile floor. *Damnable cat no doubt,* he thought, trying to convince himself that it was that easy. Cautiously, looking side to side, he walked over to pick up the scattered remains.

Then came the soft knocking on the front door once more. Chad looked over at the large grandfather clock that was the highlight of the main hallway; it was a little past three. "Who the hell is it this late?" he said softly to himself.

Again came the knock, faster, a little louder this time.

Chad walked over to his front door and looked through the peephole. He saw no one standing on his front steps. Now he started to get more and more concerned. "Who's out there?" he asked through the door.

Again silence. Chad waited a few moments, his ear pressed to the door.

Bang, bang, bang, came a loud pounding on the door.

Chad jumped back at the noise. His eyes widened, and

his pulse quickened. "I have called the police. Now please leave my premises at once."

This was again followed by a long period of silence; not a sound could he hear coming from the other side of the door. Slowly, Chad backed up across the tile floor, and just as he was about to turn and run up the steps to fulfill his promise of calling the cops, he heard the front door slowly squeak its way open. Chad knew that door was locked; he had locked it himself before he'd gone to bed. He wanted to run, but now he had to see. Turning his head, he placed one foot on the first step, prepared for his flight.

But there was no one standing in the now wide-open doorway. No madman came rushing in, no monster from the shadows, nothing. Chad was at a loss. Should he go close the door? Should he run upstairs, leaving all his possession unprotected? What about William? Should he go grab him and take him to their room and lock the door?

Finally, Chad decided on the latter. He turned and quickly fled up the stairs to his son's room. Chad could swear he heard someone or something close on his heels as he dashed all the way up the stairs. He turned only once but saw nothing. Still, he could feel it, whatever it was; it was close, so close.

As he flung open his son's bedroom door, he came to a dead stop. William was still sound asleep in his bed, but next to him stood a small boy with a large piece of broken glass from the globe held high above his head. Without warning the boy started thrusting the glass into William's unprotected face; over and over again came the unabated blows. Coming to his senses Chad ran to his bedside, slipped on his son's skateboard, and landed headfirst on top of William's stomach.

William quickly sat up. "What the fuck, Dad?"

Looking up, Chad started to cry as he saw his unharmed son looking down at him like he had gone completely out his mind.

"Dad, what the hell are you doing?"

Chad looked around. The room was empty. There was no small boy; no piece of broken glass; and no wounds on his son's young, handsome face. He grabbed his son and gave him a huge hug while weeping openly into the boy's chest.

"Dad, what the hell is going on? You're freaking me out."

CHAPTER 8

Hard Facts

Hazel was awakened by Brian's warm body being pressed against her back.

"I hope that's a pee hardon, because you aren't getting any this morning," she said, half-awake.

"It is morning wood, but I thought maybe we would put it to good use?"

"Well think again. I have to get to the office this morning." As Hazel said this, she threw back the sheets and looked over at the alarm clock. "Shit, I overslept." She stood and head toward the bathroom.

"It's Sunday. We both have the day off, for God's sake. I thought we were going to spend it together."

Hazel paid no attention as she walked into the bathroom and closed the door.

"Shit," said Brian, and he too got out of bed and headed downstairs to the kitchen in defeat. He set up the coffeepot and then returned to the bedroom, where he got dressed. Just as he was pulling on his shirt, Hazel came out of the bathroom and headed straight to the closet.

"Are you going to be there all day? Can't we get away for a little while this afternoon or something, maybe go to the track, have some beer, lose some money?"

Hazel emerged from the closet, her daily wardrobe in

hand. "I will be back as soon as I can. I promise." She kissed him on the cheek and then walked over to her side of the bed, where she started getting dressed.

"Coffee is running. Want me to pour you a cup to go?"

Hazel stopped and turned to him. "You know me so well."

With that, he was gone. Hazel finished getting dressed. She really wasn't planning on spending all day at the office or the university. She wanted to spend time with Brian today, a chance to enjoy each other's company. But first things first— she had made a promise to Nancy and the crew, and she was not one to go back on her word. First, however, she needed to check on things at the office, see if there were any other overnight attacks. "Did you tell anyone else about resigning?" she yelled from the bedroom door.

"I told Jackson," Brian yelled from downstairs.

"What did he say?" she said as she made her way down the stairs and to the kitchen.

"He said, and I quote, 'You're a damn fool,' end quote."

"Sounds like Jackson. He is just afraid I will put him with Harris."

"Yes, he did bring that up," Brian said with a big smile on his face.

"Maybe I will put him with Miller."

"If his wife found out Miller was his partner …" Brian just shook his head. "She is very much the jealous type."

"Well, I'll cross that bridge when I get to it I guess," said Hazel. She grabbed her newly filled coffee mug, gave Brian a kiss on the cheek, and walked out the door.

• • • • • • • • ● ○○○○○○○○○ ○

"Moretti, call for you on line two," yelled Miller across the nearly empty office.

"Me? No one even knows I'm here today. Who is it?"

"It's Commissioner Timberlake. He wanted the captain, but I told him she was off today, so he asked for the next in command. And that would be you, sweetheart."

"Shit. What the fuck does he want?" Vinnie said under his breath and then picked up the line.

"Commissioner, this is Detective Moretti. How can I help you this morning?" This was followed by a long pause. Vinnie thought he had pushed the wrong button for a moment, and then a voice came over the phone, so soft it was hard to hear.

"Detective Moretti, I would like to meet with you today. Is that possible?"

"Of course. Can I ask what this may pertain to, sir?"

"Just meet me at that bar on the corner of West Ave. and Ganson, say one?"

"Yes, sir. Is this about a case or something?" asked Vinnie. The tone in the man's voice was almost desperate.

"Just meet me around one, all right?"

"Yes, sir, around one."

Then the line went dead. Vinnie had a very uneasy feeling about all of this. Yes, he was planning on making contact with the man, but he never in a million years had thought that Timberlake would be calling him. As he hung up the phone, he paused, leaned back in his chair, and folded both hands behind his head. *What the fuck do you want, Commissioner?* After a few minutes of contemplation, Vinnie stood up and grabbed his coat. He no longer felt like fighting with his slow-ass computer. He needed to get out, get some fresh air. Maybe he would hunt down Bibens for a while, see what he was up to. Or maybe he'd go to the library and do a little research on their good old friend Commissioner Timberlake before their meeting.

• • • • • • • • ● ○○○○○○○○○ ○

As Vinnie was walking out the back door of the Jackson police station, Hazel was walking in through the front. That was the one thing about being captain that Hazel loved, a parking spot right in front of the building.

"Captain, I thought you were off today," said Jackson, who saw her come through the door and decided to follow her through the building and straight to her office. "I was wondering, with Hicks leaving—"

"I promise I will avoid pairing you with Harris as much as possible. Is that what you were going to ask?" said Hazel, removing her jacket and putting her purse on her desk.

Jackson just gave his patented joyful grin. "Hicks talked to you already?"

"It's no secret. No one likes working with Harris." Opening the bottom drawer to put her purse inside it, Hazel saw the magazine she had placed in there the day before. "I will do what I can."

"Thanks, Captain, you're the best," said Jackson and turned to leave the office.

"Jackson," said Hazel, still looking down into her drawer rather than looking up at him. "You went to St. Timothy's High School the same time Moretti did, didn't you?"

"Well he was three years older than me. I was just a freshman the year he graduated. Why?"

"Oh nothing. I was just wondering what he was like in school. I mean, the man never talks about himself, what he does, or who he sees."

"That's Vinnie; it's just the way he is. But what I can tell you is the man could play ball. I mean I have never seen any man, black or white, that could drive to the hoop the way that man could."

"So basically, he was a jock in school?" asked Hazel, taking a seat behind her desk.

"Yes and no. I mean, I didn't know him all that well back then, but I know he was the class valedictorian," said Jackson, rubbing his chin.

"Moretti was valedictorian?" Hazel repeated in surprise. "You have to be kidding me."

"I know a lot of people thought he went to Parksville on a sports scholarship, but I heard he went on an academic one, perfect four point."

"What about family? Did you ever meet any of them?"

"No, but that boy was poor; of that there is no doubt," Jackson said, shaking his head. "I mean, the old raggedy cloths he used to wear. Everyone at school made fun of him for it, but he would just let it roll off his back. Sorry, but that's about all I know."

"Thanks, Jackson," said Hazel.

"No problem, Captain. Anything else?"

"Anything happen last night I should know about?" she asked.

"Not a damn thing. Cheech gave me his report this morning, and last night was as silent as the grave."

"Good. Let's keep it that way," she responded with a smile. "You can go now, and please shut my door before Miller finds out I'm in."

Jackson gave a nod of his head and smiled, as if to say I know just what your mean, and then shut the door.

Hazel sat at her desk for a good hour and a half, signing time sheets she should have signed Friday, returning phone calls, and going through the mindless paperwork that came with being a boss. Her life had been so much easier just being a regular cop. Around ten, she put everything away and started walking through the office toward the door.

As she was passing Vinnie's desk she saw the brown folder he'd had in her office the night before with the pictures of those influential individuals they thought maybe somehow be connected to the case. She grabbed it off the desk and stuck it under her arm. She still needed to keep her promise and go to the university and ask those questions that Nancy needed answers to, but maybe she could answer a few of her own to help solve this case. Hopefully today would be a good day. She would get the answers from Bobby she needed and then meet Brian at the track before post time.

The drive over to the university was uneventful, but she did try and take in all the fall colors one last time. She knew it would not be long before the trees would be bare, the grass would turn brown, and the only green would be on the lonely pines. She didn't mind the winters, but they were just so damn long. Still, on a day like this, when the sun ignited the foliage in shades of brown, red, and yellow, it was hard to focus on the bitter cold to follow.

As she past the university, she was in awe of its charm, the red brick buildings towering three and four stories high, with gothic windows and vines growing up on all sides. This was the older part of the university, five or six large building scattered about in all directions and all connected with sidewalks running this way and that. The science building was in the newer part of the university. It was more modern, with all the buildings having more of a boxed look, all painted in boring tan colors, four or five stories high, with flat roofs—far less romantic than the older buildings. Just as she was about to make the turn into the science building parking lot, she noticed out her rearview mirror a large black car behind her. She knew that car; it was Bibens's. *Has he been following me?* she thought.

As she pulled into her parking spot, she looked over her shoulder to see if he was still following her, but there was no sign of him. *He must have continued further into the university.* She grabbed her purse and Vinnie's brown folder and then started walking toward the building, knowing that Nancy had left the front door open for her. Once inside, she hurried and ducked around the corner, so she could see if Bibens would double back. Sure enough, after just a few short minutes, she saw him drive by, passing the parking lot to the science building and heading back toward the main road. *That fucker followed me to find out where the kid is. How could you be so stupid, Hazel Mae?* she thought to herself.

As she walked down the hall to the lab, she caught herself pulling down upon her bra; it was getting old and rubbed in places it need not rub. She was going to throw it away, but whenever she washed it, she would convince herself she could get one more good wear. If she had it her way, she would throw every bra she had out with the trash. They had it right in the sixties, because nothing was better at the end of the day then setting the girls free.

Hazel pushed the button for the outside door and then waited patiently for someone to descend the steps to let her in. By chance, she gave a look down the hallway to the front door one more time and saw a figure peering through the front window. As soon as the figure spotted her looking back, it darted out of sight. Just then, the door opened, and Albert, out of breath from running down the steps, came into view on the other side.

"What's wrong?" he said to Hazel, who did not show any response to his arrival; she was still focused on the front door.

"Bibens—I think he is following me."

"Screw him. He has no authority over our project. We figured he would find us sooner or later," responded Albert without even a hint of concern. "We deal with the FBI and CIA all the time. They always want to know what we are up to."

Comforted by Albert's words, Hazel turned and followed Albert up the steps. "Bobby is doing a lot better this morning. He doesn't seem as tired," Albert continued.

Nancy met them both at the top of the stairs. "Hazel, I am so glad to see you. I have so much to tell you. Albert and I thought for a moment you might not show. Let's go in and have a seat. Do you want some coffee? Sorry it's not as good as Jim makes, but it is his downtime."

"No, thank you," Hazel said as she made her way over to the glass. She had to see him, make sure he was all right.

"He's been a lot more active this morning. He even got out of bed and retrieved his breakfast tray this morning, ate the whole thing," interjected Albert.

"That's great. He's getting use to this place," Hazel said, putting a hand to the glass. Turning to Nancy and Albert, who had already taken their seats at the table, Hazel saw an emptiness in their expressions. "What's wrong?"

"The agency wants a definitive answer as to whether the boy possesses a danger to the safety of civilians by the end of the day, or they will be coming and taking him away," said Nancy, refusing to make eye contact. "They are giving us until tomorrow morning to submit our report."

Hazel turned her gaze back to the boy below. "Where will they take him? Do you know?"

"No, we have some ideas, but—" commented Albert.

"Will you three still be working with him?" questioned Hazel.

"I don't know," said Nancy, standing and joining Hazel by the glass. "We are field agents, and his abilities are far beyond what any of us expected. Not only can he move things with his mind, but he can also project himself to unknown places. We still don't have any proof that he won't, or hasn't already, used his gift to harm others."

"Another cage," said Hazel, fighting back tears.

"Well we are not done yet. We still have a job to do here, ladies," spouted Albert. "Nancy has a set of questions to ask the boy. Maybe it will make a difference. Maybe we can get some answers, answers that will provide the proof we need."

Hazel smiled. She appreciated Albert's optimism, but she knew he was grasping at straws. There was no way to prove the boy was not a danger; she knew it, and so did the rest.

"I don't understand God sometimes," offered Nancy. "Why give such a powerful gift to such a beautiful young boy, knowing it would destroy his life?" Tears were now starting to form in her eyes as well.

"Albert's right. We're not done with him yet," said Hazel, returning to the table and sitting down. "If we can keep him from being taken away and locked up for the rest of his life, then we need to do it. We have to at least try."

"And if we can't?" asked Nancy.

"*Then we learn what we can while making this one of the best fucking days of his life!*" exclaimed Albert.

Both women turned and looked at Albert in disbelief. Neither had ever heard him use that tone, let alone that kind of language. In spite of their ill feelings about the boy's possible fate, they both spontaneously started to laugh. "God, sometimes you amaze me, Albert, and you are so right. Let's give it our best shot," said Nancy as she too walked over and joined Albert at the table and sat down.

"Okay, let's put together what we know. Nancy, would you mind sharing yours and Albert's findings so far?"

Nancy thought for a moment and then, twirling her coffee cup in circles on the table, she looked over at Albert, who nodded his head. "Okay, here it goes. Let me start off by saying that Bobby has powers that go beyond our scope of knowledge. He is something new. Yes, Albert, Jim, and I have all seen individuals with the ability to move objects with their minds. Believe it or not, it's not as uncommon as you might think."

"But we have never encounter anyone like this. I mean, him taking a juice box off the tray is one thing. That is not at all shocking; we have seen similar things done a hundred times. But to move a room full of furniture—that's the most power we have ever encountered," offered Albert.

"So how did he get so strong?" asked Hazel.

"We believe he was born with his gift, but maybe his confinement enhanced it somehow, gave him time to develop it," replied Albert.

"You mean some form of coping mechanism?" asked Hazel.

"Exactly," replied Nancy. "Not only was he able to develop his abilities, but when he created an imaginary friend to help deal with his situation, he also learned how to direct his power, share his energy with his new companion."

"What about that thing connecting Bobby and Richie that Albert showed me on his screen. Have you ever seen that before?"

Both Albert and Nancy shook their heads. "It is believed that siblings, usually twins, sometimes have a psychic connection that connect one individual to another. But no one has ever actually physically seen a psychic connection between two humans," said Albert.

"Bobby's connection with Richie is unique. We believe it's either because Richie is pure energy, not a physical being, or because he is nothing more than an extension of Bobby himself," added Nancy.

"Wow, this is like way over my head," Hazel said as she stood and started pacing back and forth.

"Think of two computers connected. They can pass information back and forth along a wire, only these wires no one has ever seen until now," said Albert, wiping the sweat from his forehead with the back of his sleeve. "For the first time, we have documentation of that connection; the scientific community will no longer debate it as speculation or theory, but recognize it as fact."

Nancy again broke in. "In Bobby's case, though, it's not just information being transferred. Somehow, someway, he is capable of feeding Richie his own psychic energy. We believe that's why Bobby is so tired; it takes a lot out of him to supply Richie with the power he needs to exist."

Hazel walked back over to the table and sat back down, looking at them one at a time in the eyes to make sure they could not avoid an answer. "Do you believe he killed the doctor? No bullshit, just a straight answer."

Nancy reached over and took her hand. "We don't know the answer to that. All we can say is yes, he could have; he had the strength. If he could rearrange that room down there with all that heavy furniture and equipment, then yes, he could have lifted that doctor and thrown him out the window. Do I personally think the boy has the mental capacity to commit such a crime? Again, the answer is I don't know. If Richie houses all the negative feelings of fear and anger that the boy must have from being confined for so long in that basement, if in fact Richie is in part a manifestation of his need for revenge or even self-preservation, then yes, it is possible."

"In that case, the Bobby we know may have no control over the friend he created. Hell he might even be unaware of what Richie has done," added Albert.

Nancy stood and walked behind Hazel, putting one hand on each shoulder. "Look, when he first came here, I too resisted the notion of any kind of split personality. But the fact is, we just don't know. That's why I have written these questions the way I have. And to tell you the truth, even if we get all the answers we want, there is still no way to verify the results."

It took a while for Hazel to respond, but then she simply said, "I want to thank you both for being so honest with me about all of this." Once again, she was close to tears. "But if you don't mind, I would like to see the boy now. I know it sounds crazy, but I need to be down there."

"No, it doesn't sound crazy at all," Nancy assured her.

· · · · · · · · · · ● ○○○○○○○○○ ○ ○

Sam sat in church with Linda; their oldest girl, Darlene, and the baby, Donna, were strategically placed between them. The preacher was long-winded today, and if not for the continuous nudges from Linda, Sam was sure he would have fallen sound asleep. It was by chance that he happened to look behind him and see, sitting in the very last pew, Earl Southworth. His faced showed signs of exhaustion, as if he hadn't sleep for days. But it was his eyes that kept causing Sam to repeatedly turn over his shoulder to look; they seemed distant, like a man on the brink. Sam remembered his name coming up as one of the individuals who was being harassed by the unknown forces. It was obviously taking its toll on him.

After the service, as everyone was making his or her way out the front doors, Sam excused himself and walked ahead of Linda and the girls to stop Earl from getting to his car. Just as he was opening the door, Sam arrived. "Earl Southworth, I haven't seen you in years."

"Sam, I heard you were back in town. Good to have you back," said Earl and offered him his hand.

Sam took it and was surprised at the man's grip; it was feeble, not at all the way Sam remembered it. They had gone to this same church together long before Sam ever moved away. "Yeah, this is our first Sunday back. Nice to see the old place again," he said, turning to look at the modest church. "How have you been?"

"To tell you the truth, Sam, not so good. I have a lot on my mind lately."

"Is there anything I can help you with? I don't mean to sound rude, but you don't look so hot."

Earl smiled and sat down in the front seat of his Cadillac. "I'm okay, just a little trouble sleeping is all. Not use to sleeping alone I guess. My wife left me, and I am just going through some things right now. But I do appreciate your concern." With that, he offered Sam a smile and shut the car door.

"Go home and get some sleep," yelled Sam through the open window.

Earl just simply drove off, not saying another word.

Sam turned and walked back to Linda, who was still talking to a group of women by the front door, each hand occupied by that of a child. As Sam walked toward her, he had the strangest feeling that this would be the last time he ever saw Earl. He knew Earl was mixed up in this crazy shit going on in Jackson somehow, but the man who had just pulled out of the parking lot was undoubtedly at the end of his rope.

· · · · · · · · · ● ○○○○○○○○○ ○ ○

Hazel told herself not to act as stressed as she really was. If Bobby picked up on her uneasiness, he may shut down before they ever get started. Albert had checked, and Richie was in the room, but Albert stated that he was very faint, sitting in the corner under the glass. As she walked through the door to his room, Bobby, who had been lying on his bed, got up and ran to her. He gave her a long embrace. "Hazel, you're here. I'm so happy you made it today."

"Well of course I'm here. Did you think I wouldn't come?" she said, rubbing the top of his head. "Come, let's sit on the bed for a while, okay."

"I feel just a little tired today, not as bad as yesterday. I promise I won't fall asleep."

Hazel looked down into the boy's face. He was beaming, "You still look a little tired to me."

"Not like yesterday; I promise. Did Nancy tell you I got my own breakfast this morning?"

"Yes, she did. We are both very proud of you, sweetie."

Bobby hopped on the bed and patted the space next to him for Hazel to sit down. "I am getting used to my new home," he said, grinning ear to ear.

"That's great," said Hazel, fighting back her emotions.

Here she was acting like everything was okay, when deep down, she knew the boy would be gone soon—taken to some unknown location where she may well never see him again. It was tearing her apart on the inside. "Let's play a game," she said, trying desperately to change the subject. She quickly pulled the brown folder from Vinnie's desk out of her purse. "I want to know who you know and who you don't, okay?"

"Sure, but I don't know many people."

"It's okay. It's just for fun." With that, she pulled out a picture of Agnes Prescott. "Have you ever seen this lady before?"

Bobby shook his head. "No, sorry, not that one."

"And her?" she said, pulling out a photo of Barbra Wentworth.

"No, sorry. I'm not really good at this am I?" said Bobby.

"It's okay, honey. No one expects you to know any of these people." With that, she pulled out a photo of Dr. Hendershot.

"That's the doctor from the hospital," said Bobby. "I remember he gave me a shot."

"Do you know what happened to him after the shot?" asked Hazel.

"No. What?" asked Bobby.

Hazel remembered the boy had passed out when the attack had happened. "Oh nothing, just checking to see if you were paying attention." Then she reached down and tickled him. The boy giggled. "What about this guy?" she said, pulling out the picture of Earl Southworth.

"Nope, never saw him."

"Well, that's it. That's all I have."

"Did I do good?"

"You did great, but now I want to ask you some questions that Ms. Nancy wrote down. Be careful. She's a tricky one," she said, giving him another tickle.

Bobby once again gave a giggle. Hazel could tell he was having fun. This was far from her usual interrogations, but she was getting results. She pulled out the list of questions Nancy had given her. She knew that, upstairs, Nancy would be hanging on every word that came out of his mouth. She started, "How long have you and Richie been together?"

Bobby's face lit up. At first, she thought approaching this subject would cause him discomfort, but on the contrary, he seemed elated.

"You know about Richie?"

"Yes. Nancy, Jim, and Albert heard you talking to him the first full day you were here." This she said pointing upstairs.

"I forget sometimes and talk out loud, but I don't have to. We can talk without saying anything," he responded. "It used to drive the Man crazy sometimes."

"How long have you been able to move items with your mind?" asked Hazel, still ready from the script.

"You mean my secret thing? Always I guess," Bobby offered, shrugging his shoulders.

"And how long has Richie been a part of your life? How long have you been together?"

"Always. I can't remember a time without him," said Bobby, looking at the list of questions.

This was going far better than she had hoped. "Can you always see what Richie sees?"

Primavera inolvidable

Inconscientes de la mera primavera
*   aves a nido, con ruido agradable,*
pipian a una brisa antojadiza
*   y se recogen a esperar mientras*
las querellas de unos arrendajos,
*   peleando entre sí por migajas*
dejadas al lado del sendero,
*   disturban esta escena hermosa.*

Resignado me vuelvo triste a lo
*   cotidiano sin el ánimo de continuar*
con dedicación a la tarea de ser.

Otra vez enjaulado yo, sin poder
*   olvidar primavera, el azul del*
cielo espacioso reflejado en
*   mi computadora, me distrae.*

Lo dejo y salgo fuera cuando me
*   presenta panorama del arco iris*
en las flores de abril desplegadas
*   a la vista aborrida con gris del*
invierno que me parecía incesante.

Unos vientos, ahora suaves, no
*   tempestuosos, mecen la cuna*
de la temporada al ritmo etéreo,
*   y duermo sin preocupaciones*
en los brazos de esta belleza.

Unforgettable Spring

Unaware of the arrival of spring
   birds in the nest with pleasing
noises, chirp to the whimsical
   breeze and withdraw to await
sustenance, while the quarreling
   of mockingbirds, fighting among
themselves for the crumbs left at
   the side of the pathway, disturb
this unforgettably artistic scene.

With resignation, I sadly return to
   my daily tasks without enthusiasm
to continue with dedication to living.

The expansive blue sky reflected
   in my computer distracts me,
as I am once again in my cage
   without the power to forget spring.

I leave all behind and go outside
   where a panorama of rainbow colors
of the flowers of April is displayed
   to my view, now tired of the gray of
winter which has seemed so endless.

The breeze, now soft, rocks the cradle
   of the season to an extraterrestrial rhythm,
and I sleep without worries wrapped in
   the arms of spring's exquisite beauty

Libertad

Cuando escoje el cielo ponerse
menos que azul, claro todos los
políticos, eruditos y científicos no
pueden mandarlo volverse azul.

También, aunque me echan en
una jaula con cadenas modernas
llamadas softwere y hardware, no
pueden quitarme el espíritu libre
ni hacerme callar los pensamientos
vivos que me preservan del tedio
inventado que llaman, "modernismo."

Sólo al quebrar estos grillos que me
restringen, me volaré emancipado
con águilas al sol y veré el mundo
ahora hecho cristal para revelar
a los videntes el propósito de ser.

Liberation

When the sky chooses to be less
    than clear blue, the politicians,
the erudite and scientists cannot
    command it to return to blue.

Likewise, even though they throw me
    into a cage with these modern chains
called software and hardware, they
    cannot deny freedom to my spirit nor
can they silence my resonating thoughts
    which save me from this tedium
invented in the guise of "modernism."

Only in breaking out of these fetters
    which restrain can I now, emancipated,
soar with eagles to the sun and glimpse
    a world now turned to crystal revealing
to the seers the purpose of life.

Morning Walk

The path seems somehow
    much longer today even
though we always go this way.

Max knows but cannot say
    what we both are feeling.

The cacophony of morning
    birds awakens my consciousness
with their natural harmony.

This everyday awareness
    opens discoveries hidden
in the chants of dawn that
    continue ringing in my head.

We communicate without words;
    I know the trail, Max does too.

Today the familiar feels
    strange since with age
I stop to rest much more.

Autumn Miracle

Hope and faith hidden in the last
   rosebud of autumn shines radiantly
in the rising sun of morning when an
   indifferent world ignores the brilliance
displayed above.
                        Leaves are quiet as
   a silent stream in adoration of the miracle
of dawn, a secret opportunity to breathe
   freely, to taste beauty concealed to those
who choose to be blind.
                        The mirror in
   a serene mountain lake reflects a calm sky
just like a quiet sea that awaits the storm
   which stalks the perplexed vagabond to
drown him in its menacing deep.
                        Then all nature
   gratefully kneels to plead for deliverance.

Sonata de la noche

Profundidad nocturna habla del abismo
en susurros al principio, más aumentando
despacio hasta estallarse de lo mas alto
en voz baja y recia a amonestar al mundo
liviano, embriagado en narcisismo y orgullo.

Tal pesadilla achecha tranquilidad
disfrazada en forma del fantasma infame
que molestaba la ópera ficticiosa,
captando cada ser débil y engañado
por las artimañas de la noche sutil.

Con resolución e impaciencia infantil
el hombre extraviado amenaza los cielos
con puño exigiendo respuesta inmediata
que solo viene, después de tribulación,
en forma de voz pequeña y penetrante.

Night Sonata

From the great expanse, the depths of night
speak in whispers at first, then slowly
crescendoing until it explodes from
the heights in a loud, deep voice warning
a blithe world drunken with narcissistic pride.

Such a nightmare, subtly disguised as
the infamous phantom, that haunted
the fictional opera house, stalks serenity
attracting each weak and deceived
person by the wiles of furtive night.

With resolution and infantile impatience
one unfortunate soul threatens the heavens
with a clenched fist demanding an immediate
response, which only will come after much
tribulation, in the form of a still, small voice.

Passage to Infamy

—A visit to Washington, DC's, Holocaust Muse

The unthinkable terror of Auschwitz
confined in claustrophobic cells looms
ever larger with every measured step
through corridors lined with photographs
of those extinguished by blind fanaticism.

By design like innumerable cattle thronging
toward an unknown fate, lines of curiosity
seekers mill through succeeding revelations
of inhumanity, crossing that inevitable
threshold from naïveté and indifference
to the world of stark comprehension.

Each display reverberates with unconsolable
cries against injustices which can never be
reconciled by past or present political impotence.

Maps and charts present a methodical march
of genocide inflamed by perceived racial
superiority disguised as zealousness.

Discarded shoes covered with ashes spewed
from ignominious furnaces lie ominously
silent in heaps behind fences preventing
their irreverent disturbance by sadistic
collectors of sensational memorabilia.

No less unsettling are locks of shorn hair
alongside bales of hair ravaged in mass
from the unsuspecting, dutifully entering
austere chambers fitted with death-spitting
spigots disguised as showers ostensibly
to rid the unwary of unwanted vermin.

The vision of such atrocities is surpassed
only by haunting voices of survivors preserved
to recount abuse, depravation, suffering.

The realizations engendered by the visual
images raise their heads as hideous nightmares
preserved to pique even consciences seared
by selfish youth veneered with indifference.

Repulsion comes even to those inured by
previous wars, after peering over cement
walls made to hide from tender feelings
human experiments couched in scientific
learning to enhance further warfare.

A tower of photos discovered in the remains
of a community obliterated from history,
as if instantaneously, portrays hatred
telegraphed from the eyes of invaders as
evil projectiles to immobilize resistance.

As disgust merges into feelings of
helplessness and complete abandonment,
the depiction of those last days of pain
changes all into momentary hope
when films of soldiers from the hammer
and sickle empire liberate the emaciated
thousands nearly bereft of body and soul.

Only those who have steeled themselves
in years of bigotry and apathy emerge
unchanged into the light chamber of liberation
where they pensively pause to reflect
smugly with gratitude having been spared.

Yet, those truly altered by travel
through another dimension of human
feeling struggle through a curtain
of tears leaving one, lone candle
to reflect the totality of this infamy.

       (Written on the fiftieth anniversary of the
       liberation of Auschwitz.)

Nocturno español II

El espíritu y belleza de España
  se despliega en el ritmo del flamenco,
espejo del ánimo y ardor latino,
  incorporado en esas castañetas
y las máscaras de los bailadores.

En el fuego y las piruetas se trata
  de hacerse regocijar esta alma
triste al pensar en la gloria perdida
  que gozaba España en los días pasados
de armadas, reyes y conquistadores.

Se fluyen las faldas y capas rojas
  a la música encantada y repleta,
evocando siluetas de arte pura
  simbolizada en muñecas giradas
por adonises escultos, gentiles.

Con la última inclinación y la caída
  del talón me despiertan de este sueño
a esa realidad que siempre me acecha;
  mas, guardo una chispa de esta hermosura
para inspiración futura en días ásperos.

Spanish Nocturne II

The spirit and beauty of Spain is
    manifested in the rhythm of the flamenco,
the mirror of Latin verve and passion,
    which is embodied in the castanets,
costumes and masks of the dancers.

With the fire and pirouettes the saddened
    soul attempts to rejoice, but is overcome
with the contemplation of the now lost
    glory that once was Spain of the days
of armadas, kings, and conquistadores.

The skirts and capes flow quickly
    to the haunting music replete with
the vision of pure art embodied in
    dolls spinning under the arms of
the sculpted and lively Adonises.

With the final bow and the curtain falling
    I am awakened from this artistic dream
to reality which continues to stalk me;
    yet, I treasure a spark of this beauty for
future inspiration on inevitable dark days.

A Rose Garden Reply to Darwin

I have struggled against
　　Darwinian forces to cultivate
beauty in arid Sierran soil.

Each blossom, though smaller
　　than those from richer earth,
is more precious by far.

One particular bloom eclipses
　　all others unfolding in splendor,
soft, luminescent pink, with
　　an unforgettable fragrance
which pervades summer's air.

This season is the last for this,
　　my favorite, ailing and delicate.

It will succumb to aphids, wood
　　borers that attack its weaknesses
daily, in spite of dusts I administer
　　faithfully with Hippocratic concern.

Soon, I will no longer see my
　　favorite, nor bask in its radiance,
yet I can only console myself
　　knowing that its memorable
essence will forever be indelibly
　　etched on my immortal memory.

Poesía

At last the floodgates have been
    opened again with words spewing
forth unorganized, twisted, contorted,
    yet filled with sentiment to be felt only
by one who chooses the least-worn path.

The task of aligning these fragile
    meanings into lasting treasures
furrows many a brow and ages
    a feeling heart yearning to hear again
each unleashed nuance and harmony.

Emotional orations and pleadings
    serve nothing to corral untamed
words into meaningful impressions
    which, in truth, cannot compare
to those that cannot be written.

Reflections on *Berceuse*
by Jean Sibellius

Concentric rings, reflections of immortality
in a secluded forest pool, slowly dissipate into
blackness of night, and resound throughout
universal stillness sinking deeply into those
hearts prepared for immeasurable joy.

Healing tears of gratitude briefly blur the memory
etched by enchanting strains surging from each
epiphanic moment which comforts like soft
blankets, shields from uncertainties of living.

Inevitable sadness returns when melodies
end and the symphonic grandeur ceases,
leaving only thirst for the next manifestation
mercifully bestowed upon unworthy mankind
cradled in the awesome immensity of eternity.

Transcendent Music

Longings for eternity encircle
    every thought and vision from
syncopated rhythms of haunting
    music which endures in memory
long after its final moving chords
    disappear into the humdrum
oblivion of monotony disguised
    as salvation through acquisition.

Yet, like the sun's rays awaken
    the world to one more radiant day,
music's moving, but gentle caress
    from the baton of one prepared to
inspire can elevate a soul mired
    in self-pity and discouragement.

Una visita a la pirámide *Luxor*

*Las esferas que creamos nos esclavizan
en cámaras vacías, pero resonantes
con voces de los ancianos que allí andaban
en una búsqueda infinita y enigmática
para encontrar la felicidad efímera.*

*Sólo el soberbio ignora las instrucciones
hieroglíficas inscritas con muchas
lágrimas, sudor y sangre inestimable
de generaciones difuntas gritando
ahora amonestaciones a los sordos.*

*Con asombro se contempla estas escenas
mientras cautivado en un nave encantado.*

*Al salir a la atmósfera carnavalesca
pronto se olvida el mensage de las edades.*

A Visit to the *Luxor* Pyramid

The various spheres which we create
hypnotize us in those empty rooms, which
resonate with voices of the ancients who
roamed there in the endless, enigmatic
search for evasive, ephemeral happiness.

Only the proud ignore the instructions
in hieroglyphics inscribed with many
tears, sweat, and the precious blood of
generations now defunct and trying to
warn those who, by choice, may be deaf.

With great wonderment one considers such
scenes while captive in an enchanted boat.

Yet, leaving this carnival-like atmosphere most
deliberately forget the lessons from past ages.

Sports' Mating Dance

The mating dance of feathered
   athletes after displayed prowess,
spoils the achievement from
   "showboating" antics to attract
a hoped for showering of accolades
   from conceited commentators,
all this in the revered pursuit of
   seductive, elusive fame and fortune.

The Gettysburg Address

Memorable brevity is a gift
that many writers and orators
never achieve, because
seductive words continue
to stoke inflated egos.

A Caprice

The mystery of grandma's kitchen
   alchemy remains buried with her,
although her daughters in vain
   attempted to duplicate those
delicacies only she could concoct.

She always saved a bowl of soup
   or, as I recall, a secreted slice of
meat or a piece of pastry for me.

As a child, I always raved about
   her cooking, perhaps that is why
she seemed to favor me; at least,
   my ego wanted it so, in spite of the
protests of my siblings and cousins.

Unfortunately, I guess I will never know.

Imaginación suelta

*Me asombro con boca abierta al contemplar
cielos desenrollados y desplegados en un
panorama de estrellas, planetas, y lunas.*

*En este éxtasis suelto la mente, la única
parte de mi ser que es capaz de salir
libre a explorar los universos cerrados
en imaginación sagrada, no obstante,
los deberes mundanos me llaman con
choque duro a esta realidad calderoniana.*

*Más, hago la lucha para preservar sólo
unas moléculas para otros momentos
asombrosos cuando otra vez penetro detrás
del velo a ver las perplejidades de tantos
océanos y átomos de esta existencia.*

Imagination Unleashed

In contemplation of the heavens, I stand in
awe as they are unrolled and displayed before
me in a panorama of stars, planets, and moons.

In this hypnotic trance I liberate my mind,
the only part of me that can travel freely
to explore universes locked in my sacred
imagination; nonetheless, mundane
duties abruptly call me back from my
cherished reverie to this Calderonian reality.

Still, I must fight to preserve only a few
molecules for another inspirational moment
when once again I am allowed to penetrate
the veil to see the perplexities of the many
oceans and atoms of this amazing existence.

Reconciliando a morte

A manhã seguinte não hà felicidade
  depois da morte de uma pessoa muita amada.

Parece-me que outra aurora não pasa-se mais
  pensando que uma vida dissipa tão fácil.

Eu não sinto-o mais por razão da ruptura
  de meu coracão que era como cristal antes.

Não mais brilha este sol, salvo escurece-se ainda
  o meio-dia aos meus olhos cegos por o pesar.

As tristes lágrimas vertidas desfacem-se
  nos rios fluindo aos grandes mares tranqüilizantes
para os aflitos que, com fe, recebem paz.

Agora vou ao altar de manhã a colocar
  minha alma acima, oferecendo-a como dádiva
aos cegos que não podem acreditar num céu.

Reconciling Death

There is no happiness the morning after
    the death of a loved one; it just seems
that another sunrise will never occur
    again since a life can end so easily.

I do not feel any more because of this
    broken heart that was like crystal before.

Now even the sun does not shine, while noonday
    seems dark to my eyes now blinded by sorrow.

Tears shed in sadness disappear into rivers
    flowing into those great tranquil seas from which
the afflicted, through faith, may receive peace.

For this, I must now go to the altar of morning,
    placing my soul there as an offering—a gift to
those who are blind and cannot believe in heaven.

Canto a la vejez

La caída lenta de hojas de otoño
reflejan el humor de una tierra
harta con disipaciones tantas
del verano muriéndose a pasos.

Por fin duerme el mundo tiritado
en este viento áspero del otoño,
descargándose en sueño sereno
de todos los excesos del verano.

Como el otoño anhela el reposo,
yo pateo las hojas en la acera
contemplando llegada de invierno
tremendo con canas y dolores.

Mas, sigo resignado y agradecido
por vida amplia de flores y cascadas.

Song of Aging

The leaves of autumn falling gently
   reflect the somber mood of tired
earth inebriated by the rhythms of
   dissipate summer slowly dying.

Resolutely, the world shivers in
   harsh winds of fall and sleeps
with peaceful dreams to unburden
   itself of the excesses of summer.

As autumn yearns for rest, I shuffle
   through the leaves while contemplating
with awe the arrival of winter with
   its inevitable pains and graying hair.

Yet I am content, grateful for a life filled
   with beautiful flowers and waterfalls.

La Cumbre de *Kilimanjaro*

La jornada árdua de esta vida
a través del desierto formidable
oprime alma dedicada a buscar
la belleza y majestad de existencia.

Los oases infrecuentes no satisfacen;
sólo la vista del agua del mar,
la meta fijada para él que busca,
traerá la felicidad deseada que
puede elevar hombre desconsolado
a la cima áspera de Kilimanjaro.

De evitar una caída calamitosa
se esfuerza uno fervientemente
descender del monte sagrado para
incitar a otros alcanzar la cumbre.

The Heights of *Kilimanjaro*

The arduous journey of life across this
    formidable desert discourages even
those dedicated souls who search for
    the beauty and majesty of existence.

Infrequent oases do not satisfy, only
    the sight of ocean's life-giving water,
the fixed goal for him who searches,
    brings desired happiness and will
elevate disconsolate man in his quest
    to attain the harsh crest of *Kilimanjaro*.

Avoiding inevitable perils requires earnest
    dedication and inner strength to descend that
sacred mountain, as encouragement to those
    who follow in their attempts to scale its heights.

A Remembrance from *Les Misérables*

Boisterous laughter amid friendly cheers
from poignant remembrances of happier
days gone by, become only whispers on
doleful winds chilling a soul filled with grief
for those lost in seemingly futile battles
against injustices of an upside-down world.

Each familiar, beloved face marches past
in this vision of one miraculously spared
the fate of those who sacrificed themselves
that he might live to see one more day.

Still, those empty chairs and empty tables
will forever remind not just him, but also all
who have achieved true liberation from man's
inhumanity, of the cost of such freedom and
with tears etch sincere gratitude into hearts
forever changed by such hallowed memories.

Singing Shenandoah

Those who live music
    commence nostalgic, yet
melancholy whisperings
    of eternity encrypted
on atoms of everyman's
    tears which stream into
torrents of grief, longing,
    joy, elation, anxiety.

Each unforgettable strain
    disappears on the whimsical
wind and is soon extinguished,
    extinct for a seemingly long
season patiently awaiting
    another magical intonation.

About the Author

The author was born in Logan, Utah and raised Cornish, Utah. He currently resides in Carson Nevada and has been a resident of Nevada for over years. He married Carolyn, his wife, in 1970. The follow year he graduated with a Bachelor of Arts from Utah S University in Spanish with minors in Music, English German. He speaks and reads four languages: Engl Spanish, Portuguese and German in that order of flue with reading and speaking some French and Italian. received a Juris Doctor from Brigham Young Universit 1981. The author began writing poetry while in college. hobbies include poetry, literature, gardening, music, sing and directing church choirs. He has five children and tw grandchildren.

What else can an insomniac do with all their energy, but toss and turn?

Hey, bet you thought you were tired.

This is true, you are tired, but this may be the very reason you are holding onto the energy, because you are tired. Now it's impossible to sleep because you have all this pent up energy that you're holding onto. It turns into a vicious cycle.

The Spinning Record

We have all had the experience of taking our problems to bed with us. Our mind will think about whatever problems challenged us during the day and this repeats over and over like a spinning record.

These thoughts are congested or blocked energy. Our thinking becomes jumbled and like other problems we solve regularly, these problems evade solutions. This is recognized as stress.

We all respond to stress and it is necessary to our survival, called fight or flight. The problem is without stress we would not be able to act in times of danger. Many people say they perform best under some stress. Other people are immobilized by the fear stress creates, like a deer in headlights.

The signs of stress are tight muscles, clenching or grinding your teeth, breathing rapidly and sweating profusely. Different people have many different responses to stress. The energy you release while you respond to stress is either physical or mental, so either your body will toss and turn or your thoughts spin like a broken record and you will not be able to sleep.

The first step is to recognize what is happening in your body, mind and spirit.

To solve your toss and turn or spinning record sleepless nights, sit up in bed immediately, turn on the lamp, and reach for your pen and paper you keep near the bed. Now, record exactly what your thoughts are telling you.

First, you must become aware that there is a problem.

Second, there is a group of problems that are disrupting your sleep because they are ready to be solved.

It's easy to see that our mind is presenting them to us, in an effort to remind us to write them down, *now*. If you do fall asleep you may forget the problem in the morning, but that night you are kept awake again. Our mind keeps us awake until we take charge of the situation; otherwise the problems will keep spinning round like a broken record.

By writing it down the problem is visibly on paper so that it becomes clear. In the morning you can refer to it when it's ready to be solved. As soon as you transferred the problem to paper ask your brain to bring you the necessary solution in your dreams that night.

The purpose of this exercise is first to release the energy by writing the problem on paper and second, solve it later so you can sleep tonight.

When they are arranged in order on paper, your mind can let go of that energy. Set it on the table next to the bed authorizing your subconscious mind to work on the solutions in your dreams.

It is important that you verbalize *this instruction* to your mind. Let your dreams come up with the best solution to your problem, while you are asleep. When you instruct your mind, the solutions will begin to surface from your subconscious to your conscious mind. Be aware of your dreams, because the solution that will help you sleep can come in this form.

Where does the energy come from?

The reason I write about energy, is so that you understand the basics and that energy can affect your sleep or lack thereof.

Since the Industrial revolution, we began our mad consumption of electricity and oil. Since the explosion of the technological revolution, almost everyone who owns a computer, cell phone, or electronic communication device leaves it plugged in 24 hours a day.

As human beings we have also increased our dependence on a limitless energy that powers our bodies and gives us life.

Some energy comes from an earthly source like the sun, earth, or wind. Some energy comes from earth's bounty as the food we eat. Then, some energy is manufactured from our own bodies, and some energy is pure energy that comes from a mysterious source.

Some people call it God, the creator, their higher power or their source. Acts 17:28 *It is in God we live and move, and have my being*

In the 21st century our need for the energy that comes from outside our being has expanded exponentially. Our daily activities that require us to multi-task and utilize electronic equipment grows everyday. Operating computers, cell phones, smart phones, e-mail, Ipads, and social media networks have opened up new electromagnetic frequencies of energy bombarding us continuously.

Not only do we overeat when we are tired, trying to produce more energy, we lose sleep in an effort to hold onto energy when we are tired.

Could our body, mind and spirit live without that unlimited, invisible thing we call energy?

With the use of these electronic tools to communicate and interact with each other, our bodies are transferring energy to the chakras at a velocity unlike anything similar in the history of mankind.

The other source of energy, which has a profound effect on our own energy level, is our interaction with other people or lack of contact with others, which effect our emotions.

Emotions are energy, powerful energy that can empower you or deflate you. When emotional energy is plugged into the wrong outlet it will rob you of sleep.

Emotional pain taught me a valuable lesson. An example of my own self discovery is when during an argument with my partner; I noticed how much negative energy was exchanged during these battles. After one of these battles my body was vibrating with all this energy, I could feel my chakras spinning, but still I couldn't let it go . . . I tossed and turned that night until I knew I wouldn't sleep a wink. After my self examination the cause became clear that I was responsible for creating the negative energy.

The emotional pain which turned into negative energy would not let me sleep.

I acknowledged my part and asked my partner if we can make up.

When we forgave each other, I realized by letting go of the hostility, it released the negative energy. After that, we both softened up and finally fell asleep.

The practice of the rituals in this book will help you gain control over your negative emotions and the energy it creates that keeps you from falling asleep.

The energy that comes from our emotions can either run our life or ruin our life.

Put in simple terms; negative emotional energy is a resource that continues supplying the fuel for your insomnia.

Then, there is bad emotions (energy) that are inflicted upon us from other people. Emotions or feelings, good or bad, cause a memory. Negative memories if stored (not forgiven) are trapped emotional energy in our energy warehouse, the chakras.

We cannot always control emotional pain, who or what caused it, but we can control our reaction to it. Clearing the conscience feels as good as, climbing into a freshly made bed with warm clean sheets, right after bathing. With a clear conscience you succumb to falling asleep easily and effortlessly.

We can't see energy but we know it exists. We can't see electricity either, but it powers everything we do. We are constantly receiving energy in huge quantities as much or more than the air we breathe, it's always there.

After use, energy is usually discharged automatically. When we experience pain in our back, neck or any area of the body that may indicate trapped energy is there.

Chapter 4

Pain Keeps You Awake

Pain is a very complicated part of our body's makeup. Really, what is the purpose of pain and where does it come from?

It can come from a physical, emotional, spiritual or an undefined source.

Pain is a major cause for the lack of sleep.

It's impossible to fall asleep when you have constant pain, without the use of drugs. Chronic pain of any kind will bring about big changes in your sleep patterns.

Likewise, this may be the other purpose for pain, not to keep you awake, but to cause change in your life. Maybe it's there to inform us that we are holding onto past hurts and remain unforgiving. The pain that keeps you awake is a message that needs to be examined.

Ritual #3 Release and Ship Out

Sit in a comfortable chair in a quiet place, where you can have privacy.

Gather up all the bad feelings you have about yourself, including guilt, shame, envy, anger, hate, and fear. Especially the guilt you wear around your neck, because you think you aren't doing enough for your parents, children, spouse, friends, others. This might take a few minutes . . .

Put all these feeling in a clear garbage bag so you can take it with you . . .

In your mind's eye see yourself going to the river where you will find a big blue sail boat.

Empty the clear garbage bag and fill the boat with all the bad feelings you were able to recover and launch it out to sea.

Watch as the boat finally disappears from sight. At the same time *repeat in your mind that you release* all those bad feelings that you emptied on the boat, then *invite and receive* the flow of your creative energy.

With the release and then disappearance of the boat, likely the bad feelings will change. Claim that they are far and gone out to sea. They no longer make you feel

Some pain cannot be identified. It's there and it hurts, but it eludes you. Undefined pain may be the result of our guilt-ridden world.

To Forgive is Divine

This is a biggy, after being tried and tested by experience, is one of the reasons we may find it hard to sleep. That may be why it says in the bible, never let the sun go down on your anger . . . Ephesians 4:26

Your emotions might still be tied up with past hurts. That someone broke your heart, cheated on you, abandoned you, or wrongfully accused you; make's it hard to forgive. When faced with countless painful and unfortunate relationships through-out our lives, holding onto those left over emotions will likely keep you earthbound (stuck) and unhappy.

Being able to forgive might be the hardest thing you have ever done, or the bravest, but it will expand your soul.

Even after you have forgiven others, guilt will not let you sleep, unless you forgive yourself.

The ritual I use to rid myself of the past un-forgiveness and guilt is:

There is a remedy to resolve those deep dark feelings of self doubt and despair.

It's an age old practice that is just as popular today as ever and that is called prayer.

Prayer substantiates faith, which creates a connection to your higher power. That means, when you pray, you acknowledge that you believe God hears the prayer . . .

When you make this connection a light will begin to shine on the darkness that surrounds you.

Focused prayer, like meditation can be successful at helping you sleep.

It's a fact that it alters your consciousness to rest in the alpha state and it also lowers your (frequency) vibration.

Best of all, you have now become conscious and made the connection that your higher power is there. Through the act of prayer, *you can act as if*, you are really in a relationship with your higher power.

There is no longer any reason to feel alone when life's problems try to overwhelm you.

anything, because you barely remember what caused them.

A guilt free sleep comes easily to those who can forgive themselves and others.

When we hold onto guilt it traps energy. Many of us are in a state of constant self criticism before we realize it. We are not aware of these unconscious feelings, but they probably began with our parents, teachers, and our own erroneous beliefs.

Guilt plays an important role in our sense of self. Guilt stops positive energy from expressing. It is hard to impossible to release this blocked energy without becoming aware of the reason WHY the guilt exists in the first place. When self discovery leads you to the reason for your guilt, you can forgive yourself and finally fall asleep.

Spiritual Restoration

This is so subtle that it often goes undetected as one of the reasons we haven't been able to fall sleep.

We have all experienced sleepless nights during times of great stress, when life's problems seem to overwhelm us.

During these times, sleep, may not be easily found, but there is hope.

Chapter 5

Yawning and Stretching

Humans are not the only animals that yawn, many living creatures, such as cats, dogs and fish do. A human fetus has been observed yawning in their mother's womb. Everyone knows that yawning is contagious. As soon as we see someone else yawn there is an involuntary action, an automatic reflex that kicks in, which causes us to yawn. What's that?

Scientists have no clue, but have been theorizing for years and still cannot explain, why we yawn?

I don't pretend to be smarter than a scientist, but this I do know; we all have had a good yawn at some point in our lives when we are tired.

Could be, another reason why we yawn is that our body is discarding pent up energy . . . .

Yes but, scientists want to know, exactly, what purpose does yawning serve? Once we experience a good yawn and this energy is discarded, our bodies can feel tired, bored, or very relaxed and will start tuning out. Is it possible that yawning also acts as a signal to the brain to slow the body down and fall asleep?

You can feel the satisfactory relief after a good yawn. It stretches the facial muscles and at the same time relaxes them as we open our mouth wide. We inhale a deep breathe of oxygen and exhale carbon dioxide along with pent up energy. Sometimes a deep guttural sound will accompany it to give us more relief.

The risorius muscles that are connected to the jaw at the temporomandibular joint (a small joint located in front of the ear where the skull and lower jaw meet) are also connected to the base of the brain. So that a good yawn is signaling the brain instantly. The brain also creates neurotransmitters that are sent out that can generate yawning. Could it be that the message (it's time for sleep) is being sent through-out the body.

In this chapter, a new ritual to try is the practice of yawning and stretching the jaw to send a signal to the brain.

Remember to instruct the brain (verbally) often, that every time you yawn, it will be the signal that slows down your metabolism. You're body needs rest and you want to be able to fall sleep tonight.

Ritual #4 Yawning Your Way to Sleep

Stretch your arms over your head, and then stretch your arms back behind your head. Clasp your hands together, but continue to hold them up over your head. Release those tense muscles before you lay in bed. Stretch your limbs out by extending them out as far as you can.

Even if you do not feel like yawning at the moment, act as if you do. Open your mouth wide and extend the lower jaw as if you were popping your clogged ears. Try yawning now. If this didn't turn into a real yawn keep trying, until it does. You can continue to practice this until you have really yawned four or more times or until tiredness follows.

When I use this method and stretch, I yawn every time and will yawn many times after that.

If you can't yawn then watch a video tape on youtube. com of people yawning. Yawning is contagious. Maybe it will help us send that signal to the brain that we are tired and ready to fall sleep.

Holistic vs. Drugs

Since the 60s many USA citizens have become dependent on drugs to help them sleep. These drugs mask our sleep problem rather than understand the nature of them. We all have resorted to drugs to get to sleep when sleep eludes us. If not we might be up all night, so we take action and quickly go for the drugs to get the sleep we need.

I too have walked down this road and chosen the quick fix. The problem is that after frequent use we develop a resistance to the drugs and have to take larger quantities to get the sleep we need. Finally, when we wake up in the morning we're in a fog for hours afterwards.

Now we're faced with a new set of problems, we have developed a dependency on drugs to help us sleep. Guilt follows as we blame ourselves for allowing this to happen.

After you give up the drugs, it may take awhile to get back to the place were you can fall asleep naturally.

Living at the end of the twentieth century we've re-discovered natural remedies passed down from our ancestors to help us sleep.

The powers of natural herbs have demonstrated they can successfully bring on sleep; have few side effects and no dependency issues. Melatonin is just one over the counter, natural, non-narcotic, and non habit forming sleep aid that works, and therefore is safe to take daily.

Always consult your primary physician before taking any natural supplements.

Teas to Help You Sleep

In this chapter we will address the use of teas as a temporary aid to help bring on sleep. From experience I can assure you, if the teas are prepared as directed you will get results. The blending of herbs, roots, and leaves has created formulas that will send you into a deep sleep if you drink it before bedtime.

Look for natural herbs made into teas that can restore sleep. Chamomile, Valerian root, lavender, and Jarrow to name a few. Stay away from caffeinated teas.

Whether you decide to use foods, vitamins, natural supplements, herbs, or teas, all are created by nature for the very purpose to help you sleep.

Getting enough sleep each night is crucial for the repair and replication of healthy cells.

Every night while we sleep our liver goes through a cleaning and flushing process to remove toxins, dead cells, and debris in the blood.

This is an automatic process by our body to cleanse it and keep it healthy.

Every night, before we close our eyes to sleep, we should make it a habit until it becomes automatic, to cleanse our heart and mind from the stress of the day.

Then as we sleep the stagnant energy and bad vibes that we picked up during our waking time are flushed out.

Getting a good night sleep is the purpose of this little book.

I hope by sharing some of my tried and true methods and intentional rituals you can discover how to find the way for sleep to return.

GOODNIGHT

"I don't think so. I mean, I can't keep my eye on him all the time, can I?" said Bobby, trying hard to make a joke.

Hazel gave him a smile. "Do you always know what Richie is thinking?"

"No, at least I don't think so; I'm not real sure on that one." Bobby rubbed his chin like he was giving it good thought.

"Bobby, would you ever hurt someone who is being mean to you?"

This time he looked straight at Hazel. "No. I would never hurt anyone. That's not nice."

"What about Richie? Would he ever hurt someone?" This Hazel asked not sure if she wanted to know. She knew Richie was still in the room with them.

"I know Richie has a temper," he started very nonchalantly, "but I don't think he would hurt someone on purpose. It's hard to tell with him sometimes."

Hazel gave him a puzzled look. She wanted to follow up with this but kept to her list. "Bobby, do you know where Richie goes when he leaves here?"

Bobby grinned. "You know when he is not here. How?"

"We can see him with the cameras," said Hazel, not sure if she was supposed to tell.

"Sometimes yes, and sometimes no. I saw into the room upstairs. I like Albert. He seems nice, and he works with all those cool things. But sometimes he leaves, and I am not sure where he goes. It's only when he lets me see."

"Bobby, do you sometimes get angry?"

"Sure, silly, I get mad sometimes. Doesn't everybody get mad sometimes?" Bobby got up off the bed. "Can we play something else? I like your game, but to tell the truth, it's not much fun."

"Okay, but I got a question for you now that Nancy didn't write. I just want to know."

"Okay, one more. Then can we do something fun?" Bobby said this while holding up a single finger.

"Why didn't you use your"—Hazel thought for a moment about what he had called it a few minutes before—"your secret thing to escape from the basement?"

"Richie said to never speak of our secret thing. He said we didn't know what was outside, and if people were like the men that came downstairs to look, we were better off where we were."

"Do you always do what Richie tells you to do?" asked Hazel. She knew she was pressing it, but she needed to know.

"Of course not. Now can we play?" said Bobby sternly. It was true; he did have a temper, and it was starting to show.

"Yes, yes we can play, and I think I am going to ask Nancy to get us some ice cream as well."

"Ice cream. What's ice cream?"

CHAPTER 9

The Traitor

Vinnie pulled his car into the empty parking lot. He was fifteen minutes early and debated his next course of action. Should he wait outside until he pulled up or wait for the commissioner inside the bar? Choosing the latter, he got out of his car and headed for the back door. A light drizzle had started to fall. It gave him a chill as it landed softly upon his face. *A few degrees colder and this would be snow,* he thought. Vinnie had never been in this bar. He was not much of a drinker, and the few bars he did go to were in Lansing. He was surprised at how dark it was inside, and he stopped just past the door to give his eyes time to adjust. The pungent smell of cigarette smoke mixed with beer made him uncomfortable. Straight across from him was the door to the men's room, the ladies to his right. To the left was a large old mahogany bar with stools placed every couple of feet in front of it. As he walked forward, the room opened up, and there across from the bar were small square tables turned sideways in a single row along the wall, just enough room for four people at each. Beyond the bar was a pool table, and two more tables were placed in front of the two large tinted windows facing the street. In between the windows, a front door opened out onto the sidewalk.

The bar was empty except for an older couple, mid to late

fifties, eating their lunch of hot dogs and beer and a man at the far table in front of the right window sitting alone. Vinnie knew at once that it was Timberlake. He walked past the bar and toward the table. As he made his way, he marveled at all the memorabilia hanging on the walls—old mirrors, clocks, neon signs, and pennants, all decorated with old beer adds, like Black Label, Schlitz, Falstaff, and Pabst Blue Ribbon. *I wonder what all this shit is worth*, thought Vinnie as he made his way to the lone man sitting as far away from everyone as he could get. *This place would be a collector's dream.*

Vinnie had expected someone in a suit or at least a nice polo shirt, but the man at the table was clad in blue jeans and a T-shirt. As he got closer, he noticed quite a few shot glasses lined up on the table, some empty and some still waiting to be drunk. He wondered how long the commissioner had been there, for he saw more were empty than full. "Commissioner," said Vinnie.

"Detective Moretti, I presume," said the man looking up at him.

Vinnie nodded his head. He at once noticed the puffy bloodshot eyes; either the man had been drinking all day or had just had a good cry. Vinnie's first impression was that it was a little of both.

"Sit down, sit down, and the name is Chad, for God's sake," Chad slurred this while pulling out the chair right next to him for Vinnie to sit down.

Vinnie took his seat and gave a questioning look at the table.

"Crown Royal; I love this shit."

"I can see that," said Vinnie. "Sorry I'm a little early, but you never know about traffic."

Just then the Backstreet Boys came on the jukebox. Vinnie looked over and saw the woman who was sitting at the bar picking out tunes.

"I hate this fucking song," Chad said, putting another shot to his lips. "What about you?"

"It's okay, I guess; never cared too much for boy bands."

"Now that's what I'm saying. What ever happened to good old rock and roll—Seger, the Stones, the Who? Now they knew how to make music."

Vinnie knew the man was avoiding the reason he'd called him here. But if there was one thing Vinnie had, it was patience; he knew better than to try and rush the conversation. "I am more a Pink Floyd, Yes, and Rush fan myself."

Chad smiled. "You got taste in music, young man."

"Thank you. You too."

After a short pause, Chad looked Vinnie straight in the eyes. "How long you lived in Jackson, Moretti?"

"The name's Vinnie, and I have been here my whole life, born and raised. We lived for a few years in Michigan Center, but other than that, I have lived right here."

"When I tell you what I have to tell you, it will make me a traitor. Can you understand how that makes me feel?" asked Chad. He looked down once more to the shots laid out before him.

"I'm not sure what you mean, so it makes it hard for me to answer that question."

"You know a fucking traitor—someone who betrays the

trust of those he swore loyalty to, an asshole, a Benedict Arnold."

"I guess that would depend on who you were betraying and why."

Chad smiled. "You're a smart man. I like that. Let me just start by saying I love this town. It is what I consider to be more of hometown America than any city I have ever been to. The people here, for the most part, are good people. They work hard, raise their families, and strive to be happy." Then came another long pause as he put yet another shot to his lips. "But Jackson has a dark side. Unfortunately, I have been a part of that dark side for many years."

"Every town has a dark side; it just depends on how hard you look."

Chad leaned back in his seat and adjusted his crotch with no attempt to be discreet. "Well, this is pretty fucking dark when you look at it. Have you ever heard of the Primrose Society?"

"The what?"

"The Primrose Society. Of course you haven't. Very few people have, even though they have been around for over a hundred and thirty years. Let's just say, they are responsible for some of the evilest atrocities this city has ever had to endure."

"What are they, like some kind of cult or something?" asked Vinnie, thinking about all the bizarre happenings in town.

Chad laughed. "No. Sorry, but that's not the case. That would be too easy." Rising on wobbly legs, Chad announced,

"I got to piss. Feel free to help yourself to a shot while I'm gone."

"No thank you," said Vinnie.

As he watched, Chad shrugged his shoulders and then walked toward the back door and the bathroom, leaving him sitting there by himself. A million ideas of what the Primrose Society might be hurried through his mind. Looking down, he counted twelve shots, seven gone, and one empty glass of beer. *He must have started with a chaser*, pondered Vinnie, *but didn't bother to order a second.* In Vinnie's experience as a detective, he knew that what the commissioner was saying may or may not be factual, but he also knew his inhibitions were down. Any good cop would have stopped this conversation once they saw the shots lined up, but Vinnie felt strongly it was the commissioner's way of getting the nerve to tell the truth. That made his story even more compelling. If he truly felt like he was betraying someone, then a few shots might ease the pain.

Through the tinted glass, Vinnie saw that the drizzle had now become a downpour. A young couple came running through the front door. They both smiled at Vinnie as they passed and headed toward the back of the bar. Vinnie nodded his head in a greeting and then looked beyond them to the back door for Chad. He was still not out of the bathroom.

Fortunately, the new couple placed themselves at the other end of the bar. Vinnie had a feeling that, even in his current state, the commissioner would not be as willing to tell his tale if someone else was in earshot. No sooner had the couple taken off their jackets than the very attractive girl, dressed in faded jeans and an old Lions jersey she had cut off so it ended just below her breast, came walking back up to his table. Her ears were pierced at least a dozen times on each side.

"Hi there, handsome. My boyfriend and I were just wondering if maybe you would like to party with us for a little while."

Vinnie looked past her and down the bar. The young man was looking in their direction and had a shit-eating grin on his unshaven face. "Sorry, but I will have to take a rain check on that one. You see, I'm here for work." Vinnie pulled back his jacket, exposing his badge.

This did not even faze the young woman, as she leaned in closer to him. "Well, Officer, maybe when you're off duty, the three of us could get together and have a few laughs, a few drinks." Then, reaching down, she took a shot off the table and downed it. Wiping her mouth with the back of her hand, she finished with a, "Or whatever." Slowly she rubbed the back of her hand across his shoulder and up his neck. She sneered and then started walking away. Halfway back, she passed Chad coming out of the bathroom.

This is the craziest fucking day ever, thought Vinnie. As Chad approached, Vinnie caught him turning and checking out the girl's ass as he walked by. "A friend of yours?" he asked, taking his seat.

"No. First time I've ever seen her," replied Vinnie.

"Too bad. Nice ass on that one, and those tits." Chad grabbed another shot, not even noticing that one had been drunk in his absence. "Now, where was I?"

"The Primrose Society."

"Yes, that's right. You thought it was a cult. Well, to

tell you the truth, it is more like a business contract. You see, before the Civil War ended, there were eight prominent families living in Jackson who knew the end of the war would mean extreme growth for the town. After all, the town of Jackson was well represented in the war, and all those young men would be coming home. There would be money to make, and these eight families wanted to make sure that they got a piece of the pie. Plus, they didn't want to lose their standing in the community with all that new money coming in.

"There was nothing exceptional about these families. Hell they weren't even the richest people in town, but they had all come together over business, a lost loved one, and whatever. It was my ancestor Jacob Timberlake who started the society. It started out as nothing more than group meetings highlighted with picnics and parties. But the secret business arrangements the heads of the eight families made soon started showing profits, more than even they could have foreseen. As their wealth grew, so did their stature in the community. It was then that Jacob decided to create a secret society, you see, so no one in town would ever know that all the families were really working together. Jacob believed that, with the right combination of wealth; influence; and, if need be, physical force, the new society could last forever and that each family would know nothing but wealth and happiness until the end of time." Chad looked at Vinnie and gave him a smile. He was obviously trying to get some kind of reaction from him.

Getting none, he continued. "There was an agreement, a set of rules everyone was sworn to uphold, a charter as they ended up calling it. When it was first drafted and signed by all the families it contained simple things, like only the heads of each of the eight families would be a member and privy to the true nature of their business; each family would take a turn as head the society for a period of ten years on a rotating basis, starting of course with Great-Great-Grandpa Jacob; each member had to always live within the city limits; and so on and so on. You get the point, don't you?"

"I guess, but I don't see anything malicious yet. Am I missing something?"

"Oh, but here starts the good part. You see, after a few months of creating the charter, they started adding new guidelines, ones that focused more on Jacob's desire to maintain power, like a member of the society would always have a seat on the city commission, never the major— that would be too visible a position—but at the least a commissioner."

"Influence," said Vinnie, not really taking any notice of Chad's reaction.

"Oh, you are a smart one, Detective. You catch on quick. Between the Wentworth family protecting the society family members from litigation and the Cross family protecting their investments, every one's wealth was also protected."

"And the physical threat? Who supplied that?" asked Vinnie.

"That was up to whoever held the title of chair. You see, whoever took the reins also had the responsibility of protection. It was clearly stated in the charter that whosoever ran the society needed to purchase the skills of a, to put it mildly, a professional. If anyone crossed a member of the society, he or she was dealt with. At no time were the rest of the society allowed to know who any of the chairs might have on the payroll for this particular assignment; afraid it might make them liable if anything should go astray."

"So, your so-called society ran more like the mob. Am I getting that right?"

"Yes and no. You see, to make all of this work, and to keep everyone quiet, there had to be more than just a charter or handshake. Jacob saw to that as well. One night, he invited all the society members to an all-day banquet, boasting that he had found a way to ensure that no one ever strayed from the charter or implicated another member." Chad stopped and looked down. He grabbed another shot from the table and downed it. He wiped tears from his eyes and openly started to weep.

"Look, Commissioner, we can finish this another time if you would like. I mean it doesn't have to all be said right now. Why don't you take a break?"

"No," responded Chad, wiping the wetness from his eyes once more. "No. It has to be now. I fear my family maybe in danger, Detective. I need to end this now." He took a deep breath. "I took my son to see *Deep Impact* the other day. Have you seen it?"

"Yeah, good movie."

"Yeah, we liked it as well. On the way home, my son told me that he hoped to go to Michigan State, so he wouldn't be that far away from me. Funny, because most the time he acts like he doesn't want me anywhere around. Do you have any children, Detective?"

"Me, no. I'm not even married."

"Well, I fear that is no longer a requirement, not sure

it's even a preference anymore. Let me ask you, if you did have children, would you do anything in the world to protect them? You don't have to answer that," he said, waving away the question. "You would. I can tell the kind of man you are." This was followed once more by a very long pause. "Where was I? I'm sorry."

"You were talking about Jacob having a banquet."

"Ah, yes, the banquet. You see, he made everyone agree on the menu before they even started. The best way to keep them all together and silent in Jacob's eyes was for them all to share in something so far beyond comprehension, something so terrifying, that they knew they would all spend the rest of their lives behind bars if discovered." Yet another pause. "They butchered and ate a local peasant child, consumed him entirely."

Vinnie was in shock. He could not believe what he had just heard. "Ate a child?"

"Oh, it wasn't the last time. You see, it was decided that very night that, whenever a new member would join the society, they would all share in a similar feast before he or she could become a full member. When the head of a family died, his or her eldest child would be invited to join. All new members know in advance the details of their inauguration into the society."

"And if they refused?"

"Then they were dealt with."

"How many times has that happened?"

"Only twice that I know of. You see, the society can be very persuasive. Ironic isn't it, the rich living off the poor and all that. It is in the charter that only a child born and raised within the city limits of Jackson could be chosen."

"So, you are saying you personally have …'"

Chad hung his head and avoided eye contact. "Yes, and more than once."

It took everything Vinnie had to keep from slugging the bastard right in the face, but he knew he still needed to hear more. "How does the Willmore family fit into all this? Surely they weren't part of your little social club."

"The Willmore family started out as no more than hired butchers. The Wentworth family had enough dirt on the senior Willmore to put him away for life. That's what keep him silent, but his boy," he said shaking his head. "He was a different story. The day he found out what his old man was doing he went straight to the head of the society and demanded a deal. You see the younger Willmore was a crazy motherfucker, but he was also a businessman. He knew there was money to be made in the sale of children. An ultimatum was given—the society would back his startup cost, including the house on Grinnell. There he would house children from everywhere across the country, and no members of the society would ever again have to put their necks out by snatching a child themselves. He also promised half the profits for the first ten years and a free local child when needed. He would butcher them and deliver them himself with his father's company truck. That or he would go to the police. At that point, the society had a choice to make—kill the younger Willmore or make the deal. I and a couple of others in the society refused the deal, but we were outvoted."

"Who are the other members of the society, Mr. Timberlake?" asked Vinnie in a threatening tone.

"Ho, no; that I will not tell. That will be up to you to discover, Detective. I may be a traitor, but even I have my limits. Besides, I think you can guess who some of them are already, can't you?"

Vinnie did not say a word. He just sat there, giving Chad a cold glare. "So why are you telling me all this? I mean why go through all this if it's not going to make a difference?"

"But it will make a difference, my good man. You're smart, a lot smarter than I thought you would be. You will put the pieces together from here. The society has to come to an end. I am afraid we are now paying for our sins and that of our fathers." With that, he took another shot, leaving one on the table. "Either the dead have come back to punish us, or that boy you are all hiding at the university is more powerful than you think."

Vinnie gave him a surprised look.

"Yes, Detective, everyone in the society knows about the boy and his so-called gift. But it really doesn't matter if it's the dead come back to life or if the boy is killing us one by one with his mind. You see, now that I have talked to you, I am a dead man either way. Don't think for a moment that the current head of the society does not know I have met with you. She has feared for years I would go to the police, and now I have. Her goon will kill me as soon as he possibly can. I can assure you of that."

"We can protect you," said Vinnie.

"No, no you can't. You may think you can, but you can't," said Chad, standing. Putting on his coat, he continued,

"And right now, you have nothing on me to arrest me. A Wentworth would be at your door before you could turn the key." Chad walked to the front door and opened it and then turned around one last time. "I wish you well, Detective. I truly do. I know what I have to do. I only hope you too learn the part you must play in all of this."

As Chad walked out the door, Vinnie reached down on the table and took the last shot. Out the window, right in front of him, he saw Chad stop. He pulled a revolver out of his jacket pocket and put it to his head. Vinnie ran out of the door, but it was too late.

CHAPTER 10

Order Up

The morning with Bobby was amazing. Nancy watched Hazel and Bobby play tag, wrap each other up with gauze from the one of the cabinets, and even make a tent with his blankets and sheets. Hazel appeared to do everything in her power to make the boy happy. As the morning waned and the afternoon began, it was becoming more and more apparent that she was getting far more out this day than Bobby.

When Albert arrived back from the store, Nancy walked down the steps to help him. They both walked straight to the flap to deliver the ice cream, but it was soon apparent that it simply would not fit. When Albert opened the door to hand over the tub to Hazel, it was Bobby who insisted that Nancy and Albert join them. Nancy was very reluctant at first, but Albert simply pushed his large frame past her and into Bobby's room without any hesitation. The four of them eventually sat on the floor, each with a plastic spoon and ate their ice cream straight from the tub. When they were done, it was decided that they all would move the furniture back to its original spot. The room was magically transformed into a small apartment. *We really did do our best to make the boy feel at home*, thought Nancy. The highlight of the day was Bobby's reaction when the TV was turned on. Albert had bought a two-hour long VHS filled with the *Animaniacs* and *Tiny Toon Adventures.*

With Bobby nicely snuggled in next to Albert on the couch, Nancy put her hand on Hazel's shoulder and whispered, "That will keep him busy for a while. We need to talk."

Reluctantly, Hazel said her goodbyes to Bobby, who made her promise to come back tomorrow. Walking up the stairs to the lab, Hazel gave Nancy a smile. "I know you need to do your job, but it kind of sucks, doesn't it?"

"Yeah. I guess you figured out what I am going to say. The fact he doesn't recall everything that Richie does tells me there is a good chance his confinement may have caused him to develop two distinct personalities—one the sweet child we know who interacts with his imaginary friend and the other that tells his imaginary friend to do things that the Bobby we know would never dream of."

Walking though the lab door, Hazel walked over to the table and sat down, while Nancy walked over to pour a cup of coffee. "Do you think there is a dark side to Bobby? Honestly, deep down in your heart, do you believe this?" she asked Nancy.

Nancy hung her head low, like she was checking to make sure her shoes matched. "No, I don't think so. Look at him. He is one of the sweetest kids I've ever met. But still, Hazel, we can't take the chance we're wrong. People could get hurt. I have to let them know the possibility exists."

Hazel forced a smile. "I know. It just all seems so unfair. If only we knew one of you could be with him."

Nancy walked over and put her hands on Hazel's

shoulders. "Who knows? Maybe they will move him somewhere nice, and over time, they will come to realize he is not a danger to anyone."

"Let's hope so. The thought of him spending his life locked behind doors just tears me apart."

"Me too, me too."

Hazel looked down at her watch. "Shit, I have to go. I am meeting my boyfriend at the track."

"Go. We will see you in the morning. I doubt anyone will be here to get him till later in the day, so go. Hope you have an umbrella. Albert told me it was pouring when he ran to the store."

Hazel left, and soon after, Nancy heard Albert plodding up the stairs. "He fell asleep on the couch. I think we wore him out this morning," said Albert as he entered the door. "I am going to miss him." With this, he looked over at Nancy for confirmation that this was truly the case.

"Me too," was her reply.

Albert gave her a sympathetic smile and returned to his workstation.

Within just a few minutes, Jim showed up for this shift. Nancy filled him in on all the morning activities and, finally, her decision to report that the boy could be a safety risk.

Jim sat listening at his computer. Nancy was not even sure he was paying any attention until he turned and said, "It's the right decision. We all know it." Then, turning back to his computer, he added, "I know it was not an easy one to make, but I support you 100 percent."

Albert, not even bothering to turn around, added, "Me too."

Nancy appreciated these words. She felt like she was holding the boy's fate in her hands. But she also felt a responsibility to make sure no one else was harmed. As for keeping the science building closed for another day, that would be handled from Washington. Nancy was glad for this, as the dean had not been happy with the first request.

For a good hour, the three scientists worked in silence. There was no more debate about the boy's fate; it was decided.

It was Jim who finally ended the silence. "Ozone levels are rising. Albert, where is Richie?"

"I don't see him," Albert responded, looking up at the screen.

"Well, are the cameras working? For God's sake, the numbers are going through the roof," huffed Jim.

Nancy walked over to the glass. From her location, she could see the boy asleep on the couch. His body was glowing. "Albert, move the camera over to the couch."

As Albert panned the camera over to where the boy slept, he announced. "There he is, hovering just above the boy; the bastard's already doubled in mass, and he is still growing."

Just then, Bobby's limp body started to rise off the couch, his arms spread wide.

"The connection—can you see the connection?" pleaded Nancy.

Albert tried desperately to find a good angle. "No. It's blocked by Richie. All I can see is him."

"What's that smell?" asked Nancy, covering her mouth.

"Ozone. I tell you, it is higher this time."

Bobby now hovered a good five feet off the couch. As he

floated upward, Albert could see Richie growing bigger and bigger, his hue changing from a cold to warm signature. "He's draining him," said Albert, looking over to Nancy, who still had her gaze fixed on the levitating boy.

Then, as quickly as it all started it stopped, Bobby's body feel back onto the couch, where it took a good-size bounce, the force of which caused the boy to land squarely on the floor.

"Where's Richie?!" shouted Nancy.

"He's gone. I can see the connection now. It's going out the door."

Without hesitation, Nancy ran for the door. Albert got up to join her, but Nancy insisted he stay and monitor the cameras. She almost fell descending the stairs and had to catch herself with the handrails. At the bottom of the steps, she paused, took a deep breath, unlocked the door, and went in.

Bobby lay motionless on his side. Nancy ran to him and grabbed his arm. "His pulse is low, and his breathing is shallow," she announced to the two men upstairs. Carefully, she picked him up and carried him over to this bed, where she laid him down. "He needs a doctor!" yelled Nancy.

"What doctor? I don't think we will find many volunteers from the hospital," responded Jim over the coms.

"Call Samar. Tell him it's an emergency. He'll come."

• • • • • • • • ● ○○○○○○○○○○ ○

Vinnie was still squatting near the body in the pouring rain, his hands folded together on the top of his head, leaning against the building when Sam arrived on the scene. "I take it you saw him do it?" he asked of Vinnie.

"Yeah, I saw," said Vinnie, making no attempt to stand. "Is Bibens on his way?"

"Yes, I think so," said Sam. "You know he will have a million questions."

"I wish Hazel was here. There is so much I have to tell you both."

Sam looked down at the body. Blood mixed with rainwater streamed across the sidewalk to the curb and down the road to the drain below. "Well, I don't know but I think I won't have any problem determining the cause of death," Sam said. "He still has the gun in his hand."

"Sam, do you believe in God?" asked Vinnie out of the blue.

"Of course. Do you?" Sam asked in kind.

"Yes. I mean no. I don't know. I mean, if there is a God, how could he let all of this crazy shit happen? I never want to see something like that again."

"God does not cause evil things to happen, Vinnie. Unfortunately it is man that creates his own evils. Now come on inside. We have enough uniforms on scene. Come inside and dry off."

With that little bit of encouragement, Vinnie stood and walked back into the bar, only to find Agent Bibens and his goons waiting for him.

• • • • • • • • ● ○○○○○○○○○ ○ ○

Hazel got to the track just in time for the third race. Brian was inside the main building huddled up to the bar. When he saw Hazel, he ran up and gave her a big kiss. "You made it."

"Make a million yet?" she asked sarcastically.

"Hell no. I'm down, down fifty bucks. But I say we get out of here. It's too fucking cold, and my luck is for shit."

"Oh, thank God. I was hoping you would say that," she said with a sigh of relief.

"I know it's too early for dinner and too late for lunch, but I am starving. You want to grab a bite?"

"That sounds great. How about we splurge and go to Under the Oaks? I have their flyer in my purse for a free appetizer, and you know how much I love their stuffed mushrooms," said Hazel giving him her please, please, please smile.

"Damn, you're not a cheap date; you know that."

"Shut up. If you want class, you got to pay for it. Didn't your mom ever tell you that?"

"My mother told me a lot of things, like beware of police captains with big appetites."

Hazel smacked him on the shoulder. "I don't eat that much."

Brian smiled and threw a ten spot to Denny, the bartender. "See the abuse I have to put up with?" he asked him.

"I say spring for the meal. She could throw your ass in jail." Denny gave Hazel a wink followed by a big smile when he said this.

"Thanks, Denny. See, he knows how to treat a lady."

The restaurant was only a mile away, but the drive over was slow going. The rain was falling relentlessly, the wind was picking up more and more, and the streets began to flood in all the low spots. Between the time of day and the nonconducive weather, it came as no big surprise to either of them when they pulled into a nearly empty parking.

Running to the front door, they were greeted by no one other than Mrs. Henderson herself. "Come in, come in," she said, holding the door. "Get out of this nasty weather."

"Oh, thank you Mrs. Henderson," said Brian, stomping the rain off his shoes.

"Brian, how is your brother doing? Haven't seen him in here for ages."

"Good, better now that I will be taking over the family business I think."

"Well let me take those wet jackets, and you two just go in and sit wherever you like. Sorry but Larry gave all the staff a fifteen-minute break. We haven't had much business today, but he is too stubborn to let anyone go home, afraid we will have a mad rush or something, like anyone wants to come out in this kind of weather."

• • • • • • • • • ● ○○○○○○○○○ ○ ○

As Mrs. Henderson was taking care of the restaurant's only two customers, Larry was alone in the kitchen. Usually after a Sunday lunch crowd the entire staff would be hard at work cleaning up and doing prep for dinner. But with only a handful of customers that afternoon, the kitchen was spotless and the prep work completed. For the first time ever, Larry sent his entire staff out for a break. He knew that all the waitstaff would be outside hovering under the back canopy smoking, and his all male staff of prep and line cooks, bus boys, and dishwashers would be out there with them. Breaks were the only time they could make their moves on the waitresses. He thought about sending some home, but the last time he had done this, the restaurant had been hit hard, and service was not up to his standards.

Larry checked the grease traps on both grills to make sure they were emptied and cleaned; they were. Next, he walked over to the fryers to make sure they had been skimmed; they had been. Not one piece of floating debris did he see; it was like he had just poured the oil. Thought he would never admit it to them, Larry currently had the best staff he could ever remember.

Just as he was getting ready to walk out into the dining room and take a couple of minutes with his wife, all the lights in the kitchen went dark. *Shit, now the power's out*, he thought. But looking out into the dining room area, he saw the lights were still shining brightly. *Not the fuse again*. He had just replaced that last week. As he turned to head toward the basement door, he noticed a change in the kitchen; it became misty, and everywhere—around the prep table, around stoves and ovens, and around the dishwashing area— the shadowy figures of children stood. All of them stood without making any movement whatsoever. The kitchen was as quiet as a grave. Larry tried to look at the children's faces, but they were all shielded by the darkness and mist.

Terror engulfed him. His body quivered; his legs weakened. Slowly, he tried to back up, heading out of the kitchen and into the protection of the light coming from the dining room. Still the silent children did not move, the mist forming around them continuing to get thicker and thicker.

Larry heard the demented sound of a child's laughter behind him. He turned and screamed.

· · · · · · · · · ● ○○○○○○○○○ ○ ○

Brian and Hazel had just sat at down at their table when they and Mrs. Henderson turned their heads toward the ear-piercing scream. They all stared blankly for a moment, and then Brian and Hazel both got up and, with Mrs. Henderson coming from the other direction, made a mad dash toward the kitchen.

It was Mrs. Henderson who spotted him first. Her screams echoed through the entire establishment. His body was laid out on the edge of one of the prep tables, but his face was completely submerged inside the deep fryer. Brian ran to him as Mrs. Henderson collapsed on the floor by Hazel's feet. Staff, all alerted by the screams, started pouring in from the kitchen's back door.

Brian, careful to not burn himself with the boiling grease, grabbed the man by the small amount of scalp still protruding from the oil and jerked, as he did this, Larry's body shifted on the table, and he came crashing to the floor. He landed on his back; what was left of his melting face was still bubbling from the fryer.

· · · · · · · · · ● ○○○○○○○○○ ○ ○

Vinnie was surprised that Bibens had not drilled him harder about the conversation he had shared with Chad just moments before his death. Vinnie, who was not prone to lying, instead chose only to give a condensed version of events. "He called me here and then ranted about doing the right thing for his son. He was drunk. The man was making no sense." Vinnie had told them this, knowing that the empty shot glasses would support his case. He knew that his career was on the line. But what he had learned, he needed to share with his own first—not some FBI halfwit who couldn't find his ass with both hands. Besides, he still had a profound distrust of Bibens and his motives. He did not like the man. There was something about him.

As Vinnie left the bar, Sam met him at his car. "There's a situation over at Under the Oaks that just came over the radio. I don't think anyone has notified Bibens yet, so get your ass over there now. Hazel and Hicks are on scene; it sounds messy. I will be there shortly."

Vinnie didn't say a word. He just hopped in his car and sped away. In his rearview mirror, he saw Sam walking back into the bar. He knew Sam would have to tell Bibens what was going on, but at least he had a head start.

As Vinnie pulled into the restaurant, the clouds at last gave way, the wind died down, and just a hint of sun was forcing its way through to the ground below. He quickly stopped his car, got out, and ran inside. There he saw Hazel sitting by herself at one of the tables just inside the front door.

Looking up toward him, she said, "It's Larry Henderson. He's dead in the kitchen."

Vinnie started making a move in that direction, but Hazel grabbed him by the arm. "No, don't. I will fill you in later. Trust me. You don't want to see it. Is Bibens on his way?"

"He will be shortly. Sam's with him, Commissioner

Timberlake is dead; blew his brains out right in front of me. Hazel, he told me the truth about everyone's involvement with the Grinnell house. We need to talk."

"I know, but not now, not here," she said as she got out of her seat. "I want you to go before Bibens gets here. Meet me back at the office, all right?"

"What about Sam?"

"I will tell him when he gets here. You know Bibens will have us here awhile, so just go back to the office and wait for us there."

"But, Hazel, you got to hear this," pleaded Vinnie.

"Later. Now get your ass going before Brian comes out of the kitchen and sees you here. No one else even needs to know you were here. And if Bibens sees you, he will know something's up. You suck at lying anyway. Now go."

Vinnie, who had just hurried over there, huffed as he turned around to leave. There was no use trying to change Hazel's mind, he knew. But he also knew, if he didn't tell someone soon about his conversation with the commissioner, he would burst.

• • • • • • • • ● ○○○○○○○○○ ○ ○

Since returning from church, Earl Southworth had done nothing but sit in his comfortable recliner watching football on TV. The game was not the distraction from his dark thoughts he had hoped for, but still, it helped. That boy up at the hospital was not killing his friends. They were paying for their sins; some demon from hell had come to claim the devils prize. *All those children for all those years—karma is such a bitch.* The rain outside had stopped. Somehow, he wished it hadn't; it seemed more soothing, more in keeping with his situation.

Even though he was not close to any of his house staff, he wished that at least one of them were there. The cook was in town shopping, and the maid had the day off. It was not their company he desired, simply their presence—the sound they made going about the daily duties that reminded him he was not alone.

Fucking Lions—if Sanders leaves, I'm done with these assholes, thought Earl as the game headed into the final quarter. *I have watched you bastards all these years, and for what?*

Then came the sound he had been waiting for, the sound he dreaded—the sound of a child's soft laughter in his ear. He did not even bother to turn. There was no escaping this. It was his time. "God forgive me," he said out loud.

Then as the oversize meat mallet came slamming down upon his head, all went dark.

• • • • • • • • • ● ○○○○○○○○○ ○

It was Sam who showed up at the office first. Vinnie noticed how frazzled the man looked. His usually well-combed graying hair was sticking up here and there, his shirt was untucked, his jacket was off and under his arm, and his face showed signs of exhaustion. "Bibens was still drilling Hazel and Hicks pretty good when I left. It may be awhile before she arrives," he said, sitting at the chair at the end of Vinnie's cluttered desk. "The body has been removed. It's in my office. It took both Hazel and Hicks to hold Mrs. Henderson back when they took it away. What a nightmare."

"This entire day has been a nightmare. I have so much to tell both of you."

Sam looked around the still bustling office. "Well, save it until we get behind Hazel's closed door. I'm getting a little jumpy."

"Understood," said Vinnie. "By the way, why did you come see Hazel the other day? You never did say."

"Oh, that. I came to tell her that I met with Franky Lake. I know she has this thing about him being involved with Captain Gilmore's death, but I had to see him."

"Was he any help?" asked Vinnie.

"Unfortunately, no, but there is something I need to help him with when all this is done."

"Yes, you told me the other day. Professor Parker is still missing then, I take it?"

"Vinnie, I wish I could tell you about what he is going through, but he needs help."

"Then when the time comes, count me in," said Vinnie.

"When the time comes for what?" came Hazel's voice behind them. She had just arrived, and neither man had seen her approach. Both men jumped at the sound of her voice.

"Nothing, just talking football," said Sam without missing a beat.

Hazel gave them both a questioning look. "Whatever you say. Now let's go to my office, shall we, my fine gentlemen."

Hazel looked tired. Vinnie could see the toll all of this was taking on her. "Maybe we could wait and get together in the morning. Hazel, you look like you need a break." Even though he was bursting at the seams to retell his daily adventures, he was afraid Hazel was pushing herself too hard.

"That's fine with me," added Sam, the same look of concern in his eyes.

"No. We need to talk, and we need to talk right now," responded Hazel, closing any debate. "That fucking Bibens told me that I am now implicated in two murders, and maybe it's time to step down. Can you believe that shit?" Before either man could respond Hazel continued, "Vinnie, let's start with you. It sounds like you had quite the afternoon."

Four the next thirty minutes, Vinnie retold his story from start to end. Even he was amazed at the amount of detail he remembered. It was as if the entire event, every little detail, was permanently etched into his mind. Neither Hazel nor Sam asked a single question until he was done. Vinnie could tell they were hanging on his every word.

"So, the Primrose Society—that's what they call themselves—it sounds like they are getting a major payback," said Sam. "David Willmore butchered, Barbra Wentworth boiled, and Larry Hendershot deep fried; it sounds like they are getting what they gave out."

"But what about Dr. Hendershot? It doesn't fit the profile," asked Vinnie.

"We know the doctor tried to kill the boy. Maybe he was just fighting back," offered Sam.

"Well, before we get into that, let me tell you about my day," said Hazel. She started with her time at the university and how the people Nancy worked for were going to take the boy away sometime tomorrow. Vinnie could see her tearing up when she talked about how none of the scientist working with him now would be joining him.

"Do you think all of this will end when he's gone? Do you really think the boy is behind all this?" asked Sam. "I mean, no one even knows if he has a damn thing to do with any of this. You said he had never even seen any of them."

"That, Sam, I cannot answer. I just don't know, and I have been pulling my hair out trying to find an answer. But let's stop speculating and look at what we do know. We know that the members of this Primrose Society are being targeted. Now you said that Timberlake refused to give names but did slip up and talked about how the Wentworth family took care of their legal issues and how the Cross family took care of their financial."

"That has to be Mark Cross. He is the president of the Jackson First Bank," said Sam.

"Yeah. That's what I thought too," said Hazel.

Sam stood and started to pace. "So, here's who we know might be members so far—Cross, Timberlake, Henderson, Wentworth, and Hendershot."

"Yes, but we also know that attacks have happened with the Prescotts and Southworths," added Vinnie.

"You said eight families, correct?" asked Hazel of Vinnie.

"He said eight," responded Vinnie.

As Sam finally retook his seat, Hazel stood. "That leaves one family unaccounted for. We need to do some research."

"Don't forget the society's muscle. We still don't know who it is they currently have on their payroll for protection. But there is no doubt in my mind that whoever it is took out the elder Willmore. Think about it—the one man who could finger all of them," said Vinnie.

"Vinnie, you talked about the families changing power every ten years, correct?" asked Hazel.

"Yes, that's what Timberlake said."

A look of revelation hit Hazel's face. "It's the ring. Don't you get it? We saw the ring on different family members throughout Jackson's history. What if that is their symbol for leadership? What if only the family member who runs the society wears the ring. That would explain why it was worn by the different families at different times."

"Then the head of the society now would be Agnes Prescott. The picture of her wearing the ring was only a few months old," said Vinnie.

Just then, Officer Miller came knocking at Hazel's office door. "Captain, it's important. Can I come in?"

"Come in, Miller. What is it?"

Poking her head in through the door, Miller looked around to see who was there. "They found another body, a Mr. Earl Southworth. They said his cook came home and found him stuffed into the oven." Then a look of disgust came over her face. "They said the oven was still on when they got there."

Sam stood. "Great, another one."

"Okay, Miller. We're on it. Who's on scene?"

"Harris and Chong," said Miller. Then she turned and left, closing the door behind her.

CHAPTER 11

Revelation

It was five in the morning when Hazel walked out the door of her house, taking care to not wake Brian as he lay sleeping. He did not have to get up for another thirty minutes, and the last thing she needed was him waking and questioning why she was sneaking out so early. Last night had left her shaken to say the least. There was no sleeping. Her mind just would not calm down enough for that luxury. Visions of Larry Hendershot's mutilated face and then Earl Southworth's baked remains flopping onto the floor when the oven door was open kept flashing before her eyes. *How the hell does Sam do it?* she thought.

It was agreed by Sam, Vinnie, and Hazel that all three would meet at the university around five thirty in the morning. Hazel had to have answers—no more beating around the bush with Bobby. She had to tell him what was going on. And if Richie was involved, maybe, just maybe, he would know how to end it. Then she was going to have Agnes Prescott and Mark Cross brought in for questioning.

Sam had opposed this idea from the start. "Bibens will end you," he had said. "Besides, a Wentworth would be there before you could tip your hat."

Hazel knew he was right, but she still had to try. Maybe these people had done evil things, but that was up to a judge to decide. This playing God did not sit well with her at all. To Hazel, there was no justifiable crime, only crime, and it had to be stopped.

She had given Nancy plenty of notice that she was coming. However, she'd failed to tell her that others would be joining her. She knew that this would be a problem. But damn, it she needed witnesses. She needed someone else, someone detached from the child, to evaluate the situation, and it just so happened that she had two of the brightest minds she knew of at her disposal.

All the way over to the university, Hazel checked her rearview mirror for any signs of Bibens; there was none. His statement about her stepping down still infuriated her. *Who the fuck does he think he is?* she thought. *It was on his watch that all these people have died, not mine. He's looking for a scapegoat for his own incompetence.*

As she pulled into the well-lit parking lot, she at once spotted Vinnie's car. Pulling up next to it, she grabbed her purse and got out. As Vinnie too emerged, large cup of coffee in hand, she offered, "Good morning."

Vinnie, still half-asleep, offered his morning grunt.

"There's Sam," Hazel said, pointing to the oncoming headlights. "Now remember, they don't know I am bringing people with me, so let me go in first."

"Got ya, boss," said Vinnie, moving out of the way so Sam could park on his other side.

Once all three had assembled on the sidewalk leading up to the building, Hazel said, "Okay, here we go." And with that, they all proceeded forward.

The outside door was, indeed, unlocked, and they continued on down the hallway.

"Man, this brings back memories," said Vinnie, "I haven't been in this building for years."

Upon reaching their destination, Hazel pushed the buzzer to notify Nancy they were there. When Nancy came to the door, she looked at the two men.

"Nancy, I know they are not supposed to be here, but this is very important. A lot happened last night, and I am afraid that this cannot wait."

Nancy reluctantly moved out of the way and let all three enter. "I had to call in Dr. Khatri yesterday after you left," she said, motioning the entourage up the steps to the lab.

"What's wrong with Bobby?" asked Hazel with apprehension in her voice.

"Richie, he came and drained him yesterday, shortly after you left."

Jim looked up at the new faces coming into the lab. "Nancy, who are these people? You know the protocol."

"Relax, Jim," said Nancy apparently in no mood for any disagreements from Jim. "Hazel said it's important we meet with them, so I let them in."

"Sorry," said Hazel, apologizing to Jim. "This is Detective Moretti, and this is our medical examiner, Dr. Sam Helmen."

Jim got up and shook both men's hands. "Well, welcome to the nuthouse."

Hazel took a seat at the table. "Nancy, you were talking about Richie coming to drain Bobby?"

"Yes, Samar said that Bobby was suffering from exhaustion. He fears that Richie's feedings—sorry, but I can't think of a better word for it—are literally sucking the life out of him."

"You mean Richie could kill him?" asked Sam.

"Yes, that's precisely what I mean. It won't matter if we move him or not. Richie needs to go away."

"I have to see him," said Hazel, standing and walking over to the glass. She looked down and saw that the boy was sound asleep on his bed.

"I don't know that he will even respond to you today," said Nancy, joining her at the glass.

"I have to try, Nancy. I am going to confront him with the killings."

"Dangerous move," said Jim. "Don't know if you should do that one. God only knows the reaction we might get."

"What choice do we have?" asked Hazel.

"We can wait until they take him to a safe location and then deal with it," snapped Jim.

Nancy turned and grabbed Hazel by both hands. "You do what needs to be done. More people, including Bobby, could be in danger. We don't know if Richie had anything to do with those murders, but we now know he could hurt Bobby. That's something I am willing to stop."

Jim started to say something else, but Nancy gave him such a look that he turned and said nothing more.

"Thank you, Nancy." Then turning to Sam and Vinnie, Hazel said, "Stay up here and watch from the glass. You will be able to hear over the overhead intercoms. If it gets too crazy, one of you may need to get me out of there in a hurry."

"You ready?" asked Nancy.

Hazel took a deep breath. For the first time, she was petrified to go down. "As ready as I will ever get."

"Richie is present, sitting in his usual spot. He's faint again, just a small spot on the screen," offered Jim, looking over at Albert's monitor. "Last time, it took him days to get this dim and this small."

Hazel gave no response. She turned and followed Nancy down the steps and to Bobby's door. Nancy gave her a worried look. "I have a bad feeling this time."

"I'll be fine. Please, just let me in."

Nancy swiped her card, and Hazel heard the click of the lock. Hazel stopped and took one more deep breath and then entered.

Bobby lay still, asleep on his bed. Hazel walked over and gently started rubbing his head. "Bobby, Bobby. It's Hazel. I came to see you."

"Hazel?" asked, Bobby not yet fully awake.

"Yes, honey. It's me. I need to talk to you."

"Hazel, can we talk later? I'm really tired."

Hazel sat in the bed next to Bobby's feet. She lifted the boy so that he was now sitting on her lap, his face buried in her chest. "No, honey. I'm sorry, but this can't wait. Be a big boy now and wake up for me."

• • • • • • • • ● ○○○○○○○○○○ ○

Upstairs, Nancy offered Vinnie and Sam coffee, which both enthusiastically accepted. She walked over to the coffeepot and filled two Styrofoam cups. "Sorry, we are out of cream."

"Black's fine with me," said Sam.

"Me too," said Vinnie.

"She really is amazing with him. She seems to have a gift with children," said Nancy, delivering their drinks. "She just seemed to have a connection with him from the start."

"Hazel has a big heart," said Vinnie. "She always has.

"We all think the world of her," offered Jim from his desk.

• • • • • • • • ● ○○○○○○○○○ ○ ○

After some prodding, Hazel final got Bobby to open his eyes and look at her. "Bobby, we think your imaginary friend might be hurting some people. Do you know anything about that?"

"Richie?" said Bobby rubbing his eyes.

"Yes, Richie. We think he has been doing some bad things."

"Why did you say that about Richie?" said Bobby, a little upset by this information.

"Well, people in town have been getting hurt and—"

"No. You called him my imaginary friend. What's that?"

"That's when someone is so lonely they make up a friend to keep them company," said Hazel, somewhat taken aback by his remark.

"I didn't make him up. He's my brother," said Bobby.

"Well it's nice to think of Richie that way, but really, honey—"

"He is my brother. The Man said we were"—then he paused for a moment, looking for just the right word— "twins; he called us idelical twins."

"You mean identical twins?" said Hazel, coming to the realization that they boy was telling the truth.

"Yes, that's it—identical twins. I know Richie is mad. You would be mad too if they ate you, wouldn't you?" asked Bobby.

The comprehension of what Bobby was telling her hit her full force. For a moment, she was lost for words. Robert and Richard—it all made sense. "Who ate Richie, Bobby, do you know?"

"I don't know. He won't tell me. It's all my fault," said Bobby, and he started to sob relentlessly into Hazel's arm. "It's all my fault. It was supposed to be me. They came to my cage first, but I was so scared when they opened it to take me away, I had an accident in my pants. So they took him instead."

Was that why he was being punished? thought Hazel. *Was that why his cage was so empty?*

"So, all this time, Richie was your actual brother. Why didn't you say something?"

"I thought you knew. I thought all of you knew." He looked directly up at the glass, his eyes red with tears.

"How long ago did this happen?"

"I don't know. They took him away a few days before they took me to the hospital I think."

"It wasn't your fault, honey. You didn't know what they were going to do."

"Yes, it's my fault. After Richie died he came back to me, he used his secret thing to stay and talk to me. He said that I would need to give him some of my secret thing if I wanted him to stay. After I gave it to him, I heard the Man screaming upstairs. But now he just keeps taking and taking." This was followed by another outburst of tears. "Hazel, what has he done?"

Hazel didn't know what to say other than, "He may have hurt some people, real bad, honey."

"Richie!" yelled Bobby to an empty part of the room. "What did you do?"

A strange odor started permeating from the direction in which the boy had just yelled. Hazel had to cover her nose and mouth. And then from the intercom, she heard Jim's frantic voice. "The ozone is rising. Hazel, get the hell out of there."

"Richie, I will not help you any more. You've been bad. I hate you," said Bobby as he jumped off the bed. "You promised me you would not hurt people. You fibbed, and I won't forgive you for that."

Before Bobby had finished his sentence, Jim's voice came blaring once more. "Hazel, the connection is growing, and Richie has already doubled in size. Get the hell out of there now."

"Bobby, is Richie draining you now, taking your secret thing?"

"Yes, but this time I am fighting back. He can't have it if he is using it to hurt people."

"Richie, leave him alone. You have done enough. Stop!" yelled Hazel, just before she was sent flying across the room. Her head hit the wall hard, and she fell in a heap upon the floor.

"Richie, no!" yelled Bobby. "Take your new friends and leave me alone."

Just then, Bobby had the reaction of someone who had

been hit by a bolt of lightning; he threw his arms back and arched his chest outward, and his body started shaking uncontrollably.

"My God, the connection is incredible; he is draining the boy dry," came Jim's voice once more.

"No!" shouted Hazel, getting to her feet. "Leave him alone."

Suddenly, an explosion of air burst through the glass on the second floor, knocking everyone upstairs to the floor. Everything electrical exploded into blue flames; all their computers, tape recorders, cameras, monitors—everything was destroyed. All of the team's hard work, gone in seconds.

Then as quickly as it had all started, it stopped, and Bobby's limp body fell hard to the floor. Hazel rushed to him and put her head to his chest; the boy had stopped breathing. "Nancy, he stopped breathing," she yelled through the broken window.

Nancy was still brushing broken glass off as she got up. She could feel pieces of glass stuck in her face and arms. But ignoring them, she ran toward the steps, with Sam close behind.

By the time they got there, Hazel already had him laid out on the bed.

"Call for an ambulance," Hazel yelled once more upstairs.

"Got them on line now," came Jim's voice.

A few seconds later, Hazel looked up and saw flames dancing up from the broken windows. The lab was on fire.

"Jim, Vinnie, get the hell out of there," yelled Hazel, just as another explosion ripped through the lab and the rest of the broken glass exploded, now in the opposite direction, toward Bobby's room. Nancy, Sam, and Hazel all covered their heads as glass rained down on them from above. *My God, this can't be happening*, thought Hazel.

"Vinnie!" she yelled, but there came no answer. "Vinnie, please tell me you're okay."

Still there came no reply.

In the meantime, Sam had started CPR on the boy. "Come on, you little bastard, breathe," he yelled while pushing on the boy's chest.

A few moments later, and to everyone's relief, the outside door opened, and there Jim stood with Vinnie. "Let's get him out of here. This place is going to burn," said Vinnie.

Hazel turned. The flames were now halfway across the ceiling of Bobby's room. "Doesn't this fucking place have a fire system, for God's sake?!" she yelled.

Without a moment's hesitation, Sam had Bobby in his arms and was heading for the door.

"Take the back door. It's closer," instructed Nancy.

But when they got there, they saw the door was blocked by a large picnic table, moved to keep it from being used as an exit. "What the hell? That wasn't here this morning."

"The other door," pleaded Hazel. "We need to get out of here."

Nancy was the first one to come bursting out of the front door. And thus she was the first one shot. Jim, not noticing her fall until it was too late, came out right behind her. He, too, ended up on the ground, only inches from Nancy.

Sam was the next one out the door carrying Bobby in his arms. Seeing the other two lying on the ground just in front of him, he stopped. The shot came from directly in front of him, knocking him off his feet in the doorway. Looking down, he saw that the bullet had gone through Bobby's skull, missing him completely. Vinnie grabbed him from behind and pulled him back through the door, the boy's body rolling onto the sidewalk.

"My God, now what?" exclaimed Hazel.

"It's the society's muscle," said Vinnie, landing on his butt.

"They have us pinned down," said Sam. "Hazel, Bobby—"

"I know. I saw," said Hazel. She had a look of stone-cold determination.

"Fuck this," said Vinnie, rising to his feet. "I think I have a good angle on the shot. There's a side door in the basement, hard to see from the outside. I know because I used to go down there for cleaning supplies when I worked here as a janitor—part of my work study; let me go down there, and I will circle the asshole."

"Let's move back a little," said Hazel, "and out of sight of the door."

The moment they started moving back, a new set of headlights pulled into the parking lot. Hazel jumped up. "Albert, my God. Albert is out there. Nancy told me he would be in shortly. We have to warn him." She ran to the door and started pounding on it to get Albert's attention. If it had not been for Vinnie pulling her back just in time, the next shot would have hit her squarely in the chest.

Through the now shattered glass door, Hazel continued to yell, "Albert, no!"

Whether it was her loud screams, the bodies lying on the lawn, or the sound of the gunshot, she was not sure, but the car backed up and sped off. Hazel now heard a series of shots, and from her vantage point, she could see the car being struck multiple times. This was immediately followed by a welcome sound—the sound of sirens. *Help is on its way,* thought Hazel.

A few minutes later, the parking lot was illuminated with flashing red and blue lights. Hazel, Vinnie, and Sam remained siting on the floor. The sprinkler system, all of a sudden, kicked in. Water came raining down from the ceiling.

Looking up, Vinnie said, "You have got to be fucking kidding me."

The first one through the door was Brian, brandishing his weapon. He ran to Hazel and helped her to her feet. "Are you okay? I was scared to death."

"I'm fine," said Hazel, brushing off her backside. "Did you get the shooter?"

"They're conducting a sweep right now."

"What about Albert? Is he okay?"

"You mean the big guy in the car? Yeah, he's fine. But he's one shook up son of a bitch. The EMTs are with him."

As they made their way toward the door, yet another car pulled up—one they all dreaded seeing.

"Shit," said Vinnie as Bibens got out of his car and approached.

"Captain Cowan, funny how you seem to be in the wrong place at the wrong time so often, wouldn't you say?" said Bibens.

"Hey there, Agent. So what's new?" replied Hazel sarcastically.

Bibens ignored her and leaned down to examine the boy. "Well, it looks like we have ourselves a situation here. I suppose this is the boy from the hospital."

"Yes, that's Bobby," said Hazel.

Standing up once again, Bibens smiled a taunting smile. "Let's see. That makes, what, five killings you were there for?" Then in his own sarcastic tone, he added, "And you still haven't managed to stop a one."

Vinnie's temper flared, and he took a step toward Bibens. It was Sam who held him back with a hand to his chest.

"Really, Moretti, you think you got what it takes?"

"Look, Agent. I will go back to my office and type up my whole report and give it to you. Or we can just stand out here while you try and take your cheap shots."

"You can go back to your office when I am done with you, Princess, and not before. And as for you," he said, turning his attention on Sam. "I called in my own forensic team. We will be occupying your office for a while. I hope you don't mind."

"And where am I to work?" asked Sam.

"Well, with a little persuading from me, the county has agreed to give you a little time off." Bibens snickered. "Seems they have the impression that you're incompetent, not having found anything to aid in the case and all."

Now it was Sam's face that was burning red with anger.

"As for you two"—Bibens turned to face Hazel and Vinnie—"I am working on getting both of you suspended for interfering with a federal investigation. Now, if you don't mind, and even if you do, I have a few questions about what the hell happened here. I will start with you, sweetheart, since you're currently the captain."

• • • • • • • • ● ○○○○○○○○○ ○ ○

While Hazel once again was forced to tolerate Bibens's useless line of questioning, Mark Cross was emerging from this back door. It was mostly by accident that he noticed the lights on down in the barbeque area. The sun had not yet begun to rise. And if not for the need to grab his clubs out of the shed in back—he had a noon tee time with the mayor— he would have simply walked out the front door, gotten into his car, and been on his way to the office.

Mark was very upset when he saw this. It was not the first time his son had held an event and then forgotten to turn off the lights. The party was Saturday, which meant the lights had been on all night Saturday, all day Sunday, and Sunday night. His first thought was to wake his son up and make him march down the steps in his BVDs and then run out and shut them off. This, however, would take time he didn't have. He had several meetings lined up for the morning and needed to get to the office. So Mark started walking himself down the pathway to the illuminated barbeque area.

Halfway there, he started to remember the last time he had been here—the figure of a child underneath the tarp. *What foolishness*, he thought, *a grown man afraid of his own shadow*. If he had taken the time to sit for a while with his wife, who was watching the morning news, he would have known about the murders and may have reconsidered his decision.

At the end of the path, Mark reached up and flipped the

switch to the lights. The woods went dark, and he had just turned to make the track back up to the house when, all of a sudden, the lights turned back on. *The damn switch must be bad*, he thought and turned once more to turn them off. Instead of using the switch, he reached down to the cable running from the house and unplugged the power. *There. That takes care of that problem.* Again, the area turned dark. But half a minute later, the lights once again turned on. *Maybe the generator is still on.* He would need to check the shed.

Then came the sound of rustling in the trees nearby. Mark strained his eyes to see, but beyond the lights, it was simply too dark. An uneasiness came over him. Every instinct was screaming for him to run. Then came the sound of a child giggling, only this sound came from behind him, blocking his route to the house.

""What the ..." he said. "Who are you and what do you want?"

Again, giggling came from the same direction, only closer this time. Then came more just off to his left, and yet again from his right. They were all around him—unseen children messing with his mind. Mark started backing up toward the middle of the barbeque area. "I will have the law on you. You can trust me on that one."

Suddenly, the barbeque pit used for his pig roast erupted into flames. Then came the feeling of hands, small hands, grabbing at his ankles. Mark looked down, but there was nothing there. With one swift pull, Mark went face first into the dirt. He could feel his body being drug along at a rapid speed. Instinctively, he started clawing at the ground but to no avail. He felt the tight, tiny grip release him just in front of the generator shed. The door was open. From his position on the ground, it was obvious the generator was not running; it was loud, and he had thought many times of replacing it for that very reason.

Mark, his body screaming from being so roughly dragged to this location, hurriedly stood and started making a dash toward the house. As he passed the burning pit, he noticed the rotisserie rod was gone. As he reached the path to the house, hope started to rise in him; a few more feet, and he would be in the backyard.

That was when he felt something trip him. Again, he took a header into the dirt, and again, he felt the small hands on his ankles.

Mark struggled with all his might, but the force dragging him once more to the shed was overwhelming. This, time the force stopped just short of its destination, stood him straight up, and slammed him hard into the front of the shed. Mark could not move. He felt his body being crushed against the wood siding. It felt as if an elephant was leaning against him, preventing his escape. From the open door, an ax came flying out. It flew a good ten yards and then circled like a boomerang and came directly at Mark.

He tried to move, but the hidden figure held him tightly. The ax severed his right arm before impaling itself squarely into the side of the shed. Mark watched in horror as his arm hit the ground. Pain engulfed his entire body. He tried to scream, but a small hand was strategically placed over his nose and mouth. The ax began to wiggle. It moved with an indefinable intensity until it was as last freed. Once again, it went flying through the air. Once again, it circled. Once again, it came straight for him. Only this time, it was his right leg that was the target of the ax. Still, though he now had only one leg, the force held him tightly against the wall. Again, he was hit with a new round of overwhelming pain. Then as the blood rushed from his body, everything started to fade to black. The last sound he heard was the ax, once again, trying desperately to remove itself from the side of the shed.

· · · · · · · · · ● ○○○○○○○○○ ○ ○

The moment that Hazel walked into the office, she started to bark orders. "Hicks, Jackson, I want Agnes Prescott and Mark Cross brought in for questioning on suspicion of murder."

"But—" started Brian.

"No buts. Now Hicks." Then turning to Sandy, she added, "Miller, I want you run a profile on both individuals. Vinnie has done some upfront work so check his files first. I need everything you can get on them."

"Yes, Captain," responded Sandy.

"Moretti."

Vinnie unwillingly stood. "I know, in your office. But what about Sam?"

Hazel turned and saw Sam sitting at Vinnie's desk. "Yes, have Sam come in as well."

Once everyone was in the office and seated with the door closed, Hazel started talking, "Look, you can both save your lectures about how I am fucking up by bringing in Prescott and Cross. I know Bibens will have my ass." This she said directly to Sam. "And, yes, I know that their legal team will be breathing down our necks. But this may be our last chance."

"Last chance for what?" questioned Vinnie. "Bibens will have our badges; Sam may lose his job. So last chance for what, Hazel?"

Hazel stood up, leaned over her desk, and looked Vinnie right in the eye. "To warn them. They may be nasty people, Vinnie, but they are still ours to protect. Bibens will be coming after us regardless; he made that perfectly clear. But someone has to try and keep them safe."

Sam crossed his legs. "I kinda agree with Vinnie on this one. Maybe it's Bibens's game to play."

"Maybe it is," said Hazel, returning to her chair. "But if I don't get a chance to warn them, and we find them both dead, then no badge will be worth the guilt I would feel for the rest of my life. We don't know how long Richie's powers might last, but maybe we can outlast him."

"Did you hear Bobby mention Richie's new friends? What do you think he is talking about?" asked Vinnie.

"Maybe he's found the others," said Sam.

"What others?" questioned Vinnie. "You mean the other children that the Society has eaten? What? Do you think he's leading some kind of legion of lost souls who didn't have the strength to do it themselves? Isn't that a little out there?"

Hazel and Sam both looked at him like he was crazy. "Really?" said Hazel. "Like everything we have gone through isn't a little out there?" Then Hazel started to laugh. "At this point, I would believe the Pope is a fucking Jew."

Both men started to laugh as well. It was a release—a

release of pent up frustration and feelings of helplessness. When the laughing subsided, it was Sam who spoke up once more. "You're right, Hazel. If we don't at least try, then everything we have done up to this point has been for nothing."

"Besides, there is still a madman out there with a gun who has already killed Nancy and Jim," said Hazel, hanging her head, "and taken away any chance we had of saving …" In a matter of moments, Hazel's laughter turned to tears. For the first time, she allowed her feelings to come to the surface.

Both men looked at each other, neither one quite sure what to do. Finally, Sam offered her the hankie from his coat pocket.

"Let's review here for just a few moments. We know that it was Richie who killed Henderson, Southworth, and Wentworth, and probably Hendershot," said Hazel, regaining some of her composure.

"So much for the thought of him protecting Bobby. He was probably just protecting his power supply," added Sam. "And don't forget David Willmore."

"Willmore junior, yes, but not senior. That too must have been whoever Agnes Prescott hired to do the society's dirty deeds," said Vinnie, "him, Nancy and Jim, maybe even Bobby."

"Who knows? Maybe we were on the list as well; he just didn't get the chance," said Hazel.

"I don't think so. I think we were a surprise," said Vinnie, "I think he went there to kill the boy and all the scientists, but when he saw our cars there, he had to change his plans. I think he waited for the three of us to come out. He was going to pick us off one by one and then move in on the lab. It just so happened that they came running out first. After that, he was at a loss. He knew we were still inside and armed."

"How do you think he was planning on getting past their security?" asked Sam.

Hazel shot out of her chair. "Shit, Albert. I forgot about Albert. Did any of you see him before we left?"

Both men shook their heads.

A look of panic came over Hazel's face. "If he was after Nancy and Jim, he was after Albert as well; he was waiting for Albert to arrive—him and his security badge."

"I'm on it," said Vinnie, getting up. "I'll run by his hotel first. Maybe he's there. I doubt Bibens is allowing him to leave town."

"What about me?" asked Sam.

"Well, it doesn't sound like you got anything else to do for a while," joked Vinnie, putting his jacket back on. "Might as well ride along."

CHAPTER 12

A Warning Unheeded

The hotel that the group of scientists were staying at was just off US 94, across from the mall at Jackson Crossing. Vinnie had gotten Albert's room number before he'd left the office, though he still had not worked out exactly what he was going to say. He had just parked the car when he looked at Sam. "Just a minute. I have to put my shoes back on."

"You took off your shoes while you were driving?" asked Sam.

Vinnie, busy reaching under his seat to find his other shoe, gave him a look, "What? They're new, and they're hurting my feet. I can feel a blister on my heel." Then when he was done, "Okay, let's go."

"Wait," said Sam. "Look."

Bibens's car was just turning into the parking lot as the two looked on. He pulled into a spot a few rows in front of them. "What the fuck is he doing here?" asked Sam.

"Damn," said Vinnie, "it all makes sense. Why do you think he was in such a hurry to remove you from your lab? Maybe it wasn't the fact you weren't finding results but the fear you would—results that would point back to him. Think about it. He shows up out of nowhere after the Grinnell house was discovered. Next thing you know, old man Willmore is dead, and I find him going through his shop the next day with a fine-tooth comb. Then he leaves an active crime scene, and who does he go see? Agnes Prescott."

"So, he wasn't trying to get information. He was getting his marching orders. Is that what you are thinking?"

"Damn skippy that's what I'm thinking," said Vinnie. "It's all coming together."

"And that day in my lab, all he cared about was Willmore. He wanted to know about the ballistics report," added Sam.

"More than likely because it was his gun—not the one he carries for work, but a high-powered sniper rifle of some sort. Bet he knew you would find similar bullets from that type gun used on the rest."

"Oh, come on. We're talking about a federal agent," said Sam.

"Who better to hire for a hit man than someone who has control over all the evidence?" said Vinnie, taking no notice of Sam's objection. "Did you notice how independently he works from his team, them doing minor investigations at one location while he is always off somewhere else? Of course he wants Hazel and me gone. He knows we've been working this case behind his back." Vinnie removed his gun from it holster. "Stay back, Sam. Use the radio and call for backup."

Before Sam could protest, Vinnie was out of the door and heading toward the hotel lobby, hiding his gun inside his coat. As the automatic doors opened with his approach, he saw, for just the briefest of moments, Bibens getting on the elevator on the opposite side of the lobby. Vinnie rushed in. Looking around frantically, he spotted the doors to the stairs. As fast as he could, he dashed through the doors and up two flights of stairs. He stopped and cracked open the door on the third floor just in time to see Bibens exit the elevator; his gun, equipped with a silencer, was drawn. Vinnie quickly ducked back behind the door. He heard Bibens footsteps approach and then pass him in the hallway. When Vinnie looked out through the small pane of glass just above the door handle, he saw Bibens stop in front of room 306, the room occupied by Albert.

With his gun still drawn, Bibens knocked on the door. "FBI," he shouted.

Just as the hotel door started to open, Vinnie made his move. He flew out of the door and into the open, "Hold it right there, Agent. Drop the gun."

Bibens turned and looked at Vinnie. It was obvious Vinnie had the draw on him. Regardless, Bibens turned and shot, but not before Vinnie let out a round of his own. Vinnie felt the bullet as it tore through his left shoulder. A moment later came the pain. Trying hard to stay focused, he turned to face Bibens, who was lying on the floor. Blood was gushing from his neck. Vinnie let out a moan as he started walking toward him. Without warning, Bibens rose to a sitting position and tried to get off another shot. But Vinnie was too quick and beat him to it, this shot landing straight between the agent's eyes.

Sam now came rushing out of the elevator and straight up to him. "Vinnie, for goodness' sake, are you all right?"

"I'm okay," said Vinnie, holding his shoulder, blood oozing between his fingers. "Check on that Albert fella, will ya?"

There was no need. Sheepishly, Albert's head came poking out of the door.

"It's okay. We're police officers," said Vinnie.

• • • • • • • • ● ○○○○○○○○○○○

Jackson knocked on Hazel's door. "We got Ms. Prescott in the interrogation room, Captain. She is not happy; let me tell you. Hicks and I are off to go pick up Cross."

"Good work, Jackson. I will take it from here. Do you know if Moretti has checked in yet?"

"Not that I know of," said Jackson. "You want me to check with Miller?"

"No. That's fine. I will check when I'm out there."

"Okay, Captain. Be back in a few."

Hazel was still reviewing the work Miller had put together on the two suspects. There was nothing more than what Vinnie had already uncovered. Cross had been questioned a few times for lewd behavior and public nudity, but no arrest. Prescott had absolutely nothing other than parking tickets; there were a large number of these, but there was nothing incriminating. Still, Hazel gave them one more look. She was in no hurry. Best to make a perp sweat a little before talking to him or her. Besides, from everything she'd heard about Prescott, maybe it was time someone made her wait for a change.

After a few minutes, however, the anticipation became too great. She got up and walked through the office to the interrogation room. Miller was gone from her desk, so she made a mental note to check on Vinnie on her way back through.

As Hazel entered the room, she was taken aback with just how old Agnes Prescott truly looked. She obviously had not had time to put on her face this morning, and her hair looked like a disheveled bail of straw. Agnes at once asked for her lawyer and demanded to know what she was being charged with.

"Ms. Prescott, my name is—" started Hazel in the most polite and calm tone she could manage.

"I know who you are, Captain Cowan. And I can guarantee that, after this, you will be lucky to find yourself walking the beat on the worst section of Francis Street for the rest of your pathetic career," snapped Agnes.

"Please, Ms. Prescott, I have had enough threats to my career for one day. Nothing you can say at this point will make any difference. Now, I brought you here for a reason."

"I am not saying anything without my lawyer," said Agnes defiantly.

Hazel took a seat directly across from her. "Ms. Prescott, people are getting hurt—a lot of people. Your little society is falling apart." Hazel noticed the change in Agnes's poker face at the mention of the society. "I fear your own life maybe in danger."

Agnes sat there not making a sound. She started examining her nails in a clear attempt to annoy Hazel.

"Look, Ms. Prescott, any information you can give me might just save your life. Do you understand that? The society is already down five members. I don't want to see a sixth. You can help prevent that. All I need is just a little information."

Agnes, still refusing to acknowledge Hazel's presence, continued rubbing her right thumb over the nails on her left hand, as if she was polishing them.

"Damn it, woman. Don't you care? Do those people who have died mean nothing to you?"

Agnes finally looked up at her and gave a cynical smile. "I have no idea what you're talking about?"

"Enough games," said Hazel. "People are dying, and you are most likely on the list. We can offer you some protection."

Agnes, ignoring everything that Hazel had just said, returned to her nails.

A knock came on the interrogation room door, and then Officer Sandy Miller entered. "Sorry, Captain. You have a very important call."

"Can't it wait?" said Hazel, annoyed at the interruption.

Miller gave Hazel her puppy dog face. "But Sam said it was important."

Hazel got out of her chair and started walking to the door. Before she left, she looked one more time at Agnes. "I am not done with you, Ms. Prescott."

Sandy, who was close on Hazel's heels as she hurried through the office, continued to talk. "Sorry. I didn't want to interrupt, but he sounds upset. He's on line four."

Entering her office, Hazel swung the door shut, blocking Sandy's approach. She hurried behind her desk and picked up the phone. "Sam, what is it?"

"Vinnie has been shot. They took him to Foote Hospital. He's going to be fine."

"I will be there in a minute."

"Hazel, listen. It was Bibens all along. He's the one who the society has been paying to do their dirty work. Vinnie stopped him just before he had time to off that guy Albert. Vinnie told Officer Chong to make a sweep of Bibens's car.

He did. In the trunk was a sniper riffle that he most likely used on those scientists."

Hazel did not know what to say. She just stood there taking it all in.

"Wait. They are bringing him back into the room. He's wide awake if you want to talk to him."

Before Hazel could respond, Vinnie's voice came over the phone. "Hazel, man they got me on some good shit. I can't feel a thing. I don't want you running up here, okay. I am fine. As a matter of fact, I'm planning on kicking Sam out of here as well."

"Captain, sorry to bother you again," came Sandy's voice through her closed door.

"Hold on a sec, Vinnie." She turned and yelled for Sandy to come in. "What now, Miller?"

"I am really sorry, but Hicks and Jackson just called in. They said they need you at the Cross estate right away."

"Go." Hazel heard Vinnie's voice through the phone. He'd obviously heard the conversation on the other end.

"Tell them I will be right there," said Hazel, and then turning back to the phone, she said, "Vinnie, tell Sam to meet me over at the Cross estate."

"Will do. Be careful."

"I will be up to see you as soon as I can. Got to go. Bye." With that, she hung up the phone and grabbed her jacket.

"Give me fifteen to twenty minutes' head start, and then call the feds. And make sure Ms. Prescott is still here when I get back. Got that?" she growled at Miller on her way out the door.

•••••••••●○○○○○○○○○○○

Sam arrived at the Cross estate at the same time as Hazel. Brian was standing by the front door waiting for them. "He's around back. You're not going to believe this one," said Brian.

"Didn't the wife notice him gone?" questioned Hazel as they made their way to the back of the house.

"She thought he was at work. From the sounds of things, she's somewhat of a homebody. She didn't even notice his car was still here until we arrived," answered Brian. "It's down that path over there. They have a nice place for get-togethers—grills, picnic tables, a tool shed with its own generator, a nice place for a wet bar, a place for a band to set up; it's really decked out."

As they made their way down the path, Sam saw Jackson sitting at one of the tables. He looked rather shaken and a little green. "What's with him?" ask Sam, nodding his head in Jackson's direction.

"That," said Brian, pointing over to the pit used for pig roasts. Only it was not a pig on the spit; it was the naked torso of Mark Cross.

Sam saw Hazel turn away for a moment. She was not prepared for this one. Unshaken, Sam walked forward. The rotisserie rod had been inserted through Mark's anus; it ran through the length of his body and exited through his mouth. His neck had obviously been broken and bent back to make the straight corridor required for the rod. Though the flames had long been extinguished, there was little doubt that the body had been roasted; his skin was darkish brown with black burn spots at the end of his severed limbs.

"Look. They used a hand crank," said Sam, pointing to the crank still at the end of the rod. "Someone must have been out here for hours, slowly turning." Then bending down to get a look at the bottom side of the body, he added, "Look. He is evenly cooked. They left his internal organs in. That's why his gut is busted open like that."

Jackson, hearing Sam's description, made a mad rush for the bushes. Everyone could hear him losing his lunch.

Brian just shook his head. "Jackson's the one that found him. He isn't exactly taking it well."

"Who can blame him?" said Hazel.

"Has anyone called Bibens?" asked Brian.

Sam started to say something, but Hazel cut him off. "I told Miller to wait about fifteen minutes after I left and then call the feds. They should be here soon. I doubt it will be Bibens, though. He's officially off the case. I want you two to stay on location until they show up."

"Bibens is off the case? What happened?" asked Brian, surprised by this revelation.

"Because he's dead," said Hazel in a very matter-of-fact way. "I will fill you all in when I get more of the facts. But for now, we need to deal with this shit. No doubt Bibens's new forensic team will be here soon. Sam and I need to go. We can't be seen here. Both our jobs are on the line as it is."

With that, Hazel turned and started walking toward the path. Sam, taking the hint, followed.

"I'm getting real sick and tired of seeing these cooked bodies, Sam," said Hazel as she walked.

Sam did not respond until they were out of the woods and in the backyard. "Why didn't you tell Hicks everything, you know about Vinnie shooting Bibens?"

Hazel just kept walking until she got to her car. Finally

she turned around. "Look, Sam, I think the world of you, but you have to look at all this from my point of view. Those men down there are doing their job, and I am doing mine. If I told those two what happened, it would be all over the office in a matter of minutes. Rumors based on nothing but hearsay would flood this town. The press would be all over me. And I don't need that kind of distraction, not now."

Sam smiled. "And that's why they made you captain."

"Meet me at the hospital in a few?" asked Hazel, getting in her car.

"Sure thing," said Sam, getting into his. "Maybe I'll stop and get him some Coneys from Jackson Coney Island. He said those where his favorites."

"Really? I always thought he liked Virginia Coneys best."

"Nope, Jackson," responded Sam. "Ask him."

Upon arriving at the hospital, Hazel first walked into the gift shop. *If Sam is bringing him Coneys, then I can't go up empty-handed*, she thought. There was not a lot to choose from. At first, she thought flowers would be nice. But somehow, that just wasn't Vinnie. She thought about balloons. But "It's a boy" or "Get well soon" just didn't seem to fit the situation. Finally, she decided on an oversize can of peanut brittle. *Who doesn't like peanut brittle?* she thought, walking up to the register.

As it so happened, she met Sam waiting on the elevator, and they road up to the fifth floor together, only to find that Vinnie had been moved out of ICU and onto the third floor.

When they finally did reach his room, he was just hanging up the phone.

"Well, well, well, are those Jackson Coneys I smell?" he said as they entered the room.

Sam smiled and handed him the bag containing two Coneys and a large order of fries. Then Hazel handed over her bag of goodies.

"Wow, peanut brittle," he said, forcing a smile.

"You do know Vinnie is allergic to peanuts, don't you?" asked Sam.

A strange look came over Hazel's face. All this time, and she didn't even know the man was allergic to peanuts. *What kind of friend am I?*

"No, its fine. Thanks so much, you two," responded Vinnie.

"Sorry we can't stay long. I have Agnes Prescott on ice, and I have to get back."

Vinnie gave Hazel a sneer. "No. Sorry. That was Miller on the phone when you guys walked in. Said she had been trying to reach you on your radio and your cell but couldn't get through. Seems a whole team of lawyers showed up not long after you left, and they had to let her go."

"Damn it. I told them to keep her there!"

"I am sure they tried their best," said Sam, trying to calm her.

"Well, maybe Miller wasn't trying all that hard to let me know," she responded.

"She did sound as nervous as a dog shitting on a briar. But it doesn't matter. You know as well I do there was no way to keep her there," countered Vinnie.

"Shit, well it was worth a try," said Hazel, throwing her hands up in the air. "I was trying to save the old bitch's life is all. So what if it meant spending some time in a cell? Fuck her."

Vinnie sat up in his bed. "Hazel Mae Cowan, don't even try and give us that shit. You already have it in your head to go over there, don't you?"

Sam looked at Hazel, who inadvertently looked away. "I'm going with you," he said.

"No, Sam. I know going over there will cost me my job. But I still have to try. You don't need to throw away you career as well," said Hazel, taking his hand.

"Bullshit!" exclaimed Sam. "I knew you when you were a rookie, kid. Don't try and take the high road with me. I am going. If she won't listen to you, maybe I have a few photos in my briefcase at home that might convince her otherwise. Remember, I sometimes take work home with me."

"Damn," said Vinnie. "Sam is not playing."

Hazel smiled. "Okay. Let's go get your photos. Who knows? Maybe they will change her mind."

• • • • • • • • • ● ○○○○○○○○○ ○ ○

A clap of thunder startled Agnes as she sat in her bedroom all alone. The storm seemed to come out of nowhere; just a few minutes ago the sun had been out. Now she knew she would get drenched. Her bags were all packed, and in a few moments, the taxi would arrive to take her to the airport. She had not yet made up her mind where to go—somewhere in Europe most likely, Spain maybe; she had not been to Barcelona in ages. It really didn't matter, as long as she was away from here for a while. Bibens had killed the boy. His phone call that morning had confirmed it. Too bad he hadn't been able to kill them all at once.

Regardless of what Captain Cowan had spouted, she was safe, and Bibens would make sure to keep her name out of any investigation. Her only concern was making sure that the good captain and her sidekick detective didn't push too far. They may know about the society's existence, maybe even about its history. But knowing and proving were two different things. From what Bibens had told her, they might not even be around long enough to dip their toes into her pond. Agnes looked over at the Charter lying on her bed. Maybe someday she would return. And who knows? Maybe sometime in the future the society could be reformed.

Agnes looked up as the lights in her room began to flicker. *Damn electric company. The smallest storm and they lose power*, she thought. *Last time, they were out for three days.* Again, a lightning bolt lit up the night sky. This was followed with a loud thunderclap that shook the windows in her bedroom. Agnes looked down at her watch. *What is taking them so long?*

Agnes got up and walked out into the hall. "Martin, Martin," she yelled from the top of the steps. She didn't want to waste any time when the taxi got there. Martin and a couple of the maids could handle taking her luggage down to the front door. That way, it would be there when the taxi arrived. Again, the lights flashed on and off. "Martin, I need you," she yelled once more, but to no avail. No response came from anyone on the first floor. The lights flashed once more, only this time they took a good ten seconds to come back on.

God, let the lights stay on till I am out of here. "Martin!" she screamed.

Then the strangest thing happened. The lights started to flicker, but not in the same place at the same time. Continuously the lights were going on and off in every room of the house, all at different times, all at different speeds. It was like someone was in every room and simply playing with the switches. "Martin!"

• • • • • • • • • ● ○○○○○○○○○ ○ ○ ○

As Hazel and Sam pulled up to the Prescott estate, they knew at once something was wrong. The entire estate looked like a giant disco ball, lights flashing on and off in every window. "Shit," said Sam. "We might be too late."

Hazel stopped the car, and she and Sam made a mad dash through the pouring rain to the front door. Just as their feet hit the front steps of the porch, all the lights went dark. Ignoring the doorbell, Hazel went straight for the door. It was locked. "Sam, can you run around back and see if there is an unlocked door somewhere?"

Sam nodded and took off running down the steps. "Thank goodness it's not totally dark yet. I would need my flashlight."

Hazel peered through the porch window. It was too dark to see beyond a few yards into the main hall. Then came the scream. Hazel had never heard such a petrifying scream in all her life. It was coming from inside the house. Hazel took her gun from her gun belt. Using the handle, she started busting out the window. She only hoped she did not cut herself trying to go through.

• • • • • • • • ● ○○○○○○○○○○ ○ ○

Sam, who had reached the back of the house, came to the back patio that led to the kitchen. Inside, he saw all of Agnes's staff pounding on the back door to get out. They all seemed to be in a panic when he approached. "I'm here to help. What's wrong?"

It was Lilly who finally answered him. "We were all celebrating Martin's birthday, but when we got ready to leave, all the doors were locked. It's like they're jammed or something."

Sam thought for a moment, debating his options. "I will be back for you," he finally said to the group locked inside. He knew that his priority at this point was simply getting into the house. With water dripping in his eyes, he started looking around the backyard for something to pry open the door, bash in a window, something.

• • • • • • • • ● ○○○○○○○○○○ ○ ○

Hazel managed to get through the window unharmed. As she made her way farther inside, yet another scream occupied the room. It was coming from the far end of the hall, the staircase. Moving closer, gun drawn, she saw nothing, until at last the source of the screams became undeniably clear. She watched in disbelief as Agnes was being dragged by the leg down the main stairway. She was kicking with her free leg and grabbing for anything she could get ahold of with both hands. An unseen entity was methodically pulling her down, one step at a time.

As a bolt of lightning suddenly lit up the entire room, Hazel saw, for just the briefest of moments, a boy holding tightly to the woman's leg. He looked like Bobby, but Hazel knew at once it was not him. His head was shaved, his eyes were sunken deep into his skull and encircled with black spheres, and he wore a blank expression on his bone white face. Then, as soon as the lighting flash vanished, so did he. Now it was Hazel who screamed.

Reaching the bottom of the steps, Agnes's body made a sharp U-turn to the right, toward the back of the house and the kitchen. Hazel did not know what to do. She simply stood there, watching the scene unfold.

• • • • • • • • ● ○○○○○○○○○○ ○ ○

Sam found an old metal rake leaning against the side of the house. Grabbing it, he ran back toward the patio. Instead of the back door, he ran to the large picture window in the middle of the kitchen. He motioned for everyone to back up and then brought the rake crashing through. The glass exploded inward, and then Sam took the rake and scraped it along the bottom of the window, removing all the still clinging glass out of the way. Finally, he threw the rake to the side, "Get out of there. It's not safe," he yelled.

He stood outside, offering his hand to assist as, one by one, Agnes's staff stepped over the windowpane and onto the patio. A bolt of lightning hit close by as Martin, the last to come through, was just lifting his last leg over.

"Oh my," said the old man. "I fear Ms. Prescott will have our jobs for this."

"Don't worry about that. I need you all to go find help. Have someone call the police."

Sam watched as the group hurried out of sight, and then Sam took a deep breath and stepped through the window and into the kitchen just as the door from the main hall opened. Sam instinctively ducked down behind the kitchen table. From his vantage point, peeking over the top of the table, all he could see entering the kitchen was a single stiletto and part of a leg.

"No, Richie, no!" It was Hazel's voice coming from the main hall.

Sam stood, giving away his hiding place. "Hazel, I'm in here!" he yelled. Sam heard Hazel's footsteps running across the tile of the main hall toward the kitchen. That's when the kitchen door slammed shut, ending her approach. "Sam," he heard her yell from the other side of the door.

"Help me. Please help me," came a new voice from the floor.

Sam looked down and saw Agnes lying there, her arms reaching out to him for salvation. A mist slowly started to appear out of nowhere, soon hiding the entire kitchen floor. Sam made a move toward Agnes, who was quickly disappearing in the mist. But as he took his first step the kitchen table slid across the floor, blocking him from reaching her. "Help me please," she cried once more.

Sam watched in utter horror as apparitions started rising from the mist. They all resembled the decaying corpses of children, their gray wrinkled skin hanging loosely on their skeletal remains. Then he—Richie—appeared, his eyes glowing in the darkness. "You have no place here," came his unnervingly voice.

Sam froze. He knew the boy was talking directly to him.

"There are worse beings than me that you must soon face."

Out of the corner of his eyes, Sam caught just a glimpse of the rake he had discarded moments before flying directly toward his forehead.

• • • • • • • • ● ○○○○○○○○○ ○ ○

Hazel started pounding on the door. "Richie, you know Bobby wouldn't want this. Richie?"

There came no reply.

"Sam, Sam, are you okay?" She put her ear to the door, hoping beyond hope to hear his reply.

But what she heard was a cry of pain. It was Agnes. "Stop, please stop." Then all went silent.

Hazel took a step back. She had to think. *If Sam was in the kitchen, that means he found a way in.*

Hazel dashed toward the front door. Jumping off the front porch, her feet hit the wet grass, and she slipped, falling hard on her backside. In the blink of an eye, she was back on her feet and running as fast as she could, circling the house to the back. Just as she leaped onto the back patio, all the lights in the house came back on.

Hazel came to a dead stop. The house looked like any other. Aside from the broken picture window, one would never know anything out of the ordinary had taken place. Entering through the window, she accidently stepped on

Sam, who was lying motionless on the floor. Hazel hurriedly finished climbing in, and at once, she knelt down to grab Sam's head in her hands. "Sam, Sam!" she yelled frantically.

Blood dripping from his forehead, Sam slowly opened his eyes. "Hazel?"

"Oh, Sam. Thank God. We need to get you to the hospital."

"Where's Agnes?" said Sam, trying to sit up, something that he needed Hazel's assistance to accomplish.

Hazel stood and looked around the kitchen. Agnes lay on the floor in a pool of blood just in front of the stove. From what Hazel could deduct, she had been cut from her sternum to just above her pelvis; the bloody butcher knife guilty of this dirty deed lay right next to her head. Hazel also noticed one of the burners lit on the stove with a frying pan placed on top. Pushing the kitchen table to the side, she walked over to turn it off. Looking down into the pan, she saw a piece of meat frying. She shut off the burner and walked quickly back to Sam. "She's gone, Sam. He cut her up pretty badly. Now let's get you out of here. Do you think you can stand?"

Sam reached up and grabbed Hazel's outreached hand with one of his own and his forehead with the other. "Yeah, I'm good."

With Hazel's assistance, they got him off the floor and onto his wobbly legs. "Just a minute." He said leaning against the table. After a short pause, he put his arm around her neck. "Okay, let's get the hell out of here."

Walking past the stove, Sam looked down into the pan. "He forgot the onions," he said.

"What in the hell are you talking about?" asked Hazel.

"Can't have liver without onions," responded Sam.

• • • • • • • • • ● ○○○○○○○○○○ ○ ○

It was just past midnight when Hazel finally pulled into her own driveway. As she shut off her car and reached for her purse, she noticed a book siting on the passenger floorboard. She did not remember ever putting it there but grabbed it along with her purse and got out of the car. She noticed Brian's car in the driveway. Thank God he was here. Whether he knew it or not, he was the one thing keeping her sane. As she walked through her back door, she plopped her purse on top of the table and made her way through the kitchen and dining room into the living room. There Hazel flung the book on the coffee table, took off her gun belt, sat down, and kicked off her shoes. She glanced down at the book. In the light, it resembled a journal more than an actual book. Putting her feet up on the coffee table, she let out a sigh and then heard a creaking. She knew this sound because she heard it every time someone used the stairs. She turned her head to find Brian, naked as the day he was born, eyes red from being woken, leaning over the banister. "Hey, honey, you're in late. Sorry I didn't wait up, but I have the early shift in the morning."

"It's okay. Go back to bed."

Brian just stood there for a moment, staring down at the living room. "You sure?"

"Yes, trust me. I will up in just a minute."

Brian did not say another word. He simply turned and went back up the steps. Hazel took a deep breath and leaned back on the couch. She needed to unwind. For the first time all day, she started to let the day's events slip away—that is until she heard a sound coming from her enclosed front porch. It sounded like some large animal scurrying from one end of the porch to the other.

Hazel got up and looked out the front window. There was nothing there. *You are letting all this get to you*, she thought. She wondered how long it would take to stop jumping at every little sound.

She had just returned to the couch and was ready to sit down when the sound came again; only this time, it came from the direction of the kitchen. She was just about to make the turn into the dining room when she felt a sharp pain on the left side of her lower back; the sound of the gunshot was still ringing in her ears.

Hazel turned and saw Brian on the stairs, his gun pointed straight at her. Quickly, she ducked into the dining room just as he was discharging a second round. The bullet just missed her head and chipped a good chunk out the oak door frame.

"I loved you, Hazel. It didn't have to end like this," came Brian's voice from the other room. "Why couldn't you just let this go? It was Bibens's case, not yours."

Hazel ran into the kitchen, a million thoughts running through her head. *I could run out the back door, hide in the basement, rush past him, and grab my gun.* The gripping pain in her side made the decision for her. She knew she could not run; she had to hide. She could hear his footsteps entering the dining room. Quickly, she ducked into the small broom closet by the refrigerator.

"The fucking society's charter; you ended up with the fucking society's charter."

What the hell was he talking about? What charter?

Then it dawned on her. The book she had found in her car; it was on the coffee table. That's what he had been staring at while on the stairs. She could hear the sound of him entering the kitchen. Hazel fought the urge to scream. She knew one sound and she was done for.

"We could have had a good life together, you and me. But I will be damned if I am going to prison over one snot-nosed little kid."

Hazel was starting to feel a little woozy. She was losing blood, too much blood, and quickly. She would need to do something and do it fast. Then she heard the basement door open. Hope rushed through her. *If he goes down in the basement, I will have time to go for my gun.* Standing and listening intensely in the dark, she knew this was not the case. The basement stairs squeaked worse than in the living room. If he was going down in the basement, she would have heard it by now.

"Tell me, Hazel. Did you see my family name listed there right after Hendershot and Henderson?"

In that brief moment, all came clear. She could hear Brian's own words milling around in her head: *Well, she wasn't my real aunt. I grew up with her nephew Brice. They lived next door. He always called her Aunt Barbra, and so I ...*

My family is rich, not me.

Better now that I will be taking over the family business I think.

How could she have been so blind? The Hicks were the

eighth. When his dad died, Brian would have been inducted into the society. *That means he would have gone through the ceremony, the feast.* Good God, Richie. He was eaten so that Brian could become a member.

Just then, the door to the closet flung open. Hazel did not hesitate. She pushed Brian's hand that held the gun to the side and, with the other, punched him straight in his bare nut sack. Brian went down hard but did not relinquish his weapon. Hazel made her way past him, slowly moving forward. She needed to reach her gun. Stumbling through the dining room and into the living room. She kept turning back, waiting for him to come running at her. When she finally reached the couch, she fell to her knees; her gun belt was gone.

"Looking for something?" came a voice behind her.

She did not bother to turn. Brian walked across the room, so she could see him. He stopped and leaned against the wall just below the banister. "Look," he said, pointing his gun at her. "If it's any consolation, I have no intentions of restarting the society, with all the members except for me being dead. I don't see the point. And now with Bibens dead, that only leaves the two of us knowing all the members, and I'm not telling. Thank God he managed to kill that kid before he was offed; he was a handful."

"You fool. It was never him," said Hazel. Her voice was weak, and blood was starting to gurgle in her throat."

"Yeah, right," said Brian.

Just then, the scurrying sound Hazel had heard earlier returned; only this time, it came from upstairs.

"What the ..." said Brian, turning to look up the stairs.

That's when the boy appeared just above him, standing on the stairs. He placed one hand on the top of Brian's head.

"Now you get yours, you prick!" shouted Hazel in full voice.

As soon as the boy touched Brian's head, Hazel noticed Brian's belly starting to swell.

"Oh God, my insides are burning!" yelled Brian.

Hazel watched as his legs, feet, arms, hands, and face all started swelling. She could actually see his blood starting to boil under the skin. She shielded her eyes just before he burst, blood and flesh flying across the room. Her skin was instantly scalded everywhere the splatter made contact with her bare skin. She screamed in pain and then lay down on the floor. *If death is coming, then for goodness' sake, make him hurry.*

She looked up and saw Richie still holding his hand on Brian's head, his body nothing more than bone and dripping flesh. Richie looked at her. "I have done nothing more than was done to me." With that, he was gone, and Brian's body hit the floor.

Hazel started to feel herself lose consciousness, the light fading in and out. That's when she felt the gentle touch of a child's hand in hers. "I tried to help you, Hazel. I put the book in your car."

Through her now misty eyes, Hazel looked up and saw a glowing figure leaning down toward her.

"It will be all right. I promise." It was Bobby. She knew it. She could tell from the voice. "Richie's power is gone. He has to leave now."

"Bobby, is that you?" Hazel spoke just above a whisper.

"You would like it here, Hazel. It so beautiful, and there are no cages, not one."

Then the glowing figure faded and was replaced with flashing red and blue lights outside her living room window.

AFTERWORD

Two months later

Hazel made her way into the office. A new year was only a stone's throw away, and she was glad. This year and all its terrifying memories needed to be over. Her body had healed, though she was now one kidney short of a pair. At least she'd had Sam and Vinnie as hospital roommates for a brief time; they'd both spent more time in her room than their own. It was in the hospital that they had all decided their course of action. The charter was to be burned. There would be no more Primrose Society in Jackson's future. None of them ever wanted the true story of the society's atrocities committed in their hometown to get out. Jackson was a great place to live. There was no reason to bring shame upon it and all the family members that had no knowledge of the society. It was agreed to let them grieve in peace.

For hours, they had gone over the story they would give the feds. They all knew the true tale of Bobby and Richie would never be believed. And if they were not careful, they might all end up behind bars, especially Vinnie, who had killed one of the feds' own. Thanks to Albert, they could pin all the gruesome meals prepared by Richie on Bobby. Albert knew nothing about the fact that Richie was, indeed, Bobby's dead twin. Hazel hated the fact that Bobby would take the blame, but it was the only way. As for Bibens, the ballistics from the gun found in his trunk proved he'd killed Willmore, Nancy, Jim, and Bobby, even if they were not really sure Bobby was still alive when he was shot.

Just before putting a match to the charter, Hazel did look inside and confirmed that one Thomas Hicks was, indeed, one of the original signatures. She still had problems dealing with that part of the ordeal. *How could I have been so stupid?*

To make matters even more perplexing, the strip she had used that morning was, indeed, positive; she was pregnant. The life she now carried inside of her was causing a mix of emotions. She had already made up her mind to keep the baby, even if it was the offspring of a madman. Her mind raced as she walked toward her office. *Should I tell the child inside me who its father really was? Does a child deserve to know the truth? Does he or she need to know Brian's side of the family?* Hazel pushed all of this to the back of her brain. There would be time to make these tough decisions later. For now, all she knew for certain was she was keeping the baby and it would be Cowan, not a Hicks.

Just outside her office, Sandy came running up to her. "Captain, I want to warn you before you go in. There's a group of people in your office. They have been waiting for you all morning."

"Who, Miller? Who's in my office?"

"Well, it's Moretti, Sam, and some good-looking

redheaded guy I've never seen before. Said his name was Lake, Professor Frank Lake."

"Damn it," said Hazel, not yet ready to deal with anymore bullshit. Taking a deep breath, she opened the door and walked inside.

ABOUT THE AUTHOR

Rodney Wetzel was raised in Michigan, graduated with high honors from Western Michigan University, and attended Spring Arbor College. Today he resides outside of Tampa, Florida, where he is currently working as a grant writer. With the success of this first two books Fritz and Banthom, Rodney is continuing to terrorize his fans with his latest creation Bobby's Cage.